DID THE FRAIL HAVE A HEATER?

LARRY KAHANER

Also by Larry Kahaner

AK-47

Competitive Intelligence

Value, Prosperity and the Talmud

Cults that Kill

On the Line

Naked Prey (pseud. Larry Kane)

Visit the author's website at www.Kahaner.com

This is mainly a work of fiction, but not all of it. The part about *Moneystan* is absolutely true. So are other parts. Let me start again. This novel is inspired by true events and real people. I'm sticking with that.

Published by Bay City Publishers

Cover design by Jonas Perez

CHAPTER 1

"Did the frail have a heater?"

"What?"

"The dame. Did she have a gat?"

"What the hell's the matter with you? Speak English."

"Did the woman have a gun?"

"Why didn't you say so? Yes, she had a gun. Why do you talk like that? And by the way, frail is a sexist word. You know that, right?"

Yeah, I know, but it's not my fault. Ever since the accident the words in my head don't come out the same way from my mouth. There are well-documented medical cases of people getting hit on the head then begin speaking in a foreign accent. It's called *Foreign Accent Syndrome* and check Wikipedia if you think I'm making this up. In my case the foreign accent is a 1930's private detective. Go ahead and laugh.

My name is Sam Marlowe. I know, like a mixture of two literary gumshoes, Sam Spade and Phillip Marlowe. One neurologist seemed to think that it influenced my particular affliction and my decision to become a real-life gumshoe. I'm not saying either way.

I will say this. Some people find the way I talk charmingly retro like listening to vinyl records or taking photos with non-digital cameras. Others find it confusing and think I'm being a jerk on purpose. As for me,

I find it often annoying, sometimes embarrassing, but there's not much I can do about it.

"Sorry. I got a pill to the noggin."

"A what to the what?"

"A bullet grazed my head. It did some damage to my wiring."

"Look," she said, "My name is Helen Boston, like the city. You come highly recommended. I need your help."

"Ok shoot, baby doll."

She sighed heavily. I didn't want to lose the job so I concentrated on my words and spoke them slowly. "Please," I said. "Start at the beginning." All that effort made my head hurt. I don't usually talk to myself like an old-time dick, but I have to work hard not to sound like Humphrey Bogart in *The Maltese Falcon* when I'm talking to other people. "You mean someone is trying to kill you."

"I'm the one who speaks English here. I meant what I said." Her lip curled, and she crossed her legs. She was wearing a white blouse, knitted skirt and strappy black shoes with dangerously high heels. I caught a whiff of Xanax and chardonnay.

"Spill" I said. "It's your nickel." For whatever strange reason, she understood what I meant.

"It all started a week ago," she said. "I got a text on my phone from a number that I didn't recognize. The person on the other end wrote: "Stop. I'm not the one you want. Stop trying to kill me."

"Why not just ignore it?"

"Well, I did until last night – I live alone – I heard a noise in the front hallway. I walked downstairs and saw that the door was wide open. A woman in her 30's was standing there. She had a gun in her hand and screamed: 'Stop trying to kill me!'

"I ran back upstairs and opened my nightstand where I kept a gun."

"What's with the rod?"

"I had a boyfriend who was a cop. He said everyone should have a gun next to their bed. He gave it to me. We broke up after a month, but I kept the gun."

"Sounds jake to me."

She rolled her eyes. "He also told me never to count on the D.C. police coming fast when you call 911 but to take care of yourself. He should know. I went back downstairs, hoping that the woman would be gone but when I returned she wasn't. She was lying on the hallway floor. The gun was beside her. That's when I called the police. I went upstairs again to put some clothes on. They arrived in about two minutes."

"Guess your boyfriend gave you some bad dope about the coppers."

"Like I said, they came fast and as I was walking down the stairs to let them in. She was gone, but the gun was still there. I hid it under the couch along with my own gun. They walked around the house, checked the windows and doors, and said that their siren may have scared away whoever was trying to break in. I didn't sleep that night. About an hour later I got the same text. 'Stop trying to kill me.' It was from the same number."

"So, what's the lay?" I said, realizing that what came out of my mouth was so very wrong.

"I hope that means 'what's the job?'" she said.

"Exactly," I replied. I leaned back in my chair.

"Isn't it obvious?" she said. "Find this woman and see if I've been trying to kill her."

She handed me a brown paper bag. I looked in and saw the gun. "Pennies from heaven," I said.

She ignored my comment, and I watched her walk out of the office. Her stems were aces in my book.

CHAPTER 2

My third-floor crib is decorated in early penury style. The office holds an oak desk with scratches large enough to be seen from space and a goose-neck lamp that fights for its God-given right not to bend. The top drawer holds gimcracks including snow globes of cities I've never visited and photos of people I used to know. A herd of loose .38 caliber slugs roams the bottom drawer. They sound like wind chimes when they clank against the bottles of bourbon and whiskey that move lonely nights along.

My bow to modernity is a laptop sitting squarely in the middle, and my stab at art curation is a statue of the Maltese Falcon, the blackbird dingus responsible for a slew of fictional deaths.

Tibetan monks would consider my bedroom austere save for the large, fully-packed bookcase that snugs up against the far wall. My bed is a simple platform touched by a night table. The white walls offer paintings, mostly portraits and rustic scenes, brushed by friends and previous lovers.

The bathroom is clean.

Below me is a gallery run by a woman named Gold Feather. She's been a tenant as long as I have, and we had a thing at one time. Still good friends. She sells paintings and sculptures from local artists, some photos and barely makes her rent. I help her out a bit by paying to use her studio to hide things that my client's give me. I never tell Goldie what I'm secreting so she'll have deniability if the cops toss the joint which I doubt they ever will. It's such a mess of supplies, canvases, and frames so I just find a pile of debris and place the contraband underneath. That's where I put the gun that Helen Boston gave me. I used to have a real safe but somebody stole it along with the chunk of floor it was bolted into.

On the ground floor sits a store that sells books and other items of interest to the lesbian community. I'm not quite sure how the owner knows what this particular demographic would like to buy because she isn't gay but pretends she is for the sake of her business. She goes by Sydney Redbush and I think it's a made-up name. Just like Gold Feather. Nobody uses their real names anymore.

When outsiders think of Washington, politics comes to mind. Natch. But there's more than just government here. The Washington metro area, which includes parts of Maryland and Northern Virginia, houses some of the world's leading high-tech companies. Like most of the beltway bandits around these parts, they suck off the government teat. The area just a few miles west of The District, just past the CIA, is a place called Tysons Corner which has a few upscale malls but it also sits atop the backbone of the internet. Companies want to be close to this pipe. That's why AOL started near there. Some people call it Silicon Valley East, but that's a bit of a stretch.

Privacy and secrecy are always on the minds of these companies, especially the start-ups, who fear their next big thing will be purloined. And they're right to be wary. A boatload of ex-spooks inhabit the area and supplement their government pensions by stealing from the smart and giving to the not-so-smart. Kind of like a virtual version of Robin Hood because they don't deal in tangible products but ideas and concepts. To be sure, they use old-fashioned methods of breaking into offices or people's homes but what they steal can be put on a micro-SD card.

And that's what brings me to Tysons today. I got a call from Dominick LaFarge, president, and founder of BigApp, a startup company that certifies application software for federal smartphone users. He has a problem.

I strode up to the reception desk which was commandeered like a ship's helm by a woman who I'm sure was dazzled by my good looks and cool demeanor. "I got a sit-down with the big cheese," I said.

Immediately, I could tell that my good looks evaporated and my cool demeanor turned tepid.

"Pardon?"

"The hot pillow. The chief." I handed her my card. It said I was a consultant. I keep my PI business card to impress possible dates in bars or potential clients at cocktail parties. Otherwise, I use my consultant card.

"Oh, yes Mr. Marlowe. Mr. LaFarge is expecting you."

LaFarge rose from his glass table and offered his hand. His office was too neat for my tastes. There was not a sheet of paper anywhere except for a shelf that held some file folders wedged between books. Most of them were computer manuals.

The receptionist closed the door behind her.

"You come highly recommended," he said, as he sized me up. I liked hearing that again. He wasn't what I expected for a high-tech honcho. He sported a military-type buzz cut and white shirt, no tie. His jeans had a crease sharp enough to cut your finger. He wore loafers instead of black sneakers, the Tysons footwear of choice among techies. He spoke in a matter-of-fact manner with little modulation.

"I get that a lot," I replied. "What's the wire on the action?"

He cocked his head like a dog who detected a high-pitch sound. "Yes. Yes. I heard you have a unique way of communicating," he said. "Let me tell you what has occurred." He sat down and asked me to do likewise.

"When a federal worker receives a government-issued smartphone they are not permitted to download any app that they want. There are issues of security, viruses not to mention using government property for personal use. When workers only had Blackberrys, this was not an issue. There were hardly any apps. Now that they're allowed to use iPhones and Androids, everyone wants to download games, traffic, weather apps and so on. We certify that these apps are secure, work as they say and won't harm the phone. Mainly, we make sure the apps don't have backdoors that can hijack the phone."

"So the punks don't glom the blower."

"Uh, yes. I suppose so. Anyway, we publish a list of approved apps and monitor them so the updates are in compliance as well." He swiped his fingers over the keyboard and swiveled the monitor around so I could see it. Numbers and symbols danced on the screen like the opening credits of *The Matrix*. "Look. There's a virus on this car rental app. From what I can discern, it takes the users' information and location and sends it out of the country to an as yet undetermined third party. I've notified the app maker and they say that they're not seeing it on their end which means that the virus is injected somewhere between them and the end user possibly through a federal telecom network."

"Why not call in the G-Men?"

"There's more. We recertified this app two weeks ago, yet the virus is a month old, according to this," he said, pointing to the screen again. There's no way we could have made a mistake. Our process is meticulous."

"I'm not a computer whiz."

"Of course, you're not. That's not why I called you." He tapped his keyboard again and showed me an email from someone name Sameer

Patel. It was a short resignation letter dated two days ago. "Why'd he take a powder? " I asked.

"If you're inquiring as to why he left, I don't know. Sameer has been with us for about three years and has been a trusted and valued worker." He squinted at the screen. "He recertified the app as clean even though it wasn't. That's not an error that Sameer would make. Now he's disappeared and no one has heard from him. I want you to find him. Our company is at stake, not to mention poor Sam. I think he may be in trouble."

I couldn't tell if he was really worried about the guy or was more concerned about losing the government contract. Either way, it didn't matter to me as long as his payments cleared. One thing I learned a long time ago is that clients lie, not outright lies, but they always leave something out.

And I always find out what it is.

"I notified the government agencies who have exposure to this app. So far, they haven't received any reports of malfeasance, but I want to get ahead of the curve and find out what went wrong."

I told him what I needed to begin my investigation: employment files, government contract documents, the usual, and he said the receptionist would email it all to me. I also told him that if the feds contacted me, I would be truthful although I didn't see any particular need to help them.

On the way out, I stopped at the receptionist's desk. Just as I was about to thank her for her time and trouble, and ask her to dinner, I felt like I was hit in the head with a metal garbage can. I saw a bright green aura, the radioactive color of a road worker's vest. My legs gave way and I folded to the floor in a heap.

Dammit. Not again.

CHAPTER 3

When I woke up, she was looking down at me. I could see the ceiling lights playing peekaboo with wisps of her hair as she moved her head back and forth trying to decide if I was dead. "I read your medical bracelet and did what it instructed," she said. "At least I think I did." She was smiling now, a little more settled about my health prospects once she saw me hoist up on my left forearm. The tile floor chilled my skin.

"How long?"

"About ten minutes. One second we were talking and the next …"

"It happens from time to time. Remnants of an accident," I said. LaFarge was pushing a chair towards me, but I opted for the couch. I was able to make it on my own. The pain in my head beat in steady waves and I knew what to expect. It would be like this for at least several hours, maybe the rest of the day. I closed my eyes to keep out the lights.

"Can I get you anything? "she said.

"Coffee, tea. Anything with caffeine." I heard her walk away and then LaFarge said: "Should we call 911?"

"I'll be okay. I just need a few minutes."

"Thanks, Sarah," LaFarge said, as he handed me a cup of coffee. "Uh, well. I will be in my office."

The receptionist's name was Sarah.

"Thanks, Sarah," I said.

"Are you sure you're okay?"

"I'll be fine."

"Nothing to be embarrassed about," she said. My eyelids involuntarily closed again against the bright light.

"I get migraines," I lied. "They come unexpectedly, but I get a few minutes warning. I see a bright aura and feel nauseous. Doctors say it's from a head injury several years ago."

"I get migraines, too." Sarah said. "I know what they're like."

Thanks, but believe me, you don't. My eyes were still closed, but she must have moved closer because I could smell her perfume. Despite the pain which had changed from waves to a steady pressure, I raised myself off the couch and opened my eyes. I could see halos around the ceiling lights. Pushing through the pain of my banging skull, I stood but knew that I could drop at any time.

"I'm okay," I said. "So, you'll send me over the information?"

She looked puzzled, not at my question but probably at my back-to-business attitude. She didn't know that it was taking every inch of strength to stand upright. "Yes, of course. Are you sure you're all right to leave? We have a couch in an empty office. You can lie down for a while."

I managed a smile. "I need to get going." If my head was to explode, I didn't want to ruin her dress. I tried to focus on her eyes. There were four of them. "I realize that I made a rather dramatic first impression, but how about dinner on Saturday? You can bring the documents I need. Save you an email."

She looked shocked and blinked a few times. "I promise this won't happen again." Actually, I couldn't promise it but the odds were pretty good. These episodes were becoming less frequent. "Uh, yes. That will be…uh… fun. I'll text you my address."

My headache was now a sharp pain alternating with dull. The only good thing about these attacks is that I don't talk like a 1930's cop interrogating a suspect for a while afterwards. As I turned away, she said: "I had to search on the internet to figure out what your medical bracelet meant."

I looked down at my right wrist where the silver bracelet had been turned around. I set it right and read the inscription. "No need for the croaker. It's all swell."

CHAPTER 4

Like a drunk on a bender, I got back to the office but didn't remember exactly how I did it. I looked out the back window onto the alleyway and saw my car nosed into my usual parking space. I'm pretty sure that I hadn't hit anything or anyone along the way.

I recalled that I got a new client and a date for Saturday night. I throated a couple of pills that sometimes helped the pain, and, tumbling onto the couch, decided to sleep it off. I looked at my watch. It was six p.m.

I dreamt that I was standing in some rich guy's library, books all around, some with silver embossed spines. While trying to make out the titles, he was squirting me with a garden hose.

When I woke up, the sun was out, and a huge dog was licking my face. A large dog with a large tongue and lots of saliva. Our eyes met and he licked me even harder.

"Nice doggie," I said. I reached to pat his head when Goldie walked in the room.

"That's where you are," she said. The dog pushed against her leg, tail wagging, that twisted, folding tongue hanging out the side of his mouth.

"Lonely?" I asked Goldie, wiping my face on the bed sheet.

"I'm watching him for a friend. He's a sweetheart, a Bernese Mountain dog. Look at that face. Isn't he adorable?" She grabbed his head with both hands and pointed his nose in my direction then moved it from side to side.

"He's dreamy," I answered, which wasn't far from the truth.

I dragged myself out of bed and into the kitchen. I slept in my shorts. No need to put on a robe or pants. Goldie's seen me in far less. "Wanna cup of mud?" I asked.

"Thanks."

I wasn't in the mood to talk but I could tell that Goldie was. I know her look when something is on her mind. But I wasn't going to start something that might last for a while. I just didn't have the energy. Please, just let me have my coffee first.

We sat in silence as the water boiled. The dog lay on his side under the table. I summarized in my head my two new cases then let my subconscious work on them. I believe that the best insights always come from deep within. Some people call it gut instinct, but since it comes from the brain that never sounded right to me. No matter. Whether we allow it to bubble to the surface and trust what it's saying is up to each of us.

I French-pressed the coffee and placed mugs on the table. "Moo juice and sand?" I asked.

"Black, like my men," Goldie said

I wasn't totally black. Half and half. Sometimes it works to my advantage and sometimes not so much. What does work are my green eyes against dark skin. The chicks dig it. So do some guys. It depends upon which bar I'm drinking in.

I opened the breadbox, a shiny metal job. When you opened it, the inside of the fold-down cover revealed a well-used, wooden cutting board. It was my grandmother's and it reminds me of her. I found some English muffins. “Burn a British for you?” I asked. I didn’t really want one, but it delayed talking.

“Thanks.”

I separated one and slipped it into the toaster, retrieved the butter from the fridge.

The room was quiet, and they say that the person who talks first loses.

I lost.

“What’s buzzin’ Goldie?”

“I need your services.”

I smiled, pumped my shoulders.

“Not that kind. PI work.”

Which I knew was going to be a free job. Except for the two other paying jobs what the hell else was I doing? “I’m mostly all ears.”

A soft whine came from the floor. “Duster,” she said, pointing at the huge fluff ball lying on the floor, legs up, seeking a belly rub.

“Appropriate. Can you get him to crawl under my bed a few times?”

Goldie ignored my comment. “I’m looking for a man.”

It wasn’t easy, but I let that straight line sail past. I nodded instead and sipped my coffee.

“He bought a photograph from my gallery, refuses to pay me, says it wasn’t an original print from the photographer.”

“We’re talking fuddy-duddy print?”

“Of course. Old school.” She shot me an incredulous look. “A silver-halide photograph, not something from a digital camera printed by a machine.” She seemed to spit at the word digital.

“How much moolah we talking?”

“Seven K.”

“Why not return the dough, take back the phony-baloney and move on?”

"That's the problem. He returned the print, but it wasn't the one I sold him. He insists that it is, but I can tell it's a fake."

"Did you screw up?"

"At first I thought 'no' but now... I'm not sure. I've been trying to find the photographer but he seems to have disappeared, which is odd because it was on consignment so you'd think that he would keep my apprised of his whereabouts in case I sold it."

"Yeah, that would be off the cob."

"Can you help locate him?"

To me, missing persons cases are simple. If the person isn't intentionally trying to hide then you can find them. On the other hand, if a person doesn't want to be found, it's almost impossible to find them. It's black or white. No grey. There are so many ways to hide if you stay off the grid and hire professional help. Do-it-yourselfers usually get caught. Always hire a pro. Use cash, get new ID, and move far away. End of commercial.

"Just locate the shutterbug? That's it?" I was waiting for what we call the Columbo moment when the old TV show police lieutenant gets to the door, turns, and asks his final question after you think he's done questioning the possible suspect. You see this ploy in every cop show since then, and it works because the person is caught off guard. I use the technique, too.

"That's all. Find him so I can see if I've been taken for a ride or the buyer is a thief."

"Okay by me. Send me what you got, and I'll take it from there."

Goldie motioned for the very relaxed Duster to get on his feet. He jumped up like he was spring loaded. He offered his big head for the leash and Goldie slipped it on.

"See ya," she waved and walked out the door, fluff monster pulling her.

A second later, she poked her head back in. I looked up.

"Oh, yeah. One more thing."

"Yes, lieutenant."

"Huh?"

"Nothing."

"The photographer's name is Chuck Lasser. We used to be married."

This ain't right. Columbo is supposed to deliver the zinger last line, not the other person. I watched as the leash snapped taut and an invisible force yanked Goldie out of my vision.

CHAPTER 5

I had on my Bonobos Italian knit blazer, a light blue one. My jeans were Citizen of Humanity, a darker blue of course, and my shirt was a not-too expensive Michael Kors white cotton job with geometric microprints. I was looking crisp and expensive enough to make an impression but not come off as a clothing douchebag.

PIs from the 30's were rumpled and didn't care about it. Screw that.

I grabbed my keys from the bowl next to the front door, peeled back the three-inch steel portal that keeps the city's marauders from killing me in my sleep and headed to the back alley where my heap was berthed. Unlike my awesome ensemble, my ride is plain as a sidewalk. It's a five-year old Civic, and I consider it the perfect city tin can on wheels. It's small enough to weave through traffic but large enough to keep me from getting flattened when one of DC's trash trucks, driven by a disgruntled worker, decides not to give a shit when the light turns red. As I open the car door, my eyes scan the shiny black body with its dings and scrapes that pay homage to urban life. Doesn't bother me a bit. Sometimes I see cars with fancy rubber mats with brands like 'bumper buddy' hanging out of their trunks. They hope to keep their bumper pristine from the parkers who repeatedly try to squeeze a fifteen-foot car into fourteen-foot space. I feel sorry for these dent averse fools. They're fighting against the realities of owning a car in Gotham. They need to be more accepting of real life.

I wheeled north on Connecticut Avenue heading for Maryland where my dinner companion was waiting. Sarah.

Normally I wouldn't date a client or a client's employee, but my ethics have been loosening a tad lately. Besides, she has official info on Sameer and maybe some unofficial gossip that could help me find him. At least that's what I tell myself and the IRS.

During the day, downtown Silver Spring's business area bustles with workers. In the evening, the workers bug out and the streets go quiet. The surrounding subdivisions, like Woodmoor, where Sarah lives, consist of neat, smaller homes where families talk about soccer games, swim meets and why the EPA isn't doing enough to clean the rivers and air. They all carry their own shopping bags to the Giant supermarket.

The streets are not gridded but instead wind around and up and down. No sidewalks. I landed where the Google map lady told me and knocked on the door. While I waited, I couldn't help wonder why a young, single woman was living in a house in this family-oriented neighborhood.

With a broad smile and a low-cut dress, Sarah welcomed me in. The place was neat and sparse by choice. Real art hung on the walls, instead of posters in cheap metal frames. I suppose that some people never leave their first apartment behind, but I'm glad she did.

On the coffee table was a cocktail shaker surrounded by stemmed glasses. A file folder sat next to them. Crowning the folder was a flash drive slugged "Marlowe."

Sarah handed them to me. "This is a business dinner, is it not?"

"Er… Sure."

"It's all there. Everything Dominick, er... Mr. LaFarge asked me to give you."

"What's the low down on the chief?"

She lifted the shaker which was clothed in a thin coating of frost and poured two drinks without asking. She pointed to two small bowls one containing lemon rind and the other olives pierced by plastic toothpicks. "I'm not a fan of garnish," Sarah said, "but help yourself."

I plopped an olive skewer in my glass and sat back. The first sip went down soft as an undertaker's voice.

"His bio is in there. What you see is what you get."

Move on. Nothing to see here. "What about Sameer. What's the dope on him?"

"There's more to him than meets the eye." She took a sip of her drink, and I'm pretty certain I heard her purr.

"How so?"

"I always felt he was hiding something. Not like he murdered anyone or anything like that. Just that he walked around carrying something he didn't want others to find out."

"Did you find out about that something?"

She leaned back and crossed her legs. Then she wrapped one leg around the other. How do women do that?

"One day he was stomping around the office which was out of the ordinary for him. He was usually a calm type, never any drama, complaints, or issues. He was shouting into the phone saying things like "I won't do it," and "No way."

I laughed. "It never occurred to you that this was worth mentioning to LaFarge, I mean Dominick, being so out of the ordinary?"

"In retrospect, sure. But at the time…"

"When was it?"

"About a week before he left."

"I dig. Gentle me up another if you don't mind."

She looked at me like she didn't understand what I was saying. Which, of course, she didn't and which was perfectly normal.

I concentrated. "Refresh my drink, please."

Without saying a word, she took the shaker and walked into the kitchen. I heard the rattle of ice cubes. I scoped out the room again and my eyes were caught by a sculpture, a modern piece that looked like intermingling figures reaching up. The whole piece was soapstone. I turned it around in my hands several times. Hard yet yielding.

A voice behind me said: "Like it?"

"It's swell. Who did it?"

"That would be me."

"Are you jivin' me? Where'd you learn to sculpt?

"I was an art major in college and thought I would be the next great artist. It turns out that it doesn't matter how good you are but how lucky you are. I had a few shows, some notice in the arts and leisure sections of newspapers and magazines, but nothing seemed to stick. Long story short… I didn't want to starve. I tend the front desk, but I really work directly for Dominick. An administrative assistant you might call it. We are a small company so it's pretty flat." Sarah quickly downed the last of her drink. "I'm finishing up the dissertation for my MBA."

We spent the next few minutes making our new drinks disappear.

"Can we get back to Sameer?" I asked.

"That's really all there is… except for the material that's in the emails. I haven't read them all, and I don't think Dominick has either. There's hundreds."

"I'm in the chips."

She flinched like something stung her nostrils. I've given up trying to explain the nuances of these old phrases which made sense in their time but now sound odd and off-putting. It became clear to me that despite the martinis and low lighting, this was indeed a business dinner so I suggested that we hit the road. I also sensed she knew more about Sameer Patel and I wanted to hear it.

We parked the car and walked through an enclave off downtown that doesn't evacuate after five pm. In fact, it fills with people who want to be outside but need the company of others to feel safe. Before it was Disneyed, the area had a rundown mall and some mom-and-pop ethnic restaurants that offered tasty fare to those willing to brave the streets, which, actually looked more dangerous than they were. I never had a problem but, then again, I'm a tall, blackish man, and I can look like a hard case when I want. Now, the creepiest thing that ever happens takes place on a stage where women lead Zumba classes to throngs of other women in the pedestrian-only street. Men lean against nearby buildings and leer.

We walked through the noisy crowd and turned a corner. I took Sarah's hand as she looked uneasy. I couldn't blame her. The street was dark, almost foreboding, compared to the blistering brightly lit franchise restaurants a block away.

An orange neon sign announced "Candy's Place" and we turned in. The restaurant offered eight four-tops with a smattering of diners who looked up as we entered. They checked us out quickly and went back to their meals just as fast.

I led her to a table in the middle. We were surrounded by photos on the walls, mostly Diane Arbus-like shots of bizarre-looking folks in even odder poses. The photos grabbed Sarah's attention and we stopped several times so she could take closer looks.

"Are these original?" she asked. I nodded.

We sat down. In about a minute, a server balancing several plates scurried past and without looking at us offered a quick and friendly, "I'll be right back folks."

On his way back, he flipped the pages of his notebook as he raised his eyes. "What can I… Sam… How the hell are you?" I rose and we man-hugged. The other diners peered up from their plates again and, once more, quickly, returned to their dinners.

"This guy here," pointing his notebook in my direction, "doesn't get a menu, doesn't get a check. Not here." He held his stare on me like I had a mole at the end of my nose. "We make only special dinners for him," he whispered to Sarah. "I'm sorry. I didn't introduce myself. I'm Candy, like it says on the sign. Sam, I haven't seen you in months. Where you been hiding?"

"Busy, Candy. Just busy. This is Sarah."

He took Sarah's hand and kissed the back of it. She smiled and looked at me like the mole had grown.

"This guy here… this guy here…" he repeated, his thick gray hair still looking like an ill-fitting wig even though it was real. He leaned over and squeezed my shoulder, planted a big kiss on my cheek. Sarah stifled a laugh.

"Okay, okay. Big time detective. You watch out for this guy," he said, looking at Sarah. "I'll be right back." And sped for the kitchen.

"What was that all about?" Sarah asked.

"Nothing much. Just kept his kid from the pokey. It was a bum rap."

"Tell me."

"His son was working the bar at a joint in DC. The manager doesn't like him, thinks he's a goody two shoes because he won't play ball. You know, won't play the piano."

She eyed me like the mole was growing to epic proportions.

"Skim from the cash register. The manager, who was stealing, wants to eighty-six him but the owner likes George, that's Candy's kid, so the manager plans a swindle. Before George walks through the door for his shift, he sets the time clock on the computer one hour ahead. This only works on George's account and it makes it look like George is late. A few days of this, he figures, and he can ax the kid for not showing up on time."

Candy returns with what look like Negronis. "You're gonna love these," he said as he set them down. "Dinner's coming up."

Sarah prompted me to continue.

"Okay, so Candy lays out the deal and I talk with George. He got fired, can't get his unemployment, and, dig this, a day later the manager accuses him of glomming the lettuce to cover his own light fingers."

I took a sip. "The coppers put George in bracelets. It's George's word against the manager, the new kid against a long-time employee. This is low on the to-do list for DC cops so I'm thinking that George isn't gonna get a break." I see a quick flashback to my conversation with Helen Boston about how the local fuzz got more on their minds than a simple burglary where nothing was even taken. "I got a buddy who works ABC, the Alcoholic Beverage Control Board, and I had a feeling he'd be interested in the manager's scheme."

Sarah took a sip. "Why would he be interested? There's no alcohol laws being violated, right?"

"Not quite. Every time George slung a drink, the sale got recorded to his account and it looked like he was selling drinks outside of legal operating times. That's a big-league violation in the world of booze regs. Not only that but the manager now was liable for labor law fraud by trying to force out George. For good measure, his ABC manager license had lapsed which put the bar's liquor license in jeopardy. The beefs were piling up. The upshot is that the manager left, George took his place and charges were dropped all around. It cost the bar owner some cabbage for my ABC buddy's kid's college fund, but he was happy to pay it."

"So, you're a fixer?"

"I'm a PI, but sometimes my job description expands."

"What made you decide to become a private investigator?"

I'm not much for small talk but I can hold my own. "For many years I was a newspaper reporter. Remember newspapers?

She smiled.

"I saw it as a way to make things better. Comfort the afflicted and afflict the comfortable as one of my newsie pals used to say. I did my share. Put a couple of bad guys in the hoosgow, investigated government corruption. That sort of thing. I worked on a big piece about organized crime in Ohio. Crashed on a couch in the office most nights for a year."

She pulled the glass away from her lips. "Because it was a 24/7 job?"

"Partly. I mostly had concerns that my house might be turned into a parking lot by someone with a gas can and a match."

Sarah laughed. "For real?"

"For a year, almost everyone I spoke with went by initials, the name 'Dutch,' or an adjective in front of their name - Fat, skinny, tall, short. One guy went by 'Big Joey, alias Little Joey.' Very confusing."

Dinner plates slid on the table catching Sarah in mid-laugh.

"Special, very special for you," said Candy, in a whisper so the other patrons wouldn't overhear. "Osso Buco ala Candy. Now, I'll leave you two alone," Candy said, as he glided away like he was riding a hoverboard.

Sarah took a bite of the veal and pronounced it delicious. With the fork half way to her mouth, she asked: "How did you go from reporter to PI?"

"The newspaper business was dying because of the internet and the remaining rags were unable to sustain in-depth investigations. They just didn't have the manpower. And with mouthpieces willing to work on contingency for libel suits they didn't have the moxie either. So, I decided to see how I could use my investigative and writing skills to make a living. Being a gumshoe seemed natural. Instead of working for the public, I work for one person who pays me. It's the same kind of job. You investigate and write reports. Try to do the right thing."

"And your... what... affliction... that takes your language back, like, fifty or so years? Just a coincidence?"

"That's what the sawbones told me. Some people find it amusing, but I think of it as just plain bad luck. I have to repeat myself too many times. It gets tiring and people think I'm being a wiseass – which I am anyway. Making jokes helps to keep the demons away, ya know? I'm not really a fully formed person."

She smiled. "Do you like being a PI?"

"Like it fine. The dough's better, and I meet interesting people." I held up my glass. "I get my public service fix by working pro bono for charities that need my services to keep bad guys at bay."

"Oh, like which ones?"

"Can't disclose clients." We ate in silence for a few minutes.

"You know that it's like Smith?" I finally said.

"What is?" she asked.

"Patel. It's the most common Indian name except maybe Singh."

"Is that so," she said, casual as a falling ax.

"Tell me about you and Sameer," I said. "How long have you two been lovebirds?"

She gasped and in a higher pitch, asked, "How did you know?"

I didn't know until three seconds ago. "All the signals were there," I said in my most sincere voice. "Put me wise about your relationship."

"It was just a few months ago," she began. "We went out for a drink, just a co-worker kind of thing. Then we'd have dinners out. Nothing romantic, but we were seeing more of each other as time went on." She bottomed-up her drink, set the glass down exactly in the middle of the cocktail napkin. She pulled on a corner to even out the white space. Without looking up, she continued.

"It just happened. One night we went out for dinner, came back to my place and... We didn't tell anyone in the office, of course."

"Did you have a clue that he was going to drift?" I asked.

"You mean leave? No. But like I told you, he had been acting differently lately. Kind of like… not present, you know? Distracted."

I nodded but she was still looking down at the table.

"That phone call you mentioned, the time he was yelling. What was that about?"

"I told you the truth when I said I didn't know." She folded her arms and looked up. "He didn't tell me and I didn't pry, but I know that he was short of cash, so he took on other jobs. Maybe it had to do with one of these jobs."

People make bad choices when they need money. "Any idea where he is now?"

"Honestly, I don't, but take this. It's a key to his apartment."

The exchanging of keys spells serious relationship in my book. "Why would he need extra green? He was hitting on all eight in the salary department. LaFarge wants him found but do you want me to find him?"

She didn't answer. I didn't ask if she visited Sameer's place after he disappeared. I already know the answer to that one. I just hoped that she didn't remove anything important.

CHAPTER 6

Sameer lived in the Ballston area of Arlington, Virginia, a city within a city with all the hip restaurants and bars you could ever want. As I drove along Wilson Boulevard, the spine that kept the steel and glass buildings from wandering off, I thought about how much easier it was for the gumshoes of the past. All they had to do was walk into an apartment building, jimmy the door and have themselves a look-see into anyone's home. If the 'whatever Arms' was classy, they could slip the doorman a fin to stare away for a minute while they slipped in. Now, these modern buildings with their concierges, security cards and cameras required a different set of skills.

I berthed my heap and opened the trunk. Every PI has his bag of tricks, and I gathered what I needed.

I checked my reflection in the giant glass doors before I entered, made sure I had my gear: iPad, glasses, hipster hat, cables, tools and an 'I don't care if you let me in or not attitude.' It's all about the selling and I was primed for an always-be-closing performance. I stopped in the lobby just a few feet from the concierge desk. The woman behind the desk couldn't have been more than drinking age and seemed bothered by my lingering. I turned around and closed my eyes concentrating on getting my speech normal.

I talked on my phone in a loud enough voice so she could hear me.

"Listen, Sameer. I'm the one doing you a favor. I don't care. No. I don't… " I held up a few fingers signaling that I was sorry for the intrusion into her domain. "Yes. Well, you talk to her… He wants to talk to you," I said, as I handed her the phone. I put on my best annoyed face.

"Who… who wants to talk to me?"

"Sameer. Sameer Patel in 302. Didn't he tell you I was coming?"

"No."

I pulled the phone back. "She says you never told her" I asked gently: "What's your name?"

"Jennifer."

"Jennifer," I said into the phone. "The concierge. She said you never called her. I don't need this Sameer…" I rolled my eyes and looked again at the young woman. "Hold on, Sameer."

"I'm sorry, Jennifer," I said in my sweetest voice. "I work with Sameer and… here's my ID." I let her study my handiwork courtesy of Photoshop. "I'm supposed to set up a new VPN for his router so he can have a gateway private network link to work." I had no idea what I was saying and hoped that she didn't know either. "It will only take a few minutes."

"I'm sorry, I can't let you up."

I spoke into the phone. "She won't let me up. You're out of luck, buddy, and I have to get back to the office." I waited a beat. "Well, that's your bad luck… Okay, wait a sec." I put the phone on her desk. "It's on speaker."

The trick to doing an Indian accent is not to overdo it and my pal Arjun does a pretty convincing one. He's Indian but born in Chicago and his accent is heavy Windy City. When he wants to sound Indian, he imitates his parents. I heard him say: "He works with me, Jennifer. I gave him a key. If you could let him in, I would appreciate it."

She looked up, "Well, I don't know and..."

I held up the key like I had won it in a raffle.

"Okay, I guess so. Just this one time," she said. "Where is Sameer? I haven't seen him lately."

"Big project. He's in Toronto. That's why he needs the gateway link. Verification of the protocols, you know."

She nodded.

I leaned over the desk near the phone. "We're good, Sameer," I said. "See you back at the ranch."

I placed the phone in my pocket. Jennifer led me to the elevator and summoned it with her keycard. "Thanks. I'll say goodbye on my way out," I said.

The apartment door had a regular key lock and a reader for a keycard. Must be a retrofit.

I entered, flipped the light switch and the room went dark. Whoever hit me on the back of the brain shell was a pro. One quick bop and I was eating carpet. I didn't lose consciousness but it was damn close.

"You're not Sameer," the voice behind the gun said.

"It's not your moniker either, I'm guessing."

"Who the hell are you?" the gunsel asked.

"Friend of Sameer's," I said, rubbing the back of my head. A lump was forming. Just then another suit walked in. He was tall and slim with a big head that could've tipped him over.

"Marlowe," he said, motioning for his comrade to lower his gun. "What the fuck you doing here?"

"Same as you, Keegan. Looking for Sameer Patel." I'd known Special Agent Harry Keegan for years. He was a lawsuit magnet known in DEA circles as 'Warning Shot Harry.' He once fired a warning shot into a suspect's head instead of into the air. He claimed it was an accident. This happened at least two more times that I know of and each time he was cleared.

"Billy, wait out in the hall," he said, to the bopper. "Marlowe and me gotta talk amongst ourselves." When the door closed, he began. "What's your interest, here?"

"Patel took a powder. Friends and family are worried about his health. You?"

"Same."

"Bullshit. Who were you expecting, that I got a lump on my bean?" Before he could answer, "and what do the feds want with him?"

"All good questions," he said.

"You working under a search warrant?"

He laughed. "Good one, Marlowe." He drew a cig from his pocket and placed it between his lips without lighting it.

I massaged my head. The lump was growing.

"Yeah, sorry about that." Keegan looked out the window. "Know what, I'm gonna tell you. Maybe we can help each other. We've done it before." The cigarette bobbed up and down as he spoke but remained unlit.

It's true. In a way. It had to do with an MS-13 banger who killed a friend of mine because he drove his taco food truck into the wrong alley at the wrong time. I searched for this jamoke for weeks. I got a tip where he might be, a dead-end street where he had set up shop. I was prepared to ice him. I'm usually pretty good at clocking a tail but Keegan was even better at shadowing me that particular day. I didn't spot him, must have been off my game. Before I could pull my gun, Keegan saved me the legal hassle and fired a precise warning shot through the gangbanger's heart. I watched as the agent retrieved a switchblade from his pocket, flicked it open, wiped it on his coat jacket and tossed it on the pavement in front of the prostrate street soldier.

Keegan stared in my direction. "Pobre compañero. Él no debería haberme atacado."

"Yeah, he shouldn't have attacked you," I said. "The Spanish lessons are paying off."

"I know," Keegan smiled. "And the department is even paying for my classes."

Now, Keegan hitched up his trousers and scanned Patel's living room. "This Patel character fixed up some smartphones for an organization in which we have great concerns. He's not one of them, just a nerd trying to make a buck, but he built them a crypto app that we can't break. We've been wiretapping Patel for a while but then he went silent. We want to know where he is. If we can find him, I'm sure we can persuade him to give us the key to the app. But we have to find him first."

Keegan was not only good at firing warning shots but a master of suspect persuasion techniques as well.

"I'll keep you posted," I said, as he walked out the door. He waved goodbye with the raised back of his hand.

Sameer's apartment was cleaner than a man's apartment should be except for the dishes in the sink and the dirty laundry on the bathroom floor. Everything else was neat, which told me that he left in a hurry. Big surprise. I spent a few minutes going through some random mail on his dining room table. A guy like Sameer wouldn't have much important paper. His life was digital.

I also figured that Keegan would have found anything worthwhile. Narcs know all the best hiding places. Still, if I was Sameer, I would have left some insurance behind, an SD card or thumb drive, something that he could use to convince people not to kill him or, if that didn't work, to avenge his murder. It would be the modern-day equivalent of the envelope seen in the 1930's movies addressed to the District Attorney that read: "Open in the event of my death."

The furniture screamed rental. It was contemporary and worked together like the entire place was furnished at the same time by the building management. The tip off was the faux leather couch and matching love seat.

I walked through the apartment slowly and methodically looking for anything that didn't belong. I rummaged through his dresser, clothes closet and his bathroom. His medicine cabinet attested to a stomach that was often upset and a woman who stays over from time to time.

The bed had two nightstands on either side and I checked the one closest to the window. The drawer contained a haphazard jumble of wires and cables, nothing unusual for a techie like Sameer except that one cable had a USB connector on one end but the other end was cut revealing red and green inner wires hanging out. It couldn't connect to a phone or laptop or anything. It was useless junk.

Why not toss it away if it was unusable? Hell, you can buy these charging wires at the 7-Eleven counter next to scratch-off lottery tickets.

I held the useless six-inch cable in my hand and remembered where I had seen this sort of thing before. I was sitting in a Starbucks, actually I was surveilling a lawyer, who stopped in for his afternoon caffeination, when the person next to me plugged the same looking cable into the USB port on his laptop. The other end just hung there like a weeping willow branch as he started typing. When I asked about it, he was proud to show me how he had replaced the USB connector side with a stripped-down thumb drive. He said: "All you have to do is pry open the rubber boot take out the USB connector and replace it with the inside of a thumb drive. Cool, novelty, eh?"

Very cool, Sameer, you clever nerd.

CHAPTER 7

When my brain injury turned me into an old-time dick, I decided to work with it. I bought a trench coat and a fedora. I thought I came off pretty slick but everyone else thought I looked like a forty-something hipster. Street vendors kept trying to sell me kale chips and artisan pickles.

I figured I would only take on old-time gumshoe type cases. You know, cases like blackmail, getting back stolen art stolen for rich folks and finding and destroying nude photos of wayward wives. Well, not much call for these things anymore especially the nude photos. In fact, if you can get these pix to go viral, you might be given your own TV show.

So, I just figured to go with the flow and work whatever came my way. I still had a strong rep and that helped bring in clients. And I do have to admit that being a half white, or is it half black, dick does have its advantages. Most PIs are white because they're retired cops or federal agents which was the case mostly in DC until recently. Despite living in Chocolate City, there's still a reluctance in the black community to trust any kind of law enforcement. So, yeah, I got that bit of cachet going for me. On the other hand, because I'm light skinned, white folks aren't concerned about my talents the way they would be if my skin was darker.

What a world.

One thing I have noticed. In the old detective stories, the pending cases seemed to come together in the end somehow. Everything melded and interconnected like the finale of a *Seinfeld* episode. This has happened to me, too. More than I'm willing to admit because I don't believe in coincidences. But I'm eager to see if my three pending cases will connect. If they do.

One old dick trope that I do try to avoid is getting the crap beat out of me. Those guys could take a beating and get shot at on a regular basis. That's not for me. It didn't work out so well the other day in Sameer's apartment and, come to think of it, and it's kind of why I talk the way I do. Man, that's a crazy story.

The other thing is this. These guys had a strict code of conduct, a tenet by which they lived and acted. Me, too. I always deliver what I promise. I never screw a pal and my word is my bond. That last one puts me in the upper echelon of Washington. I am a one-percenter at something.

I also work alone.

Anyway, just like my 1930's counterparts, I have out-of-the-ordinary people who help me solve cases. They used shoe-shine boys, bookies, and corner newspaper hawkers, and I use their current day counterparts.

I'm on my way to see one of my guys, a geek I went to school with named 256-L12. That's not some made up moniker, well, actually it is, but he decided to change it legally, going to court for reasons which I never understood or inquired too deeply. I recall him telling me that when he changed his name, the telecom company he worked for reluctantly went along but had a helluva time getting the HR department to cut a check to his new name. Their payroll software wouldn't accept the numerals so he rewrote it. I still call him Horace.

I bounced down the stairs of my building, and as I hit the sidewalk Sydney Redbush appeared in front of me as if dropped from the ceiling on wires. "I hope I didn't startle you, Sam."

"Nothing startles me anymore, Syd." I kept smiling and inching away but she grabbed my arm and pulled me into her store. "C'mere. I gotta show you this new art I got for the store."

"I don't really have any tick-tock. I have a meet."

"Only take a minute." As she walked, her long strawberry hair seemed to float behind her like a small plane dragging an advertising banner at the beach. She stopped in front of a statue, an abstract work of two women embracing. You couldn't see their faces but the bodies were definitely women.

"Well, what do you think?"

I knew that if I gave a quick answer it would be rejected, so I made a squinting face that I hoped would convey that I was giving it careful thought. I even walked around the stand so I could take in all sides.

"It's a gas, Syd."

"I like it too," she said. "I think it'll sell well."

I took in the other items on display, mostly books, CDs, and art, but behind the counter there was a door that led to more intimate items for sale. Several people browsed the small shop including a teenage boy and girl who looked into the glass cabinets and giggled.

I turned to leave when she said: "The sculptor who brought this in on consignment says she knows you."

I stopped dead. I'd had my fill of coincidences for the week. I'm topped out.

"Sarah… let me see…" She flipped through a notepad.

"Felder," I said.

"Yeah, that's it. How do you two know each other?"

"We put on the feedbag once. Business."

She smiled. “Pretty lass. If I went that way, I’d …”

I didn’t want to hear the rest. I waved and walked out, headed north on Connecticut Avenue. In the middle of the block I came upon Rudy the Beggar sitting on the pavement leaning against a parking meter. That’s what I call him. His real name is, well, Rudy the Beggar. That’s how he introduces himself. For fifteen years Rudy made a home on the sidewalk in front of FBI headquarters on Pennsylvania Avenue. For all that time, only a handful of people knew that he was a special agent whose job was to watch anyone who lingered in front of the J. Edgar Hoover Building and radio security if they looked like a threat. As a bonus, he was allowed to keep the money that people dropped in his cup. Then, for reasons that nobody knows or is telling, the rules changed and he had to turn that money over to the Bureau. Pissed off at the new edict, he quit.

Now he sits on my block in front of the Teekee Bar mumbling “cheap FBI bastards” to anyone who will listen. I don’t think that Rudy’s crazy, just a tad angry that his talents were no longer valued. Happens to the best of us.

I dropped a five spot in his lap and asked if he’d seen Horace.

“Inside. Went in about a half hour ago. He was carrying a backpack and a Starbucks. He wore a Nationals cap.”

I didn’t need the surveillance details, I just asked so I could funnel Rudy some jack without it seeming like charity.

Horace bought the Teekee Bar when it was a dive. It was dark, moist, and smelled like stale beer and sorrow. He liked it that way, but soon learned that although Washington types talk about dive bars with great affection and some nostalgia, they really don’t want to drink there anymore. They say they want an authentic gin mill experience but that’s malarky. They really want the latest mixology fad made with obscure ingredients. The more foreign the liquor’s pedigree, the better they like it.

Horace had a monthly note that was knocking the stuffing out of him, so he cried uncle. He made the place presentable, even dressing it to the nines and in came a steady group of drinkers. Horace kept one homage to the dive bar tradition. You needed a torch to find your way in. Most patron used the light on their phones.

I walked past a knot of shysters high fiving themselves about winning some case or other. The tallest one of the group had already turned his tie into headwear and was be-bopping around like a Class-A dip.

He corralled my arm. "Come have a drink with us, buddy. We're celebrating."

"No dice," I said. I kept walking.

"C'mon. Have a beer. Don't you guys like to drink?"

"What kind of guy would that be?" I said, as I locked his wrist and twisted it until he fell against another guy who prevented him from hitting his dome on the bar.

"Hey," he slurred. "That's not cool." With his drinking pals on high alert, ready to provide backup, he lunged at me at high speed. Like a toreador, I stepped aside as he whiffed by but not before I grabbed his tie and pulled it down around his neck. I tugged and watched his face turn red. He tried grasping at the tie, but failed. I pulled harder until his eyes were ready to pop. With one last twist, he turned limp and folded.

"Anybody else want to buy me a drink?"

The group looked down at their shoes or straight ahead at the mirror behind the bar. They abandoned their comrade on the floor who was gurgling, coughing, and trying to rise. Some friends.

"What's all this noise?" asked a voice carrying a cardboard box of spirits and placing it behind the bar. The bottles jingled. She looked over the counter at tie-man, then to his friends and then to me. "What the fuck, Sam."

"You're a sight for sore eyes, too, Kerry."

"Get him up," she commanded the group. As they lifted him by his arms, he was just coming to. His head flopped a few times like a sleepy subway rider. "What are you, lawyers?" she asked.

"Yes," one of them said in a low voice.

"You gonna sue us or some shit?"

Kerry was only about five feet tall but she commanded the bar like it was a lunar lander. Her hair was short and brown, eyes like a green laser. She wore silver rings on every finger, as many earrings as her lobe could handle and a pentagram necklace. Kerry had a smokers' voice, but I'd never seen her holding a gasper.

"No. I think we'll just leave," one of them said.

"Okay," Kerry said in a cheerful lilt. "Drinks are on me. Come again. Tell your friends."

She pulled the new bottles out of the carton and distributed them on the shelves. She looked at me in the mirror. "Kids. Right? Just letting off some steam. What's new with you? You here to see Horace? He's in the back."

I groped my way along the wall until I could make out a door that said "Incinerator Room. No Entry." I opened it and walked into a blast of light that made my eyes hurt. Horace was sitting at a desk full of papers and three laptops. He had on his Nationals cap. "Digital age, my ass," he pronounced. "Paperless office. Bullshit."

His foot tapped the floor like a heavy metal drummer. Then it transferred to his fingers and the small portion of his desk that was empty. "It's the government. They always say they want to go computerized, but they still send me paper. All kinds of paper. My suppliers," he said, waving sheets, "want the same thing but they keep sending me paper, too. Even the ones who have gone electronic. It's like they don't trust… ah, fuck it. It's like everything else…"

Horace likes to rant. It's kind of a hobby with him. The funny thing is that he's usually right about whatever he's bent about.

"I guess you're here to talk about the thumb drive." He rooted around his several inboxes until he found it. He plugged it into the laptop on the left. "I've already given it the once-over, so let me show you what I found." He took a pull from his Starbucks cup. "Peet's is better but they're not around here."

He rolled up his sleeves like he was ready to dig a hole and jitterbugged the keys faster than I could follow.

"What's the dope?" I asked.

"First off, I really like the hidden thumb drive made to look like a broken cable. That's some smartass shit." He inched up his glasses on his nose, blinked twice and sniffed. "Now," he said, pointing to the screen, "look at this."

"Your boy laid it all out, didn't try to hide his activity, if you know where to look." He poked at a few lines that looked like computer code. It had strings of words and numbers. It certainly wasn't in any language I was familiar with.

"Bottom line is that he built an app that dropped malware on the user."

"You mean like a virus?"

"Not a bad virus, necessarily. When I say malware, I'm including stuff that you don't know you have. This app was designed to look like a weather app, but it contained a cryptography program so users with the same app could communicate with each other without anyone else being able to listen in."

"So, anyone who downloaded the app had this cryptography program?"

"Yes and no. And that's the brilliance of it. The app really was a weather app, a pretty good one, too, but unless you were given an extra code to unlock the crypto program, that's all you got."

Horace laughed. "With many users downloading the app on their phones, the feds would never know who was using the cryptography program and who wasn't because this code has another feature." He pecked the keys and a new screen appeared. "There's no trace of whoever activates the cryptography code."

"Snazzy."

"You know it," Horace said. He seemed to bounce on his chair.

"How would someone get the code to activate the crypto program?"

"If it were me, I would just give it over the phone in an innocent conversation or just drop the words in an innocuous email. Who would know they meant except the intended recipient?"

"Anything else on the wire? I asked.

"Huh?"

I focused. "Anything else about this I should know about?"

"Oh, yeah," Horace said, as he hit the keys. "I can't give you specific users who downloaded the app but I was able to generate a list of their geographic areas by looking at the ISP addresses. The app was mostly downloaded in Culiacán, Mexico. Mean anything?"

"Capital of the Mexican state of Sinaloa. HQ of the most powerful drug trafficking cartel in the world." I sounded like a Wikipedia entry. "And the second most downloaded place?"

Horace raised his eyebrows. "Here. Washington, DC. Another kind of Capitol."

CHAPTER 8

Even though it was only a few days since Helen Boston had come by the office with her tale of reverse threatening texts, it seemed like weeks. I decided to do some legwork on that case while I let the others percolate. Plus, she gave me a healthy retainer.

I slid by the 2nd District to find out more about the response to her 911 call.

"If it isn't the District's finest dick," said the desk sergeant, a large man named Hooligan which was fitting considering the state of the department these days. He sported a bulbous nose with alky blooms, slicked back hair, shoulders like rock quarry walls and fingers so thick he needed bespoke gloves. If he was sitting for a caricature at a country fair the artist would have a lot to work with.

"Sergeant," I nodded. "A woman named Boston called 911 a few days ago about someone breaking into her house. Can I see the paperwork?"

He stiffened. "Problem?"

"For her; not you. She hired me to look into some threatening texts."

"Were these texts related to the 911?" he said, as he shuffled papers in an inbox.

"Maybe."

He continued to search. "Not here. Everyone's behind in their paperwork." I got the feeling that he would much rather pull open his bottom desk drawer and retrieve his office bottle.

"Who was the responding officer?"

Now he was even more uninterested but kept up the charade. He pushed his fingers across the keyboard. How he managed to click only one key at a time I'll never know. He said: "Two officers took the call." He wrote on a slip of yellow paper and handed it to me.

"Anything else I can do for you?"

"You don't like me, do you?" I said.

He sat back in his chair and templed his fingers which didn't have any light between them. Hooligan stared up at the ceiling. It was cracked like a spider had spun his web and glued it there. Several bulbs in the fixture were kaput.

"It's not that I don't like you personally, Marlowe. I don't like PIs in general. They tend to muck up the machinery, if you know what I mean." He paused and looked directly at me. "I like PIs about as much as I like reporters."

"I get it. You don't want civilians looking into what you're doing, maybe finding out that you did something small and blowing it out of proportion." I smiled.

"Exactly."

"If I find something queer, I'll sweep it under the rug. How's that?"

"You're a good one, Marlowe."

I stepped outside and called the number that he gave me.

"Officer Selden."

I explained that I wanted to talk with him about Boston. I emphasized that there was nothing amiss and that Hooligan gave me his number. "Can we meet somewhere? I can come to you."

"Sure. I'm sitting in the station."

Fucking Hooligan.

I walked back inside. Hooligan shot a smirk and waved me through. I thought I heard a knee slap.

The room reminded me of my high school cafeteria. Plastic chairs of various pastel colors lined up under a line of Formica covered tables. Several unis had their heads down, some writing on papers, others bent over laptops. A bright face looked up and I could just read the 'S' on his name tag. I walked over and extended my hand. "Marlowe."

"Selden."

He looked about sixteen years old. I thought I saw some zits ready to make an entrance.

"What can I do for you, Mr. Marlowe?"

"Did your squad car boogie over to Macomb and thirty-fifth for a burglary in progress, complainant was a Helen Boston?"

He laughed and checked his laptop. "Call came in at 2032. Code 1... On the scene at 2034... ... private home." He read for a few more seconds and looked at me. "Another unit rolled up about a minute later. We met the woman; she said someone had broken in. We checked the downstairs, the windows, back door. The usual. Did a walk-around and didn't see anything. I gave her a card and told her to call if she had any other trouble. Then we went 10-8."

"Give me the low down on what's not in your report."

He took a step back and his body went stiff. "What do you mean?"

"I'm not trying to jam you."

"Hooligan said not to trust you. And he said you talk funny."

"He's right about the second part. It's a long story. Boston's been getting threatening texts. It might be related to the break-in. And by the way, Hooligan's a fucking twit."

"Copy that."

His face opened, and he looked even more like a teenager.

"What do you want to know?"

"Was there anything unusual about what you saw or heard?"

"There was one thing," he said. "She asked us if we saw a woman running away from the house. I told her that I hadn't. I looked at my backup and he shook his head. Then I asked if she suspected the burglar was a woman and she said 'never mind.' I gave her my card, told her to call if she thought of anything else. On my way out, I asked her again about the woman. She laughed it off and said she was thinking about something else."

"What did you make of it?"

"Nothing. People get confused during times of stress, but the next day, I saw on the lookouts that a resident living a few blocks away had seen a woman that same night standing on the corner for longer than seemed right. By the time our car drove by she was gone. It was about the same time as the break-in call."

"Nobody connected the two incidents?"

"No. I still don't. People stand on corners all the time. We live in the age of Uber."

Any description?"

He checked his laptop. "White, tall, nicely dressed. That's it."

"Can I see the complainant's name and address?"

"Public domain," he muttered, as he spun the laptop around for me.

As I turned to leave, he said: "Squad cars."

"What?"

"You used the term squad car. We haven't called our units squad cars, probably not since my grandfather pounded a beat in the 1930s. Now we call them cruisers."

"Yes, I know."

CHAPTER 9

The man who answered the door gave me the jittery up-and-down. I flashed my buzzer and ID card. Only the card is kosher, but if I show the tin quick enough, it gets the job done. The one thing I'm religious about is not saying I'm from the cops.

"Who are you with?" he said. A little dog squeezed between his legs, yapping up a storm. "Samson. Get back," he said, as he pushed the dog inside. His hands were bony and I could see the blue-green veins.

I concentrated on my words. This was going to be a tough enough interview even without my crazy talk, although this guy may be old enough to maybe know the lingo. "I'm a private investigator, and I understand that you called the police about a woman who was loitering on the street."

"Ah, yes. The police. Come in detective."

Detective. Close enough.

"Sit down," he said, pointing to a couch covered in threads of dog hair. He plopped into a rocker and Samson jumped into his lap.

"How do you like being a police officer?" He patted the dog's head.

"I am not a police officer. I'm a private investigator. A private detective some call it."

"What now? Who are you with?"

I retrieved my notebook from my jacket pocket. "Mr. Weletson. You called 911 about a woman loitering outside. When the police drove by, she was gone. Can you tell me what prompted your phone call?"

"Phone call? You're with Verizon, son?"

No, sir. I'm a private investigator. I'd like to talk about the woman outside the other night. She was tall, blonde, well dressed and … "

"Yes, yes. My wife, god rest her soul, she was blonde. Always dressed well." The dog closed his eyes, his head swaying as the man stroked it. "Would you like some tea?"

Poor soul.

"No, thank you, sir. I have to be going."

I flipped closed my notebook and started to rise when he said, "I was just screwing with you. My wife said I have a bit of mean streak. I like to think of it as being mischievous. Now," he said, "what can I do for you?"

Pretty damn funny. And convincing.

"Why did you call the cops?"

"This is a residential neighborhood. No stores or anything commercial for several blocks. It's unusual for people to be standing on the corner. Also, I know everyone who lives her. She didn't look familiar to me." His voice was steady.

"Maybe she was visiting someone."

"Could be but I doubt it." He rose after depositing Samson on the floor. He showed me to the front window. "Look. That's the only street light. It's dark here at night. No one stands outside alone when they're waiting for a ride. Most wait inside until they get a text or see the car."

He had a point.

"Well, like I said, it was dark. I could tell that she was tall for a woman, maybe five-eight or nine, slim build, blonde. I didn't see her face but I had a feeling that she was nervous. She paced, looked at her watch. And that's another thing."

"What's that?"

"She wasn't looking at her phone. Everyone takes out their phone even if they have only a few seconds to kill. It's an addiction. Not only that, but people who call Uber or taxicabs like to track the driver. She didn't do that. I thought that was… well… different."

"Did you see who picked her up?"

He rocked forward and stopped. "A 2018 Dodge Challenger SRT Hellcat. Black. 707-hp supercharged Hemi V-8. Flared fenders and wide tires. It's got some power. And the full-throated sound when it sped away. Can't beat it." He paused. "I couldn't see inside, though. Tinted windows."

"You know cars, eh?"

"I was a street racer back in the day. Shelby's, Camaros. My pals and I used to race down Route 301 in PG county. Good times. I still keep up, but my street racing days are long over. I'm glad to see that muscle cars are making a comeback. Not great for the environment, I know, but they're beautiful machines."

He pointed to photos on the wall. They were mostly teens in jeans, cigs dangling from their kissers leaning on souped-up wheels. The dollies had up-dos.

"That's me," he said, his lean finger landing on a black & white of a hep cat sitting on the hood of a car. "1953. First year of the Corvette Stingray. 327, small block V8, 4-speed. She flew."

"Sweet."

"Good times," he said. "What's your interest in the woman on the street, if you don't mind me asking?"

"Not sure. It might have something to do with an incident a few blocks away."

"The Boston woman?

"How'd you…"

"Word gets around. Tight neighborhood. Lots of gossip."

"What have you heard about it?"

"Someone broke in. She called the cops. They responded and didn't find anyone."

"Are there a lot of break-ins around here?"

"Very few. People here have alarms and barking dogs."

"And neighbors who look out the window," I said.

He laughed. "That, too." Samson yapped as I got up to leave. Muscle cars, classic Corvettes and here I was pushing my atomic-powered Civic around town. At least I never worry about anyone glomming it. I called Boston to see if she was available. She said she'd be home later so I decided to cool my heels at a gin mill named Pegasus on Wisconsin Avenue for a tightener.

I settled on a bar stool and the bartender looked up from pumping a glass into the scrubber. "Yes, sir. What can I get you?" He wiped his hands and frisbeed a beer coaster onto the bar. It was a place for serious drinkers most of whom were already at cruising altitude.

"I'll have a see-through," I said.

"Coming right up."

He reached for a glass then froze as if he had been stuffed by a taxidermist. He started up again and retrieved his phone. His fingers blitzed across the screen. "I'm sorry sir but I don't know what that is." On his forearms, he had a skull with snakes oozing out the eyes. Maybe they were worms.

"Martini, straight up, twist. Beefeater."

"Got it."

"Let the vermouth take a run-out."

"Pardon?"

"Very dry."

He laughed and proceeded to build the drink. I looked to my right, and a man and woman were cracking up. Day drinking is becoming a lost art, but these folks were at the tip of a possible revival. It's not about getting loaded but about enjoying the day with a low-level buzz. It takes skill and practice. I thought these lovey-doveys had it mastered until she slipped off the stool and landed on her keister. He helped her up, hoisted her on the perch as if it was an everyday occurrence. Probably was. He glanced over at me and smiled. She looked none the worse for wear and they continued to drink and joke around.

"The name's Clarence," the bartender said as he placed my drink on the coaster.

"Sam."

We shook.

"It's on me," he said, as he knuckled the bar. The worms or snakes slithered when his muscles flexed. "For the education."

"Mud in your eye," I said, as I took a sip. I felt the gin frost my gullet spreading cold joy as it descended.

Clarence took a towel to several glasses. He held each of them up to the light for a last check and then lined them up with their brothers and sisters. He scoped the bar up and down to make sure everyone had what they needed. He diddled the computer/cash register then turned around secure in the knowledge that everything was up to date.

"So," he said. "Did anyone ever tell you that you have a unique way of talking?"

"Nope," I said, as I finished my drink. "Never heard that. Let me have a beer. I gotta ramble."

He smirked and knew he was being had. I liked that.

"Any beer in particular?" he asked, as he rattled off the names on the tap handles.

"Whatever is the coldest."

He pulled the stick on an IPA that sported a hedgehog as its logo. "They're all cold but I think you'll like this."

He was right. It was hoppy, refreshing and as cold as a brass toilet seat in Juneau. I tossed a ten-spot on the bar, waved good-bye and wheeled for the door. The couple on the end were still trading spit.

I nosed my bucket west and found myself outside Helen Boston's cave in two minutes. It was a two-story affair where the brick facade was painted white. The lawn was bigger than a postage stamp but not by much. Pink azaleas lined the front. Green shutters bracketed the windows and a flagstone walkway guided you to the front door. The air smelled sweet.

After our initial meeting in my office we had talked on the phone a few times, but I wanted to see her in person at her house. Since talking with Weletson I harbored a longshot hunch that the break-in that ended with an extra gun in my possession and the antsy, loitering woman a few blocks away were connected. Same night, same timing… maybe the odds weren't that big after all.

I rapped on the door. No answer. I rang the bell. No answer. I stepped back from the house and dialed Boston as I watched the windows for any signs of life. My call was met by a cheery voicemail greeting.

I twisted the knob and the door opened.

"Hello... Hello... It's Marlowe… Ms. Boston?" Sometimes your voice echoes in a house. Sometimes it just dies. This was one of those times.

Most PIs lock the front door so nobody can enter and get the drop on you as you explore. My experience has taught me otherwise. I always leave the door open in case I have to lam it. I don't want to be one of those people you see in the movies with the bad guy bearing down as you fumble with the door lock. Fingers twitching, arms shaking trying in a vain attempt to make for open air. I made sure the door was wide open before I headed for the living room.

I continued to call out as I footed through the first floor. Living room, dining room, kitchen, den. Basements are not my favorite, but I gave a quick galump down the uneven wooden stairs and eyed the room. It smelled of laundry and dampness, but no sign of Boston.

As I reached the second and top floor I glimpsed into the bedroom and there she was. On the bed. Not moving. She had a towel wrapped around her body and one around her head. She was on her back. I walked in past the en-suite bathroom and felt warm, moist air.

I felt for a pulse. Faint. I gently slapped her checks. No response. I searched for bruises, bumps, bullet holes or stab wounds, anything to tell me why I was standing over her with my stomach full of creeping bugs. I spied her phone on the nightstand and I pocketed it.

I called 911 then performed CPR. It might not do any good but it kept me busy while I waited for the EMTs to arrive.

I didn't have to open the door for them.

CHAPTER 10

Dead clients are bad for business.

Not only can't they pay, but I always feel obligated to finish the job. Other snoopers close the books when a client croaks. Not me. Maybe that makes me better than the rest of the gumshoes around but not enough to brag about it. Maybe it's about closure. I dunno.

I stood in the waiting room when a doctor, who looked too young to be a doctor, pulled me aside. "Are you related?"

"No, but ..."

"This is a police matter," I heard someone growl behind me. I swiveled to see Special Agent Harry Keegan. His stooge Billy was smacking the side of the coffee machine until the security officer told him to stop. Billy flashed his badge and I heard the SO say: "Then you should know better." Stooge-boy slinked into a chair and studied his phone.

"In that case," the doctor continued, "all I can tell you right now is that the patient," he referred to a tablet, "Helen Boston, is deceased. I'd say overdose. We'll know more when the toxicology report is completed. I've notified MPD. Are you city police?"

"Federal," Keegan said.

"Well, then. You'll have to wait your turn," he said, as he excused himself.

"I know why I'm here," I told Keegan. "What's your interest?"

"Drugs. As always."

"You think Helen Boston was involved in drugs?"

"Can't say."

"How did you know that she was even here? "

"Can't say."

"What can you say?"

"That our paths keep crossing."

I looked him in the eye. "You've been tracking me, haven't you?"

Keegan laughed and snapped his fingers at his sidekick. "We're leaving."

Before he could take a step, I grabbed his arm. He gave me a 'go-ahead-and-take-a-swing- and-see-where-it-gets-you' look. The waiting room came alive and the security officer approached. He was bigger than the two of us put together. "Problem, gents?" His voice shook my eyelashes.

I released Keegan's arm, and he and Billy sauntered away without a single word. The SO gave me the once over. "We're not going to have any trouble here, are we sir?"

"Not from me," I replied.

"You on the job?"

"No. Private."

"I figured as much. Nicer clothes. I know that dude Keegan. DEA. He comes around every once in a while. I don't like his attitude. Kinda pushy, you know?"

"I dig."

"One time the EMTs brought in this teenager who had OD'd. Keegan was on him like white on rice, wouldn't leave the kid alone even as he was being wheeled into the ER. He badged me but I wouldn't have any of it. I told him that this was my house and I didn't give a damn who he was. He could wait outside like everyone else. He kept trying to push his way in so he could talk to the kid. I couldn't believe it. The kid was dying and all he kept screaming was 'where did you get the drugs?' Turns out it was more than a simple OD. The kid was a mule with about twenty bags of heroin in his stomach. One of the bags must have broken. Poor kid. He had enough trouble without this badge-heavy asshole up in his grille asking shit while he's trying to make his peace with the almighty."

"That's sounds like Keegan, alright."

"You have a nice day, okay? And sorry about your friend."

I nodded.

"By the way, next time I won't stop you from hitting him." He smiled and resumed his position against the far wall.

His words stuck in my head: 'Your friend.'

I grabbed a hack back to Helen's house to retrieve my heap. When we rolled up, the property was decorated in crime scene tape and coppers were milling about. Neighbors stood on their front lawns, pointed their fingers in the direction of the hubbub and talked in hushed tones.

I saw Sergeant Hooligan standing on the sidewalk with a cup of coffee. At least it looked like coffee might be in it.

"What brings you into the sunlight?" I asked, as we saw each other at the same time.

"That's your car, isn't it?" he said. "We checked the tags."

"That's solid police work, Hooligan."

He took a sip and squinted. "Business a little slow?" he said, as he eyed my dented and scarred chariot.

"I need to get going," I said, as I felt for the keys in my jacket pocket.

"Not so fast," Hooligan said. "Someone wants to talk to you."

A woman the size of a small box truck angled past Hooligan with her hand extended. She wore a grey pantsuit with a matching opened vest that she kept tugging to the center of her torso. She wore gold earrings that could double for hula hoops.

"I'm Detective Janice Pemberton, homicide. I'd like to ask you a few questions."

"Sam Marlowe." If her skin wasn't black, I'd swear that her hand was made of steel.

"I understand that you're a PI," she said. "You've had a few dings on your record and..."

"Nothing stuck," I said quickly.

"Be that as it may, according to Sergeant Hooligan, you have been known to play fast and loose."

"He's a schmuck," I said, as I smiled and waved at Hooligan who couldn't hear us.

He smiled back and waved.

"Everybody knows that, but what we'd like to know why your car was here and you weren't. What was your relation to Helen Boston?"

"She asked me to look into threatening texts she'd been getting."

"Now she's dead at Sibley Hospital, and ..." She raised her eyebrows and took a breath. "Mr. Marlowe," she said, pulling her vest together and crossing her arms over the gap. "I'm guessing that you were the last one to see her alive."

"Technically speaking. I wanted to get some more dope from her so I called to see when I could come over. When I got here about an hour ago, she was laying on the bed. I thought she had bought the big sleep but I clocked a faint pulse. I called 911."

"When you say 'dope' you mean information, right?"

"That's flat."

She exhaled a long breath.

"What happened next?"

"I held her paw on the way to the emergency room. You know the rest."

"Uh, huh. I want to know what happened before 'the rest." She rubbed the back of her neck.

"You think I cooled her?"

"Did you touch anything else before you checked her pulse," she asked, with a smirk.

"Maybe the banister, a few door knobs. I don't know. I didn't pay attention because I didn't expect to find her almost croaked."

'Uh, huh. You said that she was receiving threatening phone calls."

"Texts."

"Did you actually see the texts?"

"She had held the phone up to me and I piped them with my very own peepers."

"I'll take that as a 'yes.' When CSID checked the house, they found her purse but not her phone. Would you know anything about that?"

"I know from nothing."

"Mr. Marlowe," she said. "You're not an easy man to talk with."

"I get that a lot."

"Would you mind if we searched your car?"

I glanced over and saw that it was being yellow ribboned like a Christmas present. "I laughed. "Is that the price of removing the tape?"

"Pretty much."

I gave her my card. "Call when you're finished. Would you mind wiping away the fingerprint powder when you're done?"

"Absolutely. We'll get it detailed at the city's expense." She pointed to two officers then to my heap. They hoisted their evidence boxes and footed toward the curb. The cops won't find anything more incriminating other than a Kit-Kat bar and maybe a loose reefer. Both are legal in the District last time I checked.

"I know you're a busy man, Mr. Marlowe, but I would stick around town if I were you."

I nodded and hoofed it in the direction of Pegasus. It seemed as good a place as any to wait for my boiler to be processed. Besides, now I know the bartender.

The lights were dim and the lushes had arrived for their after-work numbing session. The going-at-it couple was gone, and their spots were filled by a brace of young fellows with keycards tethered to their belts. Either they were drinking fast or the barkeep was tending slow because empty glasses with foam linings were taking up a large swath of counter real estate. An older man at the other end sat alone reading a newspaper with rumpled dollar bills in front of him.

"Back again, Sam?" Clarence said. "Another see-through?"

"No. Jameson, double. Rocks."

He cocked his head. "That's a simply worded order. Problem?" He checked a glass for spots then scooped ice into it. He upended the bottle for a long count resulting in a heavy pour usually reserved for regulars and big tippers.

"Someone I know just died"

His features fell. "I'm so sorry to hear that. Did you know this person well?"

"Not really. She was a… client."

He grabbed the bottle of Jameson and filled a shot glass. "Here's to…" He looked to me for a name.

"Helen," I managed.

"To Helen," he said, as he knocked it back. "How did she.. er… go, if I may ask?"

"Murder."

His eyes widened and his back went stiff.

"Seriously. Around here?"

"Few blocks away. The police are there now. I'm watching the clock spin while they toss my buggy."

Clarence stifled a gasp. Even the snakes or worms on his arms seemed to recoil.

"Yes, I am a suspect." I announced boldly, as I let the whiskey stream down my throat. "Don't worry. I didn't do it. A drug overdose, but I know it's murder. Someone dosed her but good."

Clarence turned his head when the fellows at the end of the bar bounced their heavy beer mugs on the bar. The message was clear. Clarence pulled two more brews, walked them over and cleared the empties. He slowly moved back in front of me.

"Soooo, murder, eh?" It seemed like the best he could do.

"Dead as a log." I drained the glass. The whiskey gave me a glow. "Another."

Clarence obliged. He slid the drink in my direction. I held the glass up to the light and watched the light patterns ebb and flow for a minute. "I feel like it might be my fault. She had asked me to look into a personal situation and maybe I didn't jump on the action fast enough. I'm a private dick."

His hands twisted the bar-rag until it dripped water on his shoes. He let loose a "Geeze" and tossed the towel away.

"Private investigator." I jolted the brown liquid and tapped the bar. Before I could blink, a fresh drink appeared.

"And the fucking cops. They're useless. They couldn't find a fat man in a phone booth." As soon as I said it, I realized that he probably had never seen a phone booth except in old movies.

I was getting tight as a vault, and I liked it. I checked my phone. No calls from the cops. They're not going to jangle me. Then I touched my pocket to make sure I still had Helen's phone.

"Do you know what the closure rate on murder is in this town?" I asked. My tongue felt big as a pillow and my lips belonged to someone else.

Clarence shook his head.

"Less than 70 percent, and they only get that high because most killings are a relative or acquaintance. When it comes to those who had no connection to the victim the number swings much lower." I felt like I had mouthed a lot of words in a short time.

"Fuck it," I said, as I threw a couple of Jacksons on the bar. "I gotta hit the wind."

"You okay to drive? I can call a cab."

"Unfortunately, I'll be cold sober by the time I reach my ride."

The street was full of people, and I tried not to bump into anyone. Several blocks away, a single cop car still guarded the scene. When I peered inside my wreck, it looked like I had parked underneath a volcano. The inside sported a thick veneer of black fingerprint powder. Not only that, but the reefer was missing, and the Kit-Kat bar was wedged into the ashtray.

Fucking flatfoots.

CHAPTER 11

Despite a hangover, I was sitting at my kitchen table getting a head start on next week's drinking. Why not? I'm not only the prime suspect in a murder rap, but it may have been my fault that the person died. For good measure, a G-man is tailing me because he thinks I know more than he does.

And he's right.

I know that a seemingly innocuous weather app is getting a crypto code into the hands of Mexican drug dealers. I also know that they're using it to phone people on Capitol Hill. I'm pretty sure that I can figure out the connection if I don't get bumped off first. I'm guessing that each side would call 'dibs' if they knew what I knew.

I'm also fretting about the case that my downstairs neighbor Goldie sprung on me. Finding a photographer who may or may not be a con artist. I decided to hold off on that one in the hopes that it was all just a big misunderstanding. On the other hand, will someone else get dusted because I acted too late? Sometimes I'd like to be somebody else for just a while.

My head felt two sizes too big for my hair. I clawed a fistful of ibuprofens and drove them down my craw with a beer. I followed it with another brew just to make sure the pellets reached their destination. For now, the beer helped more than the pills.

The first order of business, other than a greasy breakfast to counter my bottle flu, was to visit Horace again and see what he could find on Helen's phone. I grabbed a BLT and a side of fries at a nearby joint and aimed for the Teekee Bar. I nodded to Rudy who was ever vigilant in his post on the sidewalk and stepped inside. Horace was sitting at the bar downing joe from a mug that read "World's #2 Dad."

I've known Horace a long time but I never knew he was a father of any ranking. In fact, I hardly know anything personal about him nor he about me, and that's how we like it. I only know that he did a nickel in Lorton and faded all but a year for a non-violent offense. The records are sealed at the highest government levels, and I never wanted to dig deeper.

"Don't bring that in here, you lunatic," Horace screamed, as I waved Boston's phone in the air.

"It's jake," I said. "I turned it off."

"Whew."

It was a rule that I had to turn off my phone or any other phone associated with me in Horace's presence. I never asked why and he never explained. Without saying another word, he led me to a room in the basement, where he turned on the lights and bolted the door behind us. The room was the size of an entry-level, storage room, the type where divorced husbands park their meager possessions because they're now living in a furnished studio apartment.

On the left was a wooden workbench loaded with more electronic gear than a moon lander. A table on the opposite wall held a fully-stocked bar and frat-boy fridge. The walls, ceiling, floor, and door were covered in sheet metal. I heard a soft hum and felt cool air.

I had never been in this room before today.

"Show me the phone," he said. He turned it on and turned it towards me. "See, no bars."

"We're in what's called a Faraday cage. Phone signals can't get in and none can get out. It allows me to work on phones without having to worry about being tracked, calling a number, whatever. Even the GPS signal can't reach us. By the way," he said, "I had a hunch that there might be more information on the thumb drive you gave me, so I had another go at it."

He hooked a beer from the fridge and offered me one. I waved him off. "Your guy Sameer installed a trap door in the crypto program."

"Come again?"

"They used to be more common than they are now, but some of my freelance colleagues still use them. When you write a program for a client, you add a subroutine that can make the program malfunction or self-destruct if you don't get paid. There are two kinds," he said.

Horace is aces, but he has a Messianic complex. He loves to explain and I listen. That's the price I pay for his technical expertise. I launched into my BLT and snatched a beer from the chill box after all.

"The first kind blows up the program if you don't get paid by a certain date. The programmer must turn off the destruction code before a designated time. The more common time bomb is open ended. At any time, the programmer has a backdoor entrance to stop the program, force the program to uninstall itself or make it misbehave to the point where the user is so frustrated that he makes his payment."

I shoveled some fries into my yap. "Can the user override this?"

"Even if he knew it was there, which he probably doesn't, the programs have a suicide feature. If someone other than the programmer tries to fiddle with it, it disappears. Have you heard of ransomware? It's similar. Hackers trick users into clicking a link or attachment, usually in an email that looks like it's from someone they know, and that installs the malware. The malware locks your hard drive until you pay up. If you don't, your hard drive and everything on it goes poof."

"What did Sameer install?"

"It was the kind where he can deactivate the program. Sameer can kill the program anytime and he can do it on line or through the phone network."

"Can you do it?"

"No. It requires a password that only Sameer knows and it's DoD hardened. Even NSA couldn't break it."

I put my sandwich down and took a swig of beer. "I'm wondering if Sameer's disappearance has to do with the trap door. Maybe the cartel didn't pay him or they had a falling out and Sameer threatened to destroy the program."

"Possible," Horace said. He retrieved another beer from the fridge, placed it under his t-shirt and twisted off the cap. "Now, let's see what's on the dead woman's phone." I saw him wince as he said the word 'dead.'

For the next few minutes all he said was 'huh' and 'so' as he fingered the phone. I took the opportunity to finish my beer. He sat back in his chair, and now it was my turn to ask 'huh' and 'so.'

"She had the weather app installed on her phone, but let me check one thing." He attached a white cable to the phone. The other end went to a laptop. He studied the screen and pointed to a jumble of numbers and letters. They meant less to me than if they were in Hungarian. "This could be why she got those crazy texts. The crypto program was activated and it looks like it destabilized the phone. She was receiving bits and pieces of texts from who knows where."

"Did she activate the crypto phone program with a password?"

"It doesn't look like it. I think it was some random event, a glitch, or maybe Sameer did something to cause the program to go nuts."

"She wasn't part of the cartel crypto-phone group? She wasn't talking to the cartel?"

"No. Wrong place, wrong time - cell phone style."

"A modern-day twist on a classic story," I said. "And she was biffed for it."

Horace reached into a white, plastic paint bucket containing wires, cables, and all manner of electronic devices. "Here, I got what you asked for. Take this flip-phone. Very retro. You'll be very popular. It's untraceable and there's no GPS." He tossed it to me.

"What about incoming calls from people who have my old number?

"Forwarded. Still untraceable."

I knew better than to push for an explanation. If Horace says it's cool, then it's straight from the deep freeze.

"One last thing," he said, as he opened the door and turned off the lights. "You know who the Sinaloa Cartel is, right?"

I didn't answer. I was busy checking out the phone, flipping it open and closed like a child with a new toy. Maybe I didn't want to hear what he was going to say next with his professorial air.

"They're the largest, richest and most powerful drug cartel in the world. They've killed thousands of people. They're not just in Mexico but all over the world. It's the organization that Joaquín Guzmán headed. You know, El Chapo. He's in prison but it hasn't slowed them down one bit. They're not afraid of anyone."

"I dig. I watched the Netflix series."

"This isn't funny, Sam. No one will think less of you if you walk away. The client is dead."

"Truth be told, Horace, I'm more afraid of the mooks in Congress."

CHAPTER 12

Before I entered the cop house, I pitched my burner phone in the trash can outside. I made my way toward the metal detector portico that led to the interrogation rooms. I tossed my keys, wallet, pen, notebook, and a pen knife in the tray before walking through. "No phones allowed," Hooligan shouted from behind his desk in his chair to which he was glued.

"Don't have one," I said.

"Times must really be tough for you. Okay, step through. Room 2. Detective Pemberton is already there." I held up the knife to make sure he saw it. "Keep it," he said.

I stashed everything back in my pockets knowing full well that if I had brought in my phone, they would have kept it for safekeeping – and gotten what they could off it. I also didn't want them knowing that I'm sporting a throwaway blower.

Pemberton greeted me in the hallway. "Thank you for coming, Mr. Marlowe."

"Did I have a choice?"

"There's always a choice, but each has a consequence."

She wore the same pantsuit style at the crime scene but in a different color. Instead of hoop earrings her lobes sported studs in the shape of tiny police shields. The room had a rectangular desk with a handcuff bar on top. Sunlight showered through the grated windows and produced long, shaggy shadows.

The place smelled of disinfectant.

"Mr. Marlowe," she said, as she tossed a file folder on the table. "Let's go over the timeline again."

I recapped my day for her, especially the part about drinking at Pegasus, seeing a woman plunge off her stool and the bartender's tattoos that were either worms or snakes. "Clarence, he's the mixer, builds a fine martini. You should dip your beak there some time."

"I don't drink."

"Of course not."

She rose and walked to the window gripping the cage as she stood looking out. Without turning around, she asked, "One thing still bothers me. Ms. Boston's phone. We didn't find it. No one is without their phone these days."

"I don't always carry mine."

I heard a laugh on the other side of the one-way glass. I knocked on the mirror. "Hooligan, is that you?"

I could see her nostrils flare as she whipped around to face me and the mirror.

"Damn it," she said, as she strode to the door, flung it open and left the room. When she returned, I asked: "Who else is out there… besides Hooligan? I don't think he likes me very much."

She frowned. "The viewing area is empty. It's just us."

"I don't know what else to tell you."

"The ME said that Ms. Boston died of a drug overdose. Heroin and fentanyl. Know anything about that?"

"She didn't strike me as a hophead."

"What did she strike you as?"

"Scared. Someone who thought the cops wouldn't take her concerns seriously. That's why she came to me."

She shot a hard smile my way, and it almost knocked me over. She put on reading glasses and opened the file folder. "You did a tour in Somali, 1993 to 1994… Air Force intelligence… blah, blah, blah… general discharge." She looked at me and raised her eyebrows. "General discharge?"

"The Air Force and I didn't see eye to eye. We agreed that it would be best for both parties to split amicably."

"What happened?"

"Isn't it there?" I knew it wasn't. The records had strangely disappeared. "What does this have to do with Ms. Boston?"

"I'm just trying to understand a little more about what makes you tick, Mr. Marlowe."

"What makes me tick is doing the right thing, and calling out those who don't." I didn't mean to raise my voice. I took a breath. "I'm sorry about Ms. Boston. Maybe if I had worked her case sooner, we wouldn't be having this sit-down."

"You think that the texts had something to do her murder?"

"Don't fuck with me, Detective. You and I both know that it's all connected… the texts, the 911 call about the intruder, and her knock off."

In an instant, she took on an angry pan. She put both mitts on the table and leaned into me. "It's no longer your concern. It's our case. You got that? So, if you have her phone, I'd… "

"I don't have it."

"I could get a warrant to search your place, but you're not stupid enough to keep it there."

You got that right. I also have a gun, a lead on the woman who might own it and, yeah, I got Boston's phone.

"Marlowe, are you listening to me?"

"My ears still have room."

I saw her nod subtly at the window, but she didn't see me clock it.

"That's all. You can go."

Outside the building, I jammed my paw in the trash can to retrieve my phone. I hadn't seen Hooligan standing there puffing on a coffin nail at the side of the building until he said, "Do you need a coupla bucks, Marlowe?" I palmed the phone so he couldn't see it.

"Things are tough all over. Hold on to your steady gig, Hooligan."

He flipped the butt into the bushes and went inside laughing and coughing his head off. I hoofed across the street and stood behind a wide tree so I could eyeball the cop shop entrance without being seen.

A minute later, I saw a man strut out, put on sunglasses and enter a car that was parked next to a fire plug.

DEA's finest. Harry Keegan.

CHAPTER 13

I'm sure that DEA agent Keegan was watching through the one-way glass, and the only way he could know I was there is if someone clued him that I was coming.

I had to get him off my tail. My new phone won't betray me, thanks to Horace, but I checked the underside of my heap by the back-right wheel well. It's a favorite spot for feds, and sure enough there was a GPS tracker held fast by a magnet. Keegan ain't dumb so I checked the other wells, the trunk and even the gas cap. Nada, but I did find another tracker under the hood. You find one, even two tailers, and you think you're safe. Did he go for three? Not that I could see. Budget cuts probably.

The solution to dumping pingers is not as simple as deep-sixing them in the Potomac. I wanted the advantage of Keegan not knowing that I knew I was being followed. It's like discovering that your office is bugged. You can feed listeners bogus info which is both useful and fun.

I decided to put one of the trackers under the back tire of a UPS truck that was making a delivery to a nearby store. When the driver pulled out a few minutes later, I watched as the device reported a satisfying crunch leaving a tortilla of transistors imbedded in asphalt. Keegan would figure that I found that one and destroyed it, but he still had the other one in play.

I held it in my hand as I watched the traffic flow on Wisconsin Avenue.

Right on time, the Chinatown Bus rolled by. It makes daily trips from DC to New York City's Chinatown. It's a cheap, no-frills tin can that was established to ferry Asian immigrants wanting to visit relatives. No bus stations, no advertising, drivers barely speak English, and the only amenity is that each aisle seat has a plastic bag hanging off the side for trash. The packed bus stopped at the light and I waved at the driver. He opened the door.

"Marlowe. What you want? Go New York?"

Billy Wong earned a sheepskin from the London School of Economics and speaks high-tone British English. I'm not sure why he put on the voice act or why he was wearing a Hawaiian shirt that was three sizes too large. He's a millionaire with geetus up the wazoo. He and a few pals started the service and some days he just wants to sit behind the big wheel and drive. Today was one of those days.

I stepped in and looked over the crowd. It used to be only Asians, but now it's cult transportation and the hepcats ride it. Everyone had earbuds except the older riders who were reading Chinese newspapers and eating pork buns.

Nobody paid any attention as I talked to Billy.

"Sure, sure. No problem," he said.

He squawked something in Chinese to a man in the first row who took the tracker and placed it under his seat then returned to his newspaper.

"You go. Bus be late," he said, as he shooed me off.

With Keegan on a wild good chase I decided to head back to the office to catch up on my paperwork.

Who was I kidding? I didn't have any paperwork. I did, however, have a solid plan to study the inside of my eyelids for a few hours.

I closed the blinds and curtains to keep out the day's remaining light. The street dinned the usual noise but that didn't bother me. I finished the glass of bourbon that had been idling on the night table, followed it with a brace of ear plugs, and I was primed to meet Morpheus.

A short nap is the best way to restart the day, unless someone rouses you with a gun barrel pressed against your left temple.

"Get up, asshole."

I opened my eyes. All I could see was a belt buckle with a bald eagle stooped to conquer on an American flag background. "Up, slowly," the voice said. He had a perfect Midwestern accent which meant no accent at all.

I pushed myself up on my right arm and sat with my legs hanging over the bed. I rubbed my face trying to focus. The gunsel had a military watch cap with eye holes cut out. There was no opening for his mouth.

"How do you eat snacks?" I asked.

"Shut the hell up and listen." His everyman news anchor's voice was muffled by the cotton fabric.

Your interest in Helen Boston ends now," he said. "You will no longer have a concern in the matter. This is your last warning."

"Last warning? I never heard the first one."

The muzzle of the gat whipped my cheek and caught a hunk of soft flesh on the front sight. I fingered the area above my mouth and came away with blood.

"Damn, it," I mumbled. "Who the hell are you?"

"If I wanted you to know, I wouldn't be wearing this mask, now would I?"

"Good point," I said. "Who doesn't want me to have an interest in who killed Boston?"

"You mean who hired me to deliver this message?"

"That's exactly what I mean." My face felt hot where the gun smacked me.

"They wish to remain anonymous." The belt buckle reflected a hint of light that sneaked through a gap in the drapes. "But I can tell you this. They don't fuck around. They will kill you if you continue the way you're going."

"Would you be the one to knock me off?"

"Possibly."

"So, we're kind of building a relationship here, you and me."

"I have the feeling that you're not taking this seriously," he said.

"It's what the headshrinkers call a defense mechanism. I'm unable or unwilling to process in an adult manner a dire or life-threatening situation so I make a joke. It's Psych 101."

I think he stifled a laugh, but it was hard to tell behind the mask. He took a roll of bills out of his front pocket and threw it on the bed. "That's for you."

I unfolded the wad and fanned the Franklins. "Five grand," I said.

"For services *not* rendered."

'Let me get this straight," I said. "I walk away from the Boston case and this is mine to keep."

"You're a quick study."

"It's not like me to walk away from a case even when the client dies."

"I've heard that about you, but you might consider changing your business model."

"It certainly is something to noodle around my think tank," I said, as I placed the bills back on the bed.

His eyes squinted. "You and I have had a bit of a laugh here and I prefer to keep things light especially when I threaten to kill people whom I've just met. It helps the day go smoother, but make no mistake. This is your first, last and only warning. Now, turn around."

I stood up and faced the window. I braced for a conk on the cranium but was shocked when instead I caught a sap to the kidney that folded me a like a cheap bridge chair.

As I lay on the floor, knees kissing my chest, I heard the door open and close before my day turned dark as a grifter's heart.

CHAPTER 14

She waltzed into my office like she owned the place. If she had, I'd be in Dutch as I barely make my monthly note, and she looked severe enough to evict me without mercy.

Her body was sleek as a gazelle with a face that had seen more bad times than good. Her hair was black, straight and licked her shoulders. Eyes blue. She possessed a rough femininity that women earn by fighting fights that men don't have to. Indeed, if she were a man, her cheek might have a dueling scar. Her ensemble consisted of painted-on designer jeans, crisp white shirt, and a hint of a scarf. The whole package teetered on black stiletto heels with more straps than an English saddle. I know, I know. I tend to think of woman as sexual objects. Can't help it but if it's any consolation I sometimes do it to men, too. That's fair, I suppose.

I'd never seen her before, but she looked familiar.

"Are you Mr. Marlowe?"

"That's what it says on the door, although the gold-leafed 'M' is starting to flake off. I need to get that repaired."

"I'm Veronica Boston. Helen was my sister."

I didn't have to invite her to sit down. She owned the client chair as well and made herself at home.

"I received a phone call from a Detective Pemberton. She said that Helen was murdered."

I waited for a suggestion of tears or even full-blown sobbing but she remained stoic.

"My condolences." I reached for a gasper in my breast pocked until I remembered that I had stopped smoking years ago. I scratched my arm to do something normal with my now- extended hand.

"What did Pemberton tell you about my involvement with your sister?"

"Only that Helen had hired you to look into a phone harassment matter and that I should get in touch." She paused a beat. "So, here I am."

I couldn't figure why Pemberton suggested that she see me. Coppers don't want private dicks meddling in their business especially when it's homicide, and she made that very clear during out last meet. What was her angle?

"She also said that you talk weird, but I'm not hearing it."

Cause I'm trying damn hard. "Did the detective say how your sister croak… er… died?"

Her ramrod body got even more rigid. She cleared her throat. "She said it was from an overdose of heroin and fentanyl. Helen never took drugs. Not even in college. She barely drank alcohol. Growing up, she was the straight edge. I was the party girl. "

The woman in front of me… a party girl? The pain from the blackjack kept me from laughing. The doc-in-a-box I visited said there was no permanent damage to my kidney but sudden movements would hurt. He also said I might piss blood for a day or two. Check and check.

"Yes, I know," she announced, with a smile that barely registered. "We all change."

"Maybe your sister changed. Maybe she…"

"No way. Not Helen." Her eyes tightened, shot arrows in my direction.

"When was the last time you spoke to her?"

"Last week. She told me about the texts and the break-in. And she told me that she hired a private investigator, because the police weren't interested."

"Until now," I added. "Do you know of anyone who would want to kill Helen?"

"She kept close, didn't share a lot of her personal life with me. I didn't share a lot with her, either." She looked at her lap. "We were sisters and we loved each other. But in our family, well, none of us were close. What I mean is that we didn't share our feelings. We kept them bottled up. Tamped down. We are products of the English class system. Our grandparents on both sides were born in England, worked in pewter factories, textiles mills, that sort of thing. You didn't rise above your station. You didn't make waves. You did your duty. Even though our parents were born in Connecticut, and worked in factories, they retained that way of thinking. Helen and I rebelled, at least when it came to education."

"How so?"

"Both of us were voracious readers when we were young. We knew that there was a larger world out there, and we wanted to see it. We were curious."

"And?"

"Even though going to college, especially for girls, was considered putting on airs, that's what we did. Our parents had no money, so we each worked our way through. Helen even went on to get her MBA. I ended up in banking in New York City, and she became a business consultant. She did work for the Beltway Bandits, I think she called them. A lot of government-related jobs."

"Did Helen talk about anyone special, romantically speaking, I mean?"

"Like I said, we didn't share a lot of our personal lives with each other, but there was one man she mentioned a few times. I think he was a congressman or something like that."

"Do you remember a name?"

"Helen never said. I remember her telling me a story about him that was kind of weird."

"Oh?"

He traveled to Mexico a lot, and I remember asking 'why would a Congressman be going to Mexico so often,' and she said he had relatives there.

"That's not unusual, I suppose."

"I guess not, but what I found odd was that he told her about a cell phone app or something that allowed him to make free calls to his family there. She asked if she could have it too, to call friends overseas, but he said it was some secret app that only Congress had access to and it only worked to Mexico. That's weird, right?"

"More than you know." Horace had already told me that she had the weather app but not the crypto code. Even so, it screwed up her phone which probably got her killed.

Her pan shifted from neutral to serious. "Did the congressman have anything to do with Helen's murder?"

"Maybe, but we need to keep that between us and the black bird."

"We don't want to tell the police?"

"Nix that."

"Huh?"

"I mean no."

"Wouldn't this information help them?"

"More than likely just confuse them."

She laughed for the first time since she walked in the door.

Then serious again. "Mr. Marlowe. I want you to find Helen's killer. I can pay you any amount you want. I'll be in town for the next few days, handling my sister's affairs."

"I promise to find who killed Helen, and you don't have to pay me," I said, as I pictured the roll of C-notes still sitting on my bed. "Somebody already did, kind of." I stood up and we shook.

Her hand was cold, and her face was perplexed.

CHAPTER 15

Veronica Boston was sitting on the front porch of her sister's house when I arrived. She looked tired. "I didn't know if I was allowed inside," she said, as she rose and straightened her skirt.

The house was still crime-scene taped. Most people think that cops remove barricade tape when they're done. They don't. They leave it, just like they leave bloodied bed sheets, pieces of shot-off body parts and mountains of fingerprint dust. It cost me a double sawbuck to tidy up my wreck, and I still hold a grudge.

'It's okay," I said. "We can go in." I used my penknife to slit the plastic tape across the front door opening. "There are companies that clean up these situations. I can call one for you."

She walked behind me like I was blazing a trail in the woods. She stepped lightly and cautiously to the living room fireplace, got down on one knee next to a pair of multicolored porcelain dogs facing each other. "Staffordshire pottery dogs," she said softly. "These were our grandparents, the ones who worked in the pottery factories. Towards the end of the 19th century almost every middle-class house had them." She picked one up, studied it and smiled. "They're called King Charles Spaniels named for King Charles II who had the real dogs roaming all over his court." She placed it back on the floor. "My grandfather made these." She wiped her cheek.

The tough dame who I met in my office didn't seem so tough anymore.

She strolled along the walls studying the artwork like a collector considering a purchase. She lingered before some, nodded and roamed on. One in particular caught her in mid-step. She aimed her index finger at a painting of three men, one in a fancy, old-time, shiny, red morning gown jawing away to two others at a table. Chess pieces haphazardly covered a playing board. From the right side, a man had just entered through a door holding a parchment cylinder. "When I was a little girl, I used to stare at this in my grandparent's house. I made up stories about the men, what they were doing and what this guy," she pointed, "who I decided was a messenger, was about to say. Look, he dropped his cane and tricorner hat on the floor because he was in a hurry to deliver some news."

"Good imagination."

"Helen and I would sometimes have heated discussions about what was going on."

"I'm going to hinge the upstairs while you continue to look around."

"Um, uh. Okay."

I'm glad I did. Bloody vomit had clotted on the pillow. I grabbed it, hid it under the bed. I also collected a few paramedic leftovers: gauzes, wrappers and sponges floating on the bed. I threw them in the trash.

Helen didn't need to see any of this. There was the usual fingerprint powder on sections of the night stand, vanity and bathroom fixtures, but I let them be. If I tried to clean it up, it would become a muddy mess.

"What are you doing?" Veronica said, from the doorway.

"Just tidying up."

She raised an eyebrow and shrugged. "Find anything of interest?"

"Detritus."

"What?"

"Paramedics pride themselves on leaving a possible crime scene with everything they packed in. Nothing is left behind, not even wrappers, unless they're in a super rush. Overdoses aren't usually rush out of the room jobs as the patient is treated and stabilized at the scene. They get to the ER fast, but not so fast that one of them can't take a few seconds to clean up."

"Why do you think they didn't... wait... "She scoped out the bedroom. "I don't see anything left behind."

"Like I said, I tidied up a bit."

I was growing immune to her puzzled looks. We ambled through the rest of the house together, not speaking as we moved from room to room.

She was looking for keepsakes and memories. I was looking for clues.

In the den, she stopped in her tracks, gripped my arm and looked straight into my eyes. "Why does Pemberton think you're a suspect in Helen's death?"

I didn't show any surprise at her bomb. "Because I am. By default. I was the last person to see your sister alive. That lifts my name to the top floor."

She back pedaled, put some air between us. "Are you really a suspect?"

"Ever watch *Law & Order* on TV? To be a murder suspect you need motive, means and opportunity. I have no motive. Your sister was my client."

"And the other two?"

"I had opportunity, I suppose, but so does almost everyone else in a twenty-five-mile radius, but drugs don't fit my rub-out M.O. Burning powder is my racket."

"Pardon?"

"A gun. I prefer a roscoe in my mitts."

Her pan turned to tile. I had to keep reminding myself that she just lost her sister. Was I talking too harshly with her? I softened my voice and began, "Did your sister ever tell you that she owned a heater?"

"You mean a gun?"

"Check. A bean shooter."

Her eyes squinted. "Why do you have so many names for guns?"

"The same reason Eskimos have so many different names for snow. Did you know about her, er… gun?"

"No, but I bet I know how she got it. She had a boyfriend who was a police officer."

"She told me."

"He was always harping on her to be careful where she walked, have an exit strategy, carry mace. It made her paranoid. Helen was smart, knew how to take care of herself, but this fellow wanted to dress her in bubble wrap and not let her out of his sight. I never met him but from how Helen described him, I didn't like him one bit." Her face turned crimson. Her voice deepened. "Jealous and possessive type. Macho. He may have even been aggressive with her."

"What makes you say that?"

"Just the way she talked about him."

"Did he ever hit her?"

She drew back her lips. "They didn't go out very long. There was a reason for that."

"Do you remember his name?"

"I sure do. Thor."

"Thor? Big hammer, makes thunder. That Thor? Was that his real name?"

"That's all I know. Do you think he may have something to do with Helen's death?"

"Maybe," I said. "How does one go about finding an ancient god these days?"

CHAPTER 16

The ME's office floundered about in a building on E Street Southwest whose outside was a cross-hatch of steel and glass. Standing in the street, you could see interior stairs, elevator shafts and escalators attached to the skeleton that kept the building from folding in on itself.

I was on the seventh floor where the sign read, "Forensic Toxicology Department."

"It has to be in writing, Marlowe. You know that." Jaime de Castro was doing his best to avoid me, and I can't say as I blame him. The refrigerated drawers a few floors below were all filled, as bodies splayed on gurneys in the hallway waiting their turn to be probed and prodded to determine how they died.

"I know that Jaime, but I'm hoping we can cut through the red tape."

He huffed around the room, and I followed like a puppy dog begging for attention. "C'mon, I'm working for the deceased's sister."

"Can't do it. Don't ask me." His lab coat fluttered behind as he hustled among desks that held fancy-looking equipment. Jaime had a head of untamable hair, black as the inside of a raven, and it framed a chiseled mug. I really dug his look. He was doing his best to leave me behind.

This is how our usual arabesque went. I begged and he turned me down. I moped. Then I would secrete a bottle of Bushmills Ten-Year

Single Malt Irish Whiskey under his desk while he looked the other way. If the past was any predictor, a few minutes later an official tox screen report would magically appear.

"Name?" he said.

"Helen Boston."

"Wait here." He marched into a room marked "no admittance" and returned holding several sheets of paper. "The IT people can't seem to get our computers synced to our iPads. Paper," he said, fanning the sheets. "It's fucking barbaric." He sounded like Horace.

I scanned the summary page, but didn't see what I was looking for.

Jaime finally stopped jostling around when he saw that I was having trouble understanding what I was seeing. He looked over my shoulder. "Problem, Marlowe?"

"Says here that she died of a heroin overdose."

He leaned in further. "That's right."

"What about Narcan? I'm not seeing that."

Jaime snatched the sheets out of my hand and flipped to the second page, then the next and the next. His face sharpened. "Umm. The paramedics attended and... well, that's weird."

"You checked for it, right?"

He looked down his nose. "We screen for every fucking chemical including Naloxone."

"Any reason why it didn't show up?"

"Yes. It wasn't in the deceased's body."

"Why not?"

"You'll have to ask the paramedics," he said, thumbing his phone. "I sent you the contact info. Now let me be."

He left like he was late for his own wedding.

Twenty minutes later, I walked into the fire station which was nestled off Connecticut Avenue against a residential neighborhood.

"What can I do for you?" a soft voice said as I entered. It came from a woman who looked like she could be Beyonce's sister. Her hair was tied back in a bun, and her uniform fit like she paid for tailoring. Her trousers were bloused into ankle-high black boots. In a different color uniform, she could pass for regular army.

"I'm looking for a paramedic named A. Starling."

She looked me up and down and took a step back. A lot of people were doing that lately. She fiddled with the volume knob on the microphone that hung over her shoulder. Behind her, a pumper, ladder and an Advanced Life Support truck were berthed. The high-ceiled room smelled like a damp cellar.

"That's me. What can I do for you?"

"I'm interested in a call you made a few days ago, an overdose named Helen Boston."

"You'll have to do better. We have a lot of ODs."

I held up a photo. She twisted her head from side to side and handed it back. "Is there a problem?"

"I'm not looking to jam you…"

She squinted her eyes. "You're not a cop, are you?"

"Private investigator."

"Then I don't need to talk to you."

"No, you don't, but I'm hoping that you'll spill. I'm working for the family."

"Nothing good can come from me talking to you. You've obviously seen the autopsy report, and I suspect that you've found something to hang on me."

Just then, another paramedic entered the picture. He stood next to Starling. He was a little taller than me, and I'm six-one. He had on the same uniform but with short sleeves. His arms looked like knotted tree trunks and were just as wide. "Problem, Amanda?"

"Carl, this gentleman is asking about the OD in Friendship Heights. The woman who..."

I held up the photo again. "I remember," he said although he hardly eyed it. "What about her?"

"Why didn't you give her Narcan? Even small-time county sheriffs carry it. Comes in a nasal spray."

"Or a pen," she said. "You don't have to lecture us. We give that stuff out like Halloween candy." She grabbed her partner's arm and pulled him away. They huddled and whispered to each other. I could tell that they were disagreeing at first until they fist bumped. They approached me.

Starling spoke. "The patient was having trouble breathing. We did everything by the book. We called to her, rubbed our knuckles on her chest. No response. Her skin was blue, pupils were small, blood pressure low and she exhibited a slow heartbeat. Along with trouble breathing these are the classic signs of opiate overdose. Carl began CPR while I radioed in.

"Then..." she glanced at Carl... "we were recommending Narcan but were ordered not to administer it."

"I mean what the fuck?" Carl added. "Naloxone is a wonder drug. It almost always works and has few side effects. It's SOP."

"What did you do next?"

"We checked again, made sure we had heard the orders correctly from the doctor. He told us to rush her to the ER. We had a discussion between us about using Narcan despite orders to the contrary but decided not to."

"We went as fast as we could to the ER," Starling said.

"And she died," Carl said. His eyes stared passed me.

"It wasn't in the report that you were told *not* to give Narcan."

"We should have put it in to cover our asses."

"Who was the doctor?"

Carl moved forward, cleared his throat. "Sometimes we know the docs; sometimes we don't. Some ERs are manned by temps or the hospital farms out the unit to a group of doctors as independent contractors. We got his name though. It's in our report. Doctor J. Nahal. I remember because neither of us knew him and his order sounded wrong, but he was the boss. When we got to the ER he had already clocked out."

They both seemed to relax as if they had spent a few minutes in a confessional and had unburdened themselves.

"One last question," I said. "Did the patient look like a junkie to either of you?"

"I've been on this job for 15 years," Starling said. "It used to be easy to identify a junkie. Not so much anymore. But no, not this one. We didn't see any indication of chronic drug use."

Carl said, "What happens when you find this Doctor Nahal?"

"You mean *if*, don't you?"

CHAPTER 17

I wafted a hack back to my office, and noodled on my bill of fare. A copper named Thor who beats up women; a congressman mixed up in the dope trade; an IT guy on the lam and on the outs with a drug cartel, a suspicious dame who lingered in the shadows of a quiet street; who the hell knows how she fits in? and a gorilla who gave me a hard shot to the kidney and five extra-large to take a long vacation. I don't know who any of these jamokes really were, but one of them may be the only thing that keeps me from a lifetime of talking to visitors through plexiglass.

Is it any wonder that I drink too much? I had more loose ends than a hula skirt.

First things first. I upended a short glass of Jameson, before setting my sights on locating this Thor character. If he killed Helen then everything else would fall into place. If not, I could cross him off my list like a shopper who squeezed a few avocados and didn't place them in their cart.

Cops are gym rats, so I made a list of all the gyms near cop shops and hoped that Helen's boyfriend made an impression on the staff.

I narrowed my search to five workout joints, jumped in my heap and began cutting around town. The District isn't as large or busy as New York, Chicago or L.A. but I match our traffic against any of theirs.

Fictional dicks always seem to find the perfect spot in front of the building they desire. Not so in real life, although parking is made easier when you're willing to park illegally and take the ticket as the cost of doing business. DC's annual budget counts on a steady stream of illegal parkers, and I consider it my civic obligation to take a few hits now and then.

Gyms nowadays seem more like places to relax with a frothy, green concoction instead of revving up a sweat. The 30-something woman behind the reception counter looked happier than a Powerball winner. In a voice so cheery that it actually caused an acute pain in my right temple, she said, "Hello, and welcome to *The Gym Mill.* How can I enhance your day?"

I produced a gym bag that I'd purchased next door with the name Thor scribbled on the outside. "Well, ma'am, I found this at the Friendship Heights Metro station, just a few blocks from here. This is the closest gym so I thought what the heck, I'll give it a try." I'm not sure why, but I rendered a Southern accent.

"What's in it?" she asked, maintaining her supernova smile. I felt like I was staring into a klieg light.

"Oh, you know, the usual clothes but there's something really valuable that I thought the owner would like back."

"What's that?"

"This." I showed her a ring that was on my finger only a few moments earlier. "It doesn't look valuable, I mean, it probably isn't worth a lot but it may have sentimental value. If it were mine, I'd want someone to return it to me." I was sticking with the Southern accent.

"Absolutely. Awesome." She beamed.

"There is one client who comes in almost every night around eight. Sometimes I work the late shift and see him. I'm pretty sure I've heard people call him Thor but I've never spoken to him. I just wave at our customers as they slide their cards through the turnstile."

Bingo. First try. Better than scoring a legal parking spot.

"I can put it behind the counter and when he comes in whoever is on duty can give it to him."

"That's real nice of you but I'd rather give it to him myself. It's not that I don't trust you, it's not that. It's just that, you know, there may be a… some kind of reward. Know what I mean, ma'am?"

"Uh, huh."

"I can come back around… what did you say? … around eight, and see if I can give it to this Thor feller myself."

The klieg light which was her face went dark. "I'm sure he will appreciate it." She managed a smile with some effort.

"Thanks, ma'am."

I stepped outside and whispered 'sorry mayor.' There was no ticket on my jalopy window. I had an hour to kill, so I winged back to my crib, parked in the back alley and scrambled up the stairs. I tilted back in my chair to study the inside of my eyelids, but my cramming came to a sudden stop when my mobile rang.

The moment I answered, I wish I hadn't. I tried a monotone 'this is Sam Marlowe, please leave a message' but the caller wasn't buying it.

"Sam, this is Sarah. Mr. LaFarge would like an update. Have you found Sameer?"

She sounded all business.

"Not yet." I caught her up but omitted tiny details like Sameer providing communications services to a drug cartel that may be connected to Congress. "I saw your sculpture at the gallery."

"It seemed like a good venue."

"There are lots of good venues."

I heard a sigh. "I admit it. I wanted to see where you lived and worked. I'm nosy. Then I saw the gallery and thought it would be a good fit for my piece."

"Aces."

"Mr. LaFarge is requesting a written report on your progress." Her voice was officious again.

"I don't do written reports until the case is over. He can jangle me any time and I'll give him the latest dope."

"Actually, I was hoping that you'd come by the office. I'd like to see you."

"You can peep at me anytime, now you know where I live and work. Third floor. Call first to make sure I'm not engaged."

"Engaged?"

"Busy with another client."

"Of course. What should I tell LaFarge?"

"The investigation is proceeding and I'm making progress."

"Sam, I... never mind. Bye."

I didn't get Sarah, but then again I'm sure she might say the same about me. I didn't feel like napping anymore so I headed outside to clear my brain pan. I sat in Dupont Circle for a while, then decided to play chess with a few of the regulars including Cherry Lane, a bike messenger. I hadn't seen him in a while, and I hoped that he had something for me.

"Sam," he said, moving at me like a kid reaching for cotton candy. "How the hell have you been? Long time, no see, not since... when was it... oh, yeah, when you tried to kill me."

It's true. I was shadowing a blackmailer, hitting speed, when Cherry ran in front of my tin can. I braked hard, hit him with my front bumper and he skidded across the blacktop. He began cursing into the air until he saw it was me. "God damn it, Sam," he had said. "You trying to flatten me?" Bike messengers have no fear of death. They zip in and out of traffic like they're invincible but sometimes, like this time, they get tagged. Even though it was his fault, I bought him a new bike, actually he wanted parts for a new bike so he could assemble it himself. Fixed gear; brakes are an afterthought and frames stronger than steel construction beams. Messengers don't go for lightweight steeds like bike racers but bodies heavy enough to handle DC's epic potholes and four-wheelers fed up with sharing the road with these maniacs.

"How's the bike?"

"Painted it pink. You like?" "Check out the knobbies," he said, pointing his fingerless gloves to the fat tires. Cherry was decked in yellow and black spandex that revealed every bodily protrusion, bike shoes that slotted into the pedals and a red rock climber's helmet with as many stickers and decals that would fit. A wide bag strap slanting across his chest looked like a bandolier, but instead of bullets it held a mobile phone in a pouch.

Messengers all know each other even though they ride for competing companies. While many of the riders are employees, most are independent contractors. All they need to be in business is a bike, a phone, nerves of steel and calves of iron. They usually stream into the Circle after work, smoke a little reefer, down an energy drink and trade near-crash stories before pedaling home.

They also trade gossip, because they see Washington in a way like no one else. You would think that with scanners and email that people wouldn't need messengers anymore but you'd be wrong. Lawyers know there are more billable hours in printing on paper. Not to mention the wise guy who wants hand delivery of a compromising video and the politician recipient sending back a stack of greenbacks. Messengers know who's sending jewelry to who and which movers and shakers are no longer moving or shaking based on where their hand-delivered party invitations are going.

Cherry and I settled into opposing sides of a concrete table imbedded with a checkerboard. He reached into his bag and retrieved a wooden box and a plastic timer. Then he spread the pieces on the tabletop and held a different colored pawn in each paw switching them several times behind his back. I chose his left mitt, and the piece was black. Gawkers started to assemble. A few smelled from cigarettes. Others from reefer. I smelled an egg salad sandwich being devoured by a kid.

Cherry began with a Spanish opening and I countered in standard fashion. Play went fast as we both slapped the top of the clock timer offering a report after each move. The crowd ebbed and flowed as they wandered from table to table to find a match to their liking. It's not like tournament golf where the watchers whisper at each other from behind a rope. It was expected for people to talk to each other, even to the players, until a player makes a dumb move and requests quiet for concentration.

By move twenty-six we had already traded one bishop, one knight, both rooks and our pawn count was equal. We captured each other's queens in succession. We were even-stevens until Cherry produced a jump with his remaining knight that caught me off guard. The crowd murmured. I sighed. My fingers toppled my king as watchers drifted away.

I spanked a ten-spot on the table. Cherry held it across his hands and snapped it smartly before stashing it in his bag.

"Again?" he asked.

"Not today, Cherry. I got a growling dog in my think tank."

He laughed. "This will make you happy. After you called me, I did some checking around." He looked to his sides like he was about to change road lanes and leaned in.

"Your hunch was right on. There's been a lot of runs between the Mexican Embassy and the Senate. More than usual. Some were regular envelopes and some were puffies, you know, envelopes with a bulge."

"About the size of a cell phone?"

"Right on."

"Which building?"

"Dirksen. Most of the envelopes went to the Homeland Security Committee, but there were no names on the outside. You know about that," he said.

It's an old trick that people use to keep prying eyes like Cherry's from knowing where an envelope will finally land. Inside the envelope is another envelope with the name of the recipient. The outside envelope is opened by a staffer who delivers the inside envelope to the individual senator's office. If it's marked personal, they don't open it.

"Give me your backpack for a minute." He hoisted it over the table and I slipped a fifty into the outside pocket.

"You know that this goes against the messengers' code, right."

"Neither snow nor rain nor heat nor gloom of night..." I began.

"That's the fucking post office, Sam."

"Oh, yeah." We both laughed.

Cherry snorted. "Let me see what I can do. If I hear anything, I'll call you, but whatever you do, it has to be done fast. These people know how long it takes to get from the embassy to the Dirksen. We can't be screwing around. What's this about anyway?"

"Drug cartels."

"Good one, Sam. That's some funny shit."

I let him think that it was some funny shit.

I watched Cherry hop on his pink bike, pop a wheelie and head off home. As for me, I have a date with a Norse god.

CHAPTER 18

Dicks have a name for lies. We call them pretexts, and I just pretexted the hell out of the guy behind the counter at the gym to let me hang out in the lobby while I waited for a person I never met and didn't know what he looked like. The story involved some expensive sneakers, tickets to the ballet and a cop named Thor. Sometimes simple pretexts are best, but in this case a more complicated story designed to bore the recipient into letting you sit quietly without droning on further seems to have done the trick. It ended with the counter person promising to give me the high sign when Thor entered.

All I had to do was sit and worry about how big this guy was and how many more shots I could take before my internal organs turned to mush. With a nickname like Thor I envisioned a Goliath with bowling balls sewn into his biceps.

I didn't have to fret too long. The door opened and the receptionist nodded in my direction.

Turning to my right, I clocked him, an Ichabod Crane look-alike with a ball cap, arms and legs like soda straws.

I approached him like a snake milker approaches a rattler. "Are you Thor?" I hoped that he didn't have some secret Ninja shit that would allow him to toss me across the room like a balled-up piece of paper. Instead, he smiled.

"Some people call me that. And you are?"

"The name's Sam Marlowe. I'm a PI. I'm looking into the murder of Helen Boston." I braced for a hand flick that could fling me into outer space.

He laughed. "I was wondering when someone would get around to me."

"Who?"

"Janice Pemberton? She's been assigned to the case but hasn't contacted me. I've been waiting. How come you found me first? It's not like I've been hiding."

"I have a smaller caseload."

"What would you like to know? By the way, I was sorry to hear about Helen but it wasn't as if we were close. We only went out a few times, and it ended amicably."

Instead of stepping back, I moved closer making it harder for him to launch a swing. "That's not what I heard."

"You heard wrong," he said, with controlled anger in his voice. "Helen and I had a thing for about a month. It just didn't work for either of us."

"Her sister said that you have an anger problem."

He smiled and thought for a moment. "I admit that I have a heightened sense of vigilance and alertness and sometimes react too quickly and with more than a measured response. That comes from being a cop"

"That sounds like something a headshrinker would say."

"Word for word," he said. "Find me a cop who doesn't have this. A cop who is still alive."

"Did that… er… hypervigilance seep over to your personal life?"

"It's one of the things, I… we've been working on." He relaxed his stance, put his gym bag on the floor and pointed to the lounge area.

Once seated he said: "I tend to be possessive in my relationships. It's another fault, but I never raised a finger to Helen. I did raise my voice when my expectations were not met, and I'm not proud of it."

More shrink-talk, but I believed he was telling the truth.

"What about the gun?"

"Not my finest hour, but I thought I was helping to protect Helen from the savages that roam our streets." He closed his eyes. I heard him whisper, counting. A few seconds later, he opened his eyes. "My shrink says that it's part of my overprotective nature with a pinch of paranoia."

"Where were you the night she was murdered?"

"For one thing, I heard that murder was only a theory, that she had overdosed. Second, I was working. When I heard what happened, I checked my log. I was at the Verizon Center doing crowd control. I worked the entrances on seventh street. I'm probably on every camera they have."

"Did Helen strike you as a hophead?"

"If you mean did she take drugs? I doubt it. Maybe some alcohol, anti-anxiety meds but nothing stronger."

"What do you think she was anxious about?"

"Anxiety doesn't always have a basis in fact, but she was probably upset about us on some level. She had more invested in making it work than me."

This guy's head was so shrunk I'm surprised that he could find a cap that fit him.

"Anything else? I'd like to get my workout in."

"Only one thing. Why Thor?"

He rolled up his sleeve revealing a tattoo of a yellow thunderbolt outlined in red. "Kids do dumb things."

"So do grownups."

CHAPTER 19

"The Mexican Embassy is on Pennsylvania Avenue and Nineteenth Street Northwest behind a façade of townhouses once known as the *Seven Buildings*. The residences were built in 1796 and President James Madison and his wife Dolly lived there after the British burned the White House during the War of 1812. Only two of the houses remained and their fronts were incorporated into a modern office building in the late 1980s. Martin Van Buren lived there, too, just after his inauguration," Horace added, catching his breath. "What else do you want to know?"

"Can I borrow your van?"

"It's full of my stuff. Expensive gear." Horace kept it in the back alley and mainly used it for storage. He purposely plastered Bondo on the skin to make it unappetizing to gonifs. Stained coffee cups and fast-food trash on the dashboard rounded out the deterrent.

"I just need it for a short blip."

He reached into a drawer behind the bar and tossed me a ring of keys that looked like they were taken from a janitor's belt. "It's on there." He proceeded to build a pina colada. "Want one?"

"Why not?"

The blender keened as he rocked the machinery back and forth to help pulverize the ice. He poured the result into a tall glass with a tiki face on it and pierced the slurry with a red straw. He tested the potion and pronounced it perfect.

"Mexican Embassy, my van… what's this about Sam?"

"More rum," I said, pushing my glass forward. Horace placed a bottle of *Sailor Jerry* on the bar. "DIY," he said. I took a big sip to form space in the tumbler for more hooch.

"The Mexican Embassy is the cut-out between the drug cartel and someone in Congress."

"You mean the cartel is working through the embassy? Well, that's a new wrinkle." He said it so matter of fact that it worried me. I just stared at him.

"Who's the someone?" he asked.

"I'm hoping to score that soon."

He downed the drink and poured what was left from the blender into his glass.

"Remember that dentist over on twentieth? What was his name?" I asked.

"Ron something or other. Zinowitz, I think," Horace said.

"Yeah, that's the bo. He's only a block from the Mexican Embassy, and he owes me a favor."

"Who in this town doesn't?"

I vacuumed my glass dry. "I'm ready to book."

"Don't put any more dents in… never mind," Horace yelled, as I faded out the door.

I legged over to see Zinowitz, one of the few one-person dentist operations left in the city. It's just him, a receptionist and a hygienist. His office is on the ground floor of an apartment building, a common sitch for professional suites a million years ago. Now, all the other doctors, dentists, one-person law firms, and CPAs have moved to cheaper digs but Zinowitz stayed. And why not? He owns half the building although it was never clear to me how he got the scratch to buy such prime real estate. I always had a suspicion that he did more than take a slant into peoples' yaps.

The wall sconces seemed mainly for decoration, barely lighting the hallway. The carpet reminded me of floor coverings in Vegas casinos. They were purposely irritating to the eye so you didn't look down but kept your attention on the money-making card tables and slot machines.

I opened the door marked Dr. Zinowitz, DDS.

Two women and a man were sitting on brown Danish lounge chairs around a coffee table. They were playing cards.

"Busy day, doc?" I said.

"Sam, how the heck are you?" Ron said. He wore a white lab coat over a Hawaiian shirt. Jeans and white sneakers finished the job. "You don't have an appointment, do you?"

"No, just thought I'd stop by."

"That's cool. You know Doris and Jeannie."

They'd been with the practice for as long as I knew Zinowitz. They both smiled and said 'Hi,' in unison. I was never too sure about his personal relationship with these employees. They could have been twins.

Ron is a dentist to the stars. Hollywood on the Potomac stars. He handles choppers for politicians, lobbyists anyone who doesn't want anyone else to know their business. You would think that dentists wouldn't gab but they do. Except for Ron. He is a dental sphinx and people pay plenty for his zipped lip. Aside from that, he is a damned good tooth doctor, and despite his layback attitude, he always shells out for the latest dental technology.

Which is what brought me in today.

You have that Nomad you were telling me about?

"I got the newest version, in fact."

Doris and Jeannie sat behind the reception desk and fiddled on their computers while Ron led me into the equipment closet. He reached onto the top shelf and retrieved a device that resembled a hair dryer but with a plastic disk at the end. He also grabbed a battery pack and snapped it on to the handle. "Should be good to go," he said. "This model is even better than the earlier one. There's less back scatter and the pictures are clearer."

Just like Horace, he could go on and on about his latest gadget. I let him.

"You don't even need to give the patient a lead apron" He pulled the trigger. "You just point and shoot. Boom. There's the X-ray. It's fabulous."

He handed it to me. "Take your time. I can use the older model until you're done."

"Thanks."

"On your way," he said, shooing me out the door. We have a card game to finish."

If that's what they were really doing.

I hoofed it back to the office and waited for a jangle from Cherry.

CHAPTER 20

I grabbed some paper towels and a plastic garbage from my office and headed into the back alley to clear out Horace's vehicle. I expected the inside to stink like a landfill in August, but the trash was all for show. There were no bits of food, just paper. Even the French fry containers from McDonald's had been carefully cleaned. I took a photo so I could put everything back where Horace had it. I knew there had to be a personal theme to his interior decorating, but I had no idea what it was. I Windexed the windshield and checked the gas.

Once the cabin was clean, I worked on the back. Among the wires, cables and parts were brand new electronic equipment, some of it with metal tags stating "Property of US Government." I cleared a space on a wooden table that was bolted to the side panel.

From the outside, I glanced back at the white Econoline with its blacked-out windows and scruffy paint job. I was glad that I wouldn't have to park near any playgrounds or elementary schools.

A call came from Cherry. "You have five minutes," was all he said. The bike ride from the Mexican Embassy to the Dirksen building takes about 20 minutes. Nobody would notice an extra five minutes, but anything longer would bring suspicion.

I parked the van in a loading zone on 18th street and texted Cherry my position.

A minute later, he fishtailed to a stop. Out of breath, he handed me a bulging envelope. "Remember. Five minutes," he said, taking a swig from his water bottle and spitting into the street.

I closed the back door, switched on a light and studied the envelope. It was a standard 9-by-12 manila Kraft with a metal clasp and Scotch tape over the gummed flap. I spritzed two seconds of butane from a lighter refill along the tape and it crinkled immediately allowing it to be removed without tearing the paper. I unbent the clasp. I sprayed along the flap to loosen the adhesive, but no dice.

Cherry knuckled the side. Three minutes left.

I swiveled a knife under the flap but still couldn't loosen it. I felt a tear coming, so I eased off. I was sweating. I sprayed again, and this time the flap separated slowly as the adhesive formed parallel gooey strings as I lifted. I extracted the inner envelope and took a photo of the recipient's name.

Another knock on the side. Louder this time. One minute left.

I took as many shots as I could with the portable X-ray gizmo. This left me thirty seconds to reglue and retape the outside envelope flap before handing it back to Cherry.

I heard a single pounding on the back door. I swung the door open and Cherry was straddling his bike. "In the bag," he said. I snuggled the envelope into his messenger bag and Cherry's legs strained as he took off like he was shot out of a catapult.

Back inside, I downloaded the X-rays into my phone then sat in the driver's seat to take a breather.

I couldn't tell if the traffic officer saw me or not. I certainly didn't clock her until a uniformed arm came of nowhere to slide a ticket under the passenger side windshield wiper. Maybe she didn't see me. Maybe she saw me and didn't care. Not surprising. There was a case last year where a police officer decided to check inside a car with a dozen tickets on it just before it was about to be hooked by a city wrecker. The ME estimated the body had been in the car for over a month. By DC standards, there should have been more citations.

I cranked the engine and made for the back alley. I felt like a dog taking a bone back to his corner where he could gnaw on it without interference from anyone.

CHAPTER 21

"Sam, did you find the photographer yet?"

I had padded up the stairs as quietly as possible, but Goldie heard me anyway and opened her door. "Well?" she demanded.

"Hold your horses. I'm working on it."

"Look, Sam. This is a lot of money to me."

"I'm wise, and I'll finger him. I promise."

She moved in on me, and her face brightened. "You know, Sam," her voice slow and smooth. "I'm not just asking for me."

"No?"

"I'm asking for us. You like having me as a downstairs neighbor. Don't you?"

I nodded.

"Without this money, I might have to move, and you and I… you know."

Yeah. I knew.

"Is this like the old joke? Are we just arguing about the price?"

"Damn it, Sam. If you don't want to do this, then I can hire Stanley Brisbane or Charles King." She named the two sleaziest dicks in town.

"You'd have to slide them some geetus. They won't work for nothing."

Her phone rang and she eyed the screen. "Shit." She shot inside and slammed the door so hard it produced a blast of air in the hallway.

I reached my desk and checked the X-Rays. My suspicions were correct. The outline of a mobile phone was clear as day. As for the recipient... I scrolled through my photos until I found the one I had taken of the inner envelope.

The name was Senator Phillip Metcalfe.

Everyone knew this highbinder's moniker. He was featured in the tabloids last year for getting wedged between his mistress and his wife. She divorced his sorry ass faster than a sneeze, and his mistress dropped him like a Husky sheds hair in August.

Thanks to a fixer named Eric Deafenhill something-or-other, he landed a soft-ball interview on *Fox News*, shed tears for the camera and declared that he was a flawed human being. He followed this with a tearing of his lapel and a vow to make an even stronger bond with his lord and savior Jesus Christ. He begged his constituents to give him a chance for redemption by re-electing him. And they did.

Now he is chairman of the Senate's International Narcotics Control Caucus which didn't sound like a big deal to me until I learned that they have the same status as a full committee. This means they have some juice and money. They also have subpoena power. One of their missions, so the website says, is to foster international cooperation between countries when it concerns illegal drugs.

I doubt that extends to using secret encrypted phones carried by bike messengers.

Surveillance is not what people outside my world think it is. On TV, surveillance never takes longer than a half hour. Usually the target does something that spurs the follower into action as he flings his coffee into the street and takes off running after his prey. He catches the guy red handed and everyone goes homes happy except for the perp.

This never happens in real life.

In my world, surveillance is long, boring and you rarely see anything that makes you feel like you're spending your time wisely. It's like a jigsaw puzzle in which you have to put together pieces without having the edges or where your next piece is coming from. If you're lucky, the person you're tailing meets another person of interest in a restaurant or bar and this allows you to join together the same color pieces which eventually fit into the puzzle as a big hunk.

And coffee? Forget it, unless there's a public bathroom nearby. Quiz any gumshoe about the best place for surveillance, and they'll tell you it's next to a McDonald's.

Unfortunately, surveillance may be the only way to learn what your person is up to. In this case, confronting a senator head-on, letting him know that you know about the special mobile phones can get you harassed or worse by the Capitol Police. Visitors to Congress see this group of uniformed officers as protecting the Capitol grounds, but they're also used as a private police force by Senators and Representatives. They keep dalliances quiet and drive lawmakers home when they've had too much to drink. They make sex crimes disappear. Sometimes their plain clothes division work as enforcers, bagmen and handle unsavory jobs that even PIs like Brisbane and King wouldn't consider - which is saying a lot. Many of their detectives retire early with a pension subsidized by wiretap printouts and photos kept in a safe deposit box.

I downloaded a photo of Metcalfe into my phone, and steeled myself for long nights of sitting on my keister, eating take-out from janky eateries and hoping for a nearby McDonald's.

The life of a gumshoe may seem exciting, but don't let the glamour fool you.

CHAPTER 22

When I'm on surveillance, my think tank goes free range. Unbridled by an immediate task, regrets bob to the top of my mind like corks, filling my head with all the things I should have done along with a barrelful of choices I shouldn't have made. Like engaging in killery.

I've bumped off a few mopes in my career and it never gave me any pleasure even when he – or in one case, she – had it coming. It's part of the job, but it doesn't mean I'm immune from nightmares about it. During stakeouts, when your brain is relaxed but alert, fixated on a restaurant window, a street, a house or maybe another car, it's impossible not to dwell on the fact that you've killed another human being. Justified or not, you've played god, and all you can hope for is that you won't ever have to do it again. At least not today.

It's self-delusion in spades, an impossible dream, as you feel the comfort and horror of your roscoe's heft under your left arm. If you really didn't want to cool someone, why would you be packing heat?

Mercifully, my brain flipped back to today's lay. Trailing a pol out of his office is not like in the movies. They can emerge from an underground parking lot or leave the building on foot. There are multiple exits, too. You need several sets of peepers and luck to cover the most-used exits so I enlisted Horace to keep a lookout on the front while I eyeballed the parking garage.

I had been parked about two hours when Horace phoned. "He's on the move, hailing a cab. I'll follow."

Horace gave me the hack's tag and as I pulled behind him a few blocks later as Horace peeled off.

Metcalfe was alone.

The cab was heading for a line of fancy grub joints along Pennsylvania Avenue, and I watched as it rolled up in front of DiRienzo's Grill. I knew the place, an upscale Italian eatery with an old-fashioned zinc bar. Steaks were good, chops were better and the cocktails were expensive.

I cozied to the end of the bar where I could hinge Metcalfe who had already been seated. He was not what I expected from his official photo. The senator had a lardy-puss and buzzcut that made him look like a gym teacher who just didn't give a shit anymore. His suit was boxy, his shoes were scuffed, and his tie looked like it was knotted by child. If he was fronting for the world's richest drug cartel it didn't show in his duds.

He was jumpy as a cat in a room full of laser pens. His eyes zig-zagged between his watch, phone and the front door. He looked like he was about to dust-out at any moment.

The bartender wasn't sure who I was but had a good idea *what* I was. I had asked for plain water in a martini glass with olives which is my standard stakeout beverage. He even played along by placing the shaker above his head and giving it a few healthy jiggle-joggles before pouring. I always leave a hefty tip for these don't-ask, don't-tell libations.

The woman who sat down at Metcalfe's table looked to be in her late 40's. Her thick, blond hair with black streaks was combed straight back like she had just left the shower. Diamond stud earrings the size of pencil erasers adorned her lobes. She wore a thick gold bracelet on her right wrist and I spied a Cartier Tank watch on her left. Her clothes cost more than my car. This was not a romantic dinner unless OKCupid was hacked.

The jittery senator finally stopped vibrating as they settled in, ordered drinks and made what looked to me as introductory chit-chat. In a few minutes I saw some serious looks coming from his dinner companion who occasionally would point her finger to emphasize what she was saying. She raised her voice several times. He sat back and took it.

Their drinks arrived and they took a breather. At least, he did. She started again, pointing her finger, raising her voice which prompted the server to return and check if the drinks were okay. The senator smiled, she stopped talking and they both looked around to determine if they had been making a scene. Metcalfe swiveled in my direction and I quickly faced away.

They continued their conversation but at a lower volume. She received another brown drink, neat. It looked like bourbon. Metcalfe had another beer.

By the time their meal came, they were both almost smiling at each other.

"Another drink, sir?" the bartender asked me. His mouth crinkled at the edges.

I nodded.

After another faux performance, I asked: "That dame with Senator Metcalfe. Do you know her handle?"

"You government?"

"Private." I slid my ID under a cocktail napkin and fingered it in his direction. He lifted the edge of the napkin, looked at me, then pushed it back.

"I knew you looked familiar. You're Horace's friend, right? Or should I say 256-L12." He laughed. "I tended bar at the Teekee for a few months when I got out of bartending school."

I didn't recognize him but I did believe him. Lots of drink slingers cycled in and out of the Teekee. Horace could be tough to work for, but he was well respected for giving would-be intoxicologists their first gig.

"Kenny," he said, as he shook my hand.

"Sam."

"She's a cop in Arizona, some border town, I think. They have dinner about once a month. She talks and he listens. They having a love thing?"

"I don't think so, Kenny. More like a business meeting."

"Yeah, I kind of figured that. Look at the body language."

I didn't look over.

"I dig. Do you know her name?"

"She always pays cash. He never pays. How about a photo? Will that help?"

"How will you manage that?"

He grabbed his phone which was next to the till. The next thing I knew he was walking into the restaurant area. He stood next to their table. "Folks, I hope you don't mind the intrusion, but we're taking some pictures of the bar for our new website. You don't need to move."

They both looked alarmed as he held up his phone.

"No need to worry. You're not in the picture." He clicked away. "Perfect. Your drinks are on the house."

He returned to the bar, mixed a few drinks for a couple who had just sat down, then came over to me. He placed his phone on the bar. 'How's this?"

The photo of Metcalfe's dinner companion was crisp and clear as the water in my martini glass. "I'll email it to you. Tell Horace I said hello."

A half hour later, they both left together in separate taxis. I followed the unknown woman's cab to the Four Seasons Hotel in Georgetown. I parked in the space reserved for checking in and threw the doorman a sawbuck which stopped him from sneering at my heap. I hadn't seen it before, but she was carrying an envelope similar to the one that had been messengered to Metcalfe. She disappeared into an elevator with several other people.

Some people might think I have a drinking problem. I don't. My problem isn't drinking; it's that I can't stop drinking. There's a difference.

I detoured to the bar and ordered a drink. A real one.

CHAPTER 23

I sat at the Teekee Bar eyeing the swiggers who were saucing their way out of whatever personal hell they found themselves in today. Some looked like they had been tippling over the long term. Several others had stretched their lunch hour until it was time to go home. Each group seemed jealous of the other.

Despite being a digerati, Horace believed in the sanctity of physical newspapers and bought about a half dozen every day which he piled on the bar. Every once in a while, some asshole would hold one up and claim that he didn't see how to click on the story. This didn't happen very often, though, because Horace left standing instructions to whoever was bartending that this person was to be cut off whether they were tipsy or not. Their buddies were to be denied booze, too. Word spread. So did the fact that anyone found filling in the crossword puzzle in pen received a free libation. Horace felt his actions were good for the community and the world at large.

I ordered a Campari and soda and glanced at the *Financial Times*.

"Kerry," I said. "I think I have a problem."

"No shit. I'm surprised your liver hasn't popped out of your belly and smacked you upside the head."

"That's not what I meant."

"Oh," she said, as my drink landed in front of me.

"You know that Horace and I work together a lot but this time I'm taking on some real bad guys and there's a good chance that things could get rough."

She put down her rag. "You've been in jams before, and he's always loved the action. He says he doesn't but you know he does. And doesn't he have some government backup or something that he never talks about?"

Horace is one those guys who can make magic happen with one phone call. I've never questioned or asked about this talent including the time a black helicopter landed on the Naval Observatory grounds to take us fishing in West Virginia for the weekend.

"Don't worry about him," said Kerry. "Nobody can make Horace do anything he doesn't want to do."

"My fucking ears are on fire," Horace said, as he sidled up to the bar. "I found your guy."

Kerry purposely moved to the other side cupping her ears and humming.

"You mean the Jane?"

"Her name's not Jane. Face recognition software is the bomb."

"So, who's the tomato?"

"Her name is Feliz Montano. She's the police chief of a tiny town adjacent to the Sonoran Desert." He produced an iPad with a map, and his fingers slid across the screen and stopped. "She's located here. A community called Piedras Viejas. Has something to do with old rock formations."

"That's queer."

"And well off."

"What do you mean?"

"For a town its size, like 800 people, they have fifteen police officers. According to an article I read, she says that they need that many people to patrol the desert area. Even then, she said, they're spread thin."

I looked at the tablet while he talked and saw that the Sonoran Desert looked like an ink splotch covering parts of Mexico, California, Arizona and the top part of the Baja California peninsula.

"A hundred thousand square miles," he said. "It's the smuggler's route north for drugs and people. The most common path, according to my sources, is north from Mexico on a beeline just west of Tucson."

"Is that federal land?"

"Not all of it. That's where Montano comes in. Some of her jurisdiction takes in a section of the route. Even if it didn't, that land is so wild and rugged that any police officer could assert themselves. The illegals wouldn't know any difference. But here's the interesting part. The cartels have their own people sitting atop the mountains watching the smugglers making their way across the desert. They supply them with radios so they can warn them if they see law enforcement patrolling the area. The trek can take a week or more in one-hundred plus heat."

"We're talking US soil right."

"Yep. There are mountains just outside of Tucson and spotters sit on top with high-powered binoculars and watch for the mules making their way through the desert. Once they get to the predetermined spot, their drugs are checked to make sure it's all there, they're paid their money and they make their way back to the Mexico border and do it again or go wherever they feel like going."

"Where do the drugs go from there?"

"Usually, the cartels hand it off to their American counterparts. They may be part of the cartel or an American gang they're doing business with. By the time the drugs reach street level, they've crossed many hands. Check this out," Horace said. "This is a death map of where immigrant bodies were found over the years. According to the legend, each orange dot indicates a heap of bones bleached by the sun. Not all were smugglers, of course, but there were several thousand people dead over a ten-year period. Any backpacks containing contraband are usually missing, taken by another traveler or sometimes law enforcement," Horace said. "These people are expendable."

"And desperate," I said.

"How do you think Montano and Metcalfe figure into this?" Horace asked.

"Money. It's always about money."

Kerry had usually stayed on the far side of the bar so she purposely couldn't hear our private conversations. Now, I saw her stand still and focus her attention in our direction when she heard Horace ask: "So, what's next?"

I smiled at her and Horace. "You know damn well what's next. We're taking a trip to Piedras Viejas, wherever the hell that is."

CHAPTER 24

"Are you United States citizens?"

The uniformed officer scoped out our rental. The car was getting barbecue grill hot, as the air-conditioned air was escaping through the opened driver side window. The roadblock consisted of several cars with Border Patrol lettering and officers milling about with automatic weapons slung over their shoulders. There was no shade.

I turned to Horace. "Did we go too far? Did we drive into Mexico?"

"You are in the United States," the officer said. "Are you both US citizens?"

"We don't have to tell you, officer," Horace said, as he leaned over. "We're in the US and you can't stop us from traveling around and you can't ask us that question." I was in between these two guys and didn't dig it one bit.

"Sir," the officer said. "Just tell me if you're an American citizen. That's all I'm asking."

"And you have no right to ask me," Horace said.

"Will you pull over there?" he pointed.

"Are you detaining us?" Horace said.

"Will you pull over there?" he repeated in a louder voice.

"Are you detaining us?" Horace repeated. "On what grounds are you detaining us?"

"I asked you if you would pull over there."

"I won't pull over unless you are detaining us. Are you ordering us to pull over? Are you detaining us?"

This exchange went on for at least another five minutes with both men repeating their mantras. The officer was getting becoming belligerent. He hefted his automatic. Horace didn't show any emotion at the move.

Finally, the officer said: "You can go."

I closed the window and put the car in gear.

"What the hell was that?" I asked.

"Harassment, intimidation, bullying. Take your pick," Horace said, leaning into the back seat and lifting the cooler lid. "Want one?"

I nodded. The cool beer slid down smooth as silk pajamas on a shaved Chihuahua. Horace downed his in one smash, crushed the can and tossed it under the seat. "We'll be in Piedras Viejas in about a half hour. Wake me if we hit another roadblock." He leaned back and lowered the brim on the Stetson he bought at the Tucson airport. I felt like I was in a cowboy movie where the confident sheriff was waiting for his high-noon duel with the fastest gunslinger in these here parts.

We drove silently except for some minor snoring and melancholic ranchero music whining from the radio. I had never been to the Southwestern desert before, and I was surprised at seeing all the shrubs, trees and other plants. I pictured it more desolate. I even saw some ranches with cattle feeding on the low grass. Still, except for craggy mountains in the distance, the land was flat and desolate save for a few gas stations, diners that probably never opened and scattered houses bleached gray by the sun. Occasionally, a cluster of houses would form a town, complete with a 'welcome to' sign and population amount. Most were in double digits. The odd kid on a bike would wave. I saw several old men walking with horses or mules on the side of the road. They waved, too. Did Central Casting import them for our benefit?

The sign read "Piedras Viejas - Home of the Rattlesnakes" which I took to mean a high school sports team but who knows? The houses were one story, usually made of concrete or adobe, with dirt yards surrounded by chain link fences. Instead of grass, residents adorned their grounds with colorful pinwheels, faded tree limbs shaped like animals and tires painted white and used as planters. Dogs on their hind legs strained against the fences and barked at everyone and no one.

The roadway emitted heat waves that distorted everything.

I grew up in the District, surrounded by street noise, yelling neighbors and the occasional gunshot, so small towns without crowds of people, blaring horns or sidewalks scare me.

I shook Horace's arm. "We're here."

He lifted his hat brim and peered out the windshield as a white plastic bag bobbed along the road and lodged itself on the front bumper for a few seconds before flying away. "If you lived here, you'd be home by now," he said. "Look."

The sign said 'sheriff's office' as if you couldn't find it on your own just by driving around the entire one block by three-block downtown area. We pulled into a slanted parking space in front of the most modern building within 200 square-mile. It was all glass and metal in contrast to the worn-out wood and brick buildings that surrounded it. There was actually a paved sidewalk in front that spanned its width, then abruptly stopped. It had a wheelchair accessible ramp. The building to the right said "Jim's Mother's Restaurant" and had honest-to-goodness swinging doors. The building to the left said "Hardware," with a wooden Indian in front.

As I looked down the street, the *Gunsmoke* theme was repeated and I felt like walking behind the structures to see if it was real or a movie set.

What stood out most was a line of brand-new police cars parked across the street.

Before we walked in, I turned to Horace. "Ten bucks?"

"You got it."

The inside was cool as a cave, but brighter than a Florida beach. There was a bullpen surrounded by offices and a reception desk. The desk sergeant, or whatever they call them here, smiled as he looked us over. "You must be the gentlemen from the TV."

"Netflix," I corrected.

"Right, Netflix. I get that on my cable. Good shows. Good shows." His face got brighter. "My wife watches the ones about that Scottish woman who goes through time. She loves it. Me, I like the movies. Pretty much anything except romance. But you're not here to talk to me. You want Chief Montano."

He held up a finger and called on the phone with the other hand. "Hang on just one second."

He shook his head as he whispered into the phone. "Yes, ma'am."

He pointed down the hall. "Last door on the right. Enjoy your visit."

Horace looked at me. "Netflix?"

"The bigger the lie," I replied.

The door was open, and she waved us in.

She walked around her desk and shook our hands. "Feliz Montano." She wore her dress uniform complete with medals.

We introduced ourselves. "Chick Gomez," I said.

"Brent Peterson," Horace added. "Nice to meet you."

We handed her our business cards, and she placed them on her desk.

She looked at Horace's business card and asked, "What exactly is 'Prime Location Services?'"

"We're an independent company that scouts locations for filming. Production companies hire us to do the preliminary work before they make their decision on where to shoot. They tell us what they're looking for, we make some phone calls, do some searches on the internet and try to match up a location with their needs."

"You must visit some interesting places."

"Absolutely," I said. "Brent and I have been all over the world."

She turned back to Horace. "So, what can I do for you fellows today?"

"Well, chief, as we said on the phone, we're not just interested in how a place looks but how the people in the area might respond to having a film crew in the area, sometimes for an extended period of time."

She swiveled her chair and looked out the window at the line of police cars and then back to us.

"Funny things happen when a shooting crew shows up," I said. I focused hard on talking like a normal person. "Let me give you an example. There's so much filming around Los Angeles that when a shooting occurs in a residential neighborhood, the outstretched hands come out."

"I don't understand."

"All of a sudden, everyone has to mow their lawn, if you know what I mean."

"Actually, I don't."

"The noise would ruin the shoot so the director has someone pay off people not to mow their lawns, not to play loud music or work on cars in their driveway. Did you ever see the phrase 'best boy' on the credits?"

"Yes, I've always wondered about that."

"He or she is kind of a gopher. One of their jobs is to hand our fifties to neighbors to keep the noise down." I had no idea what the hell I was talking about.

"Interesting," she said. "If I'm reading you right, you are here to not only check on the area but to see if our residents will cooperate."

"Yes, kind of," said Horace. "And crowd control. I know that your population may be modest but you'd be surprised how many miles people will travel to see celebrities."

"I see. Well, we certainly can handle crowds. We have 15 officers just for our town and we can pull from the county and state police if necessary."

"That's the downside, if you will," I said. "The upside is how much money a production crew drops. They're looking at a two-week shoot which could mean… let's see…" I read from my blank notebook. "Maybe a hundred-thousand dollars and that's just for food, rentals of public space, and we pay your officers for crowd control. And that doesn't include if, say, they want to shoot in someone's restaurant or home. That could mean two or three grand a day to that owner."

"Interesting."

"And," Horace said, "there's the free publicity for your town. News crews often do stories on the sets of movies. That could mean more money for your town. It may even bring in tourists. What do you think?"

"Let me talk to the board of supervisors and get back to you."

"Sure," I said. "We'll be around for several days."

The chief looked at me and squinted. "By the way Mr. Gomez, have we met before? Your face looks familiar."

"I have that kind of mug," I said. Damn it. I was doing so well with my normal person's banter up until then. I can hold it together for just so long. I hope she didn't take notice.

As we walked out, Horace handed me a ten-spot, and I detected a low-level growl.

"Like taking candy from a baby," I said, pocketing the sawbuck. "They always jaw with the white guy first."

CHAPTER 25

We checked into the hotel then went next door to Jim's Mother's Restaurant. There were license plates on the walls, business cards pinned to a corkboard and rusted metal yard sale crap hanging from the ceiling. The door to the men's bathroom sported a stag head and the women's had the rear end with a white tail that stuck straight up. We sat at the bar.

The place was full which wasn't surprising. I think there were only two restaurants in town. Several servers in jeans, T-shirts and black aprons with dozens of pens in the front pocket weaved around the tables and called everyone 'hon' or 'pard.'

The bartender introduced himself as Jim and asked if we were the TV fellers they had heard about. We nodded our heads simultaneously. Horace commented to Jim how friendly everyone seemed even though we were strangers. He replied that except for border patrol officers they didn't see many outsiders but that everyone was welcomed here except for coyotes. It took me a second to realize that he wasn't talking about four-legged animals.

We ordered beers.

"Is that a problem?" Horace asked.

"Well, sir. It is. These folks come across the border and they bring other illegals and drugs and all kinds of diseases. Let me show you something." He reached behind the bar and retrieved a paper tube. He moved our glasses to either side and unrolled the paper revealing a map. He placed our beers on either end to keep it from curling. "See, this is the Buenos Aires National Wildlife Refuge. It kind of forms a notch." He moved his finger in a 'U.' "And we're right smack in the middle. The Refuge goes right to the Mexican border. The Feds put up fences but they just climb right over them. They walk through the Refuge and make their way north." He pointed to a town called Three Points which was southwest of Tucson. "Once they get there, they're home free. They can go anywhere in the US.

"What's the Refuge like?" I asked.

"It's beautiful. Rugged, mind you. Mountains, desert. You name it. It's God's country."

"Including the dead bodies," a voice from behind us said.

It was Chief Montano in fancy cowgirl clothes including a bolo tie and boots.

We swiveled our stools to face her.

"Jim," she said, "send a beer over." She directed us to a table in the corner.

"I was thinking about your proposition, gentlemen. And I have to tell you that it may be a hard sell to the board."

"Why's that?" I asked.

"We kind of like our town the way it is. We don't want a lot of hoopla and we certainly don't want any tourists. We can't handle it. There's only one hotel. Besides, money-wise, we're doing fine. Believe it or not, we run a surplus every year."

"Do tell," Horace said.

"Why don't we go for a ride-along tomorrow? I can show you around personally. Maybe you'll decide it's not suitable anyway and a meeting with the board of supervisors would be a moot point."

"That sounds solid to me," I said. "Out of this world."

Fortunately, she laughed. "I will pick you up outside your hotel at eight. We want to get an early start while there's still some coolness in the air." Her beer arrived and she downed it in two gulps. She tossed a fiver on the table, and I handed it back.

"Thanks." She looked at me again and cocked her head. "Are you sure we haven't met?"

"I would remember," I said, focusing all my might to talk like everyone else. "What was that about dead bodies?"

"You'll see tomorrow," she said and walked out.

Horace ordered another round. "Did she spot you at the bar when you were tailing Senator Metcalfe?"

"I was very careful. By the way, I got a call from Goldie. A woman who didn't leave her name asked to speak with us. Goldie said we were out of town on a location search in Arizona. The caller didn't leave a message and didn't ask for our mobile phone numbers. Montano was checking up on us."

"She's a cop," Horace said.

* * *

The next morning, we sat at the same table as last night and ordered breakfast.

"Somebody went through my bags last night, probably when we were at the bar." I said.

"Mine, too," Horace replied. "Sure you want to go into the desert with her? She could kill us and leave us with the rest of the dead bodies."

"Why would she do that?"

"Why wouldn't she?"

We ate in silence for a few minutes. "How are your eggs?" I asked.

"This is serious, Sam. She may have made you; they went through our bags. What else do you need to know?"

"Why someone murdered Helen Boston. Why a senator is sending encrypted messages to Mexico and why he met with a cop who is more crooked than the number three."

Outside a police siren chirped. "Our ride's here," I said.

We walked outside. It was already close to ninety degrees, according to the bank thermometer.

"Mr. Gomez, why don't you sit up front with me," Montano said. "Let's hit the road first. On the way back, I can show you around town."

"Sounds like a kick," I said.

"Why do you talk like that?"

"Like what?"

"Like an old black & white gangster movie."

"He got hit on the head," Horace said, laughing.

"If you say so," Montano replied, as she turned down the volume on the police radio. "I'm officially out of service. The day is my own."

We drove south.

"We're only five miles from the Mexican border as the crow flies," she said. "Most of it is federal land." We pulled over to the side of the road next to a dry river bed. She stepped out of the SUV and put on a wide brimmed straw hat. "Let's walk."

The land was flatter than day-old beer and looked like a giant had haphazardly tossed around rocks, cactus and small bushes in an angry fit. In front of us was about forty feet of a split rail fence. One of the posts had staples in it like it once held a paper sign. We walked around it.

We followed behind Montano on a well-walked path about a foot wide. I was surprised to see plastic bags, a sock, a backpack strap and other random debris along the trail. Except for the road, our vehicle and a tower on a faraway mountain top there was not a man-made structure as far as I could see.

Our footsteps crunching the parched ground were the only sounds. Even the birds that flitted from cactus to cactus went about their business quietly.

We saw the dust in front of us rise like a dirty geyser before we heard the sound. Montano flattened to the trail first and we did likewise. She calmly turned her head and said "sniper."

She pointed to a berm a few feet to our right and ran there in a crouch. "C'mon," she yelled. Our desert foxhole provided cover as three more shots pinged around us. I peeked my head up and couldn't see anyone.

She mounted her pistol on the top and peered out. It was clear to both of us that there was no shot to take. All we saw was desert. She slid down and looked at us.

"Who?" I said.

"Don't know. Border patrol doesn't use snipers as far as I know. Could be ranchers. They get pretty pissed at illegals crossing their land."

"But we're on federal land," I said.

"They think they own that, too," she said.

A bullet buzzed our heads like a mosquito and hit a cactus with a thunking sound.

Horace wiggled his phone out of his pants pocket. "Don't bother," the chief said. "No service here." Lying on his side, Horace checked his phone anyway. "Not a fucking bar," he said.

More bullets flew by in evenly spaced succession. "Looks like we may be here a while," I said. "What was it that you wanted to show us anyway, chief?"

"That," she said, pointing toward the hit cactus that was now bleeding a white liquid.

At the foot of the saguaro lay faded clothes – pants, shirt – in the shape of a person, like they had simply melted away. Above the shirt was a skull. The jeans still held a bit of its original blue. There were no shoes. Next to the clothes was an opened backpack surrounded by food wrappers, shards of aluminum foil and a strips of duct tape.

"One of my deputies reported this last week. I wanted to check it out."

"And you just leave it... them... here?" Horace said.

"This is not an unusual find," the chief said, giving a quick prairie dog up-and-down peek over the dirt rim. "We find many people, what's left of them, on this trail. Other illegals find them, too, strip them of what they can use and leave the bodies. There are so many that the feds don't even take them away. They just let Mother Nature do its thing. For a while, there was a church group that gathered the remains for Christian burials but I haven't seen them in a while."

About ten minutes later she rose. "I think they're done." The chief brushed her clothes, took out a notebook and wrote on a black page.

I stood up and looked in the direction of the gunshots. I thought I saw some dust in the air about 400-hundred yards away.

She smiled. "You don't seem all that shaken up. I would think getting shot at might rile a person from Hollywood."

"I'm originally from Brooklyn."

Horace kept squinting into the vast empty desert as we hoofed it towards the car.

The chief started the engine, and offered a self-assured smirk. "What do you think so far?" she asked.

"I'm wondering if the rest of the town will be this inviting toward strangers," I said.

CHAPTER 26

Horace sat in the backseat constantly checking his phone. He let out a tiny yelp of joy when he saw a few bars appear as we neared Piedras Viegas.

Montano turned up the radio and grabbed the microphone. "Headquarters this is Unit One."

A voice responded: "Go ahead, chief."

Montano described the location where the shooting took place and told the dispatcher to send out a car to check the area where she thought the shots came from. She hung up the mic and looked at me. "They won't find anything," she said, as she kept her eyes straight ahead. "But it's protocol."

"You seem pretty calm about it, too," I said.

"I served in Iraq and Afghanistan," she said. "The fear of being shot dead is gone from my body - and my mind. I just react out of my instinct for survival. Then I move on to the next situation."

"Just another day in the desert?" I said.

She didn't answer.

"Tell me about your overseas tours."

"Marines. Chopper pilot. Evac mostly. Two tours in each theater. Total of three years. You?"

"Air Force. Not much to tell."

She began: "I was proud to serve, but this country's going to hell in a handbasket. You saw a little of what goes on at the border, but it's not half of what's really happening. Most of the country thinks that we're rednecks and we don't like immigrants. That's not the case. We have ranchers here who've owned their properties for many generations, some of it from Spanish land grants. You can argue about whether that was right or wrong, but they do own the land legally according to the courts. Every day, they see parades of people crossing their property." Her eyes went cold; her face tightened.

"This one rancher, Rob Frantz was his name, he and his family have about thirty-five thousand acres just north of the border. His family's one of the oldest in the area. Frantz and his son, Rob Jr. have been complaining to the feds over and over but nothing ever happens. All they hear from the media and those do-good groups is that they are racists." The last words spat from her mouth.

"Their land is between two mountains which forces people to walk on a narrow strip as they head north. There's a well-traveled trail there, just like the one we were on. It goes right through their property."

"Why not just let the people pass through?"

"For a long while, they did. But a few years ago, the situation got ugly. The migrants, smugglers, whatever you want to call them, began cutting irrigation and cattle-drinking pipes instead of drinking from spigots, ones that Frantz actually installed for the thousands who walked by each year."

"Thousands?" I said.

"No lie. And I'm not even talking about the hundreds who died on his land that he and his family had to deal with. Frantz was more compassionate than other ranchers. He once told me: 'Nobody should die of thirst no matter who they are.' But when they started spooking the cattle and cutting the pipes from drilled wells installed on the property Frantz had had it. He would lose thousands of gallons every time a pipe was cut. These breaks would occur far from their house and it could take days before they found it. Thirty-five thousand acres is huge. He was starting to lose his patience and sympathy.

"One day, Frantz takes his ATV and his dog Diablo along with tools to fix a broken pipe that his brother-in-law had discovered. That was the last anyone saw of him."

Horace perked up. "What happened?"

"We called in ground search teams and choppers. The next day Border Patrol found him face down in a wash near highway Thirty-Nine. His dog was lying on his body, shivering, almost dead, but he had enough energy to growl and bark at the officers every time they tried to come near Frantz's body. An animal control officer had to put down the dog right there."

I saw her knuckles turn white against the steering wheel. "Frantz was dead from three gunshot wounds. His rifle was still in the scabbard on the side of his ATV. We investigated along with the border patrol but the only lead we had was footprints left in the muddy soil near the pipe. We got some phone calls over the following days but nothing concrete. One of the calls was very interesting, though. It came into our office about a week later."

"Oh?"

"It was from a woman who said that the Sinaloa cartel had executed her husband because he was the one who shot Frantz."

"They wanted to fade the beef?"

"Uh, yes," she said, looking at me sideway. "I guess so. They figured they could square this by taking care of the guy themselves. She didn't give a name or any details. The call came from Sinaloa, according to Mexican authorities."

"Do you believe it?"

"Who knows? If they could kill this guy to keep the heat off them, it certainly fits their MO. Life is cheap in Mexico."

She made a right turn onto Main Street. "Here we are again. Downtown Piedra Viegas." She forced a smile that was almost close to genuine.

I saw trailers on otherwise empty lots, TV dishes pointing skyward and more chain link fences than a reformatory. Rocks placed in designs – circles, squares– adorned hard-packed, dirt yards. Wooden wagon wheels leaned against low trees with bare limbs. Pickup trucks sat in front of shacks, their doors a different color than the body. The air still smelled hot.

Every once in a while, I clocked a house that stood out. They were neat, pueblo style with golf-course type lawns. They had long driveways ending in two-car garages. Walkways of fitted pavers in serene curves led to large main entrances. One in particular caught my attention because it was two stories high and larger than the others. Glass traveled from top to bottom and a balcony surrounded the second level. It was built into a rock formation that appeared not to be naturally occurring. I thought I saw a pool house behind a board-on-board fence.

"That's my digs," Montano said. "Real estate's a lot cheaper here than where you live."

It took ten minutes to tour the entire town including a stop in front of three boulders the size of fifty-gallon drums and about the same shape. They were in a perfectly straight line.

"We're named for these rocks," Montano said. "The story is that the first Spanish explorers saw these lined up as they are and believed it was divine intervention that put them there." She swept her hand. "See how they line up? They point to sunrise on the spring equinox, probably a coincidence. We tried calling it 'The Arizona Stonehenge,' even had a sign made, but nobody seemed to care." She laughed. "Some teenagers stole the sign."

She drove us back to the sheriff's office and led us inside. "Anything else I can do for you fellows?"

"I think we've seen enough," I said. "We'll be in touch."

"Thanks, sheriff," Horace said.

As we reached the door, I turned. "No offense, but how can a town this size afford all those new police cars. And this building; it's new."

Montano squinted. "Federal dollars," she said. "The government pays us to patrol border areas so they don't have to. We're actually saving the taxpayers money."

I wondered how much cabbage the taxpayers shelled out for her pool.

CHAPTER 27

"What do you think of Chief Montano?" Horace said, as we sailed the I-19 super slab north to Tucson International.

"She's as dirty as a roach motel in a fast-food restaurant," I said. "You don't have to be the Continental Op to see that." Horace started to ask, then stopped.

"All the new police cars in a shitty town like that? That ain't on the square. And here's a news bulletin: those cars and that new cop house didn't come from the feds."

"How do you know that?"

"Before we left DC, I checked. They get almost zilch in federal monies."

"So where…"

"Drug forfeitures." I pointed to a diner that promised the world's best cup of coffee. I didn't think that was on the level, but even second best would be dandy. "Pull in here." We entered and slid into a booth where the red pleather seats were cracked and slit at the edges. The Formica table had more chips than a Vegas casino. A substantial waiter whose name tag identified him as 'Doug' appeared out of nowhere with a coffee pot in each hand.

"High test or decaf," he said, with a smile wider than a hippo's yawn. He raised each hand as he spoke. We both pointed to the caffeinated choice. "Anything to eat, fellas?" I thought I detected a flirt but it may have just been the heat.

We each ordered the breakfast special touted on the blackboard behind the counter as offering 'your choice of eggs, your choice of meat and your choice of toast.' He scribbled our preferences in her notebook. "Coming right up."

I had no doubt of his promise. We were the only customers.

Horace looked at me. "Talk."

"Let's say that the coppers suspect you of drug dealing. They stop your car and search it. If they find money, drugs, whatever, they get to keep it. They can even search your crib. Whatever they find, they can glom. Here's the kicker. Even if you're found innocent, they still can keep the loot."

"You're kidding," Horace said.

"This goes for any kind of traffic stop. As long as the flatfoot has probable cause, like speeding, they can take your shit, and you've got almost no recourse." I held up my phone with a newspaper article. "Dig this."

Horace read: "Since the terrorist attacks of 9-11, state and local police had seized almost three billion dollars from motorists and others without search warrants or indictments." He scrolled the story in the *Washington Post*. "Police routinely stopped drivers for minor traffic infractions, pressed them to agree to searches without warrants and seized large amounts of cash when there was no evidence of wrongdoing." He put down his coffee cup and said: "So even if you're found not guilty, they still keep what they confiscated?"

"Yes. As long as they have a reason to stop you, their confiscation is considered kosher." Doug walked over with our meals and slid them in front of us. "Enjoy," he said.

Horace blinked his eyes. "I'm still not getting this. You mean to tell me that police can keep my stuff just on suspicion of drug trafficking even if later I'm found not guilty…"

I cut him off. "Even if there's not enough evidence, and the DA decides not to indict you."

"What about the Fourth Amendment?"

I lowered my mitt below the table. "I got your Fourth Amendment right here." I tried to sound like Tony Soprano but fell short.

"Not funny, Sam."

"How do you think Montano got all those new cars and that spiffy new cop house?"

"And her home, probably," Horace added.

"All over the country, local and state cops are raking it in. I've seen them take a Mercedes off a drug dealer and turn it into a cop car. Add that to all the used military-grade weaponry they get from the feds for homeland security and these local yokels have themselves a sweet pile of goodies."

Horace picked at his eggs. "Who else knows about this?"

"Anyone who can read," I said. "You wanna feel even worse? Companies conduct seminars on how police can maximize their profits, make more busts that bring in more lettuce. I've hinged the brochures."

"So," Horace said, "Montano's border town is in the right place at the right time to make money with this loophole. With all the smugglers passing through it's like her own personal ATM. She stops a few every day and trolls for riches."

"Speaking of stops, what was that deal with the cop stopping us and asking about our citizenship?" I asked.

"That's another one. According to the law, a cop can inquire about your citizenship if they have reason to believe that you're in the country illegally. When those assholes stopped us, they had no probable cause except that we were near the border. Most people just answer but I wasn't going to play his game. They couldn't detain us without probable cause which was why I kept asking 'are you detaining us?' That's when he gave up. Most people just pull over and allow themselves to be searched or hand over a passport or something. I hate those motherfuckers." I watched as a vein popped out of Horace's neck. His face turned red.

"What would be probable cause?"

"Talking Spanish, having an 'I love Guatemala' sticker on your car. Who the hell knows with these guys? You have to listen carefully to how they talk, too. Did you notice how he said, "Would you mind moving your car over there?' or something like that. He wasn't ordering us, he was asking us, which was why I kept repeating 'are you detaining us?'"

He was now digging into his eggs with fury, jamming his white toast into the runny yolk like he was plugging a hole. We finished our meals, and I motioned to Doug for the check.

Horace downed his coffee. "You didn't tell me that we were going to be shot at."

"It was nothing."

"Nothing?"

"All for show."

"The bullets flying over our heads felt pretty damn real."

"Use your melon. The sniper could see through the scope that it was Montano. Ranchers don't want to off her. The Border Patrol doesn't use snipers and the drug cartels aren't interested in killing anyone in Arizona unless they have to, especially not law enforcement. Even then, the smugglers don't carry weapons. They're low-level mules just trying to score a buck. And that stuff about not worrying about being shot at that Montano laid on us? That's malarkey."

"Then who's left?"

"Someone Montano paid off. Ex-marine sniper, probably someone she served with. If he wanted us chilled, we'd have as much chance as finding hips on a snake. We were in the middle of nowhere. A couple of hard boys with AK's could've turned us into dust. The idea was to scare us."

"It worked pretty well on me," Horace said.

"She doesn't want any outsiders snooping around especially people with cameras. She's got a lucrative grift."

"Cops making money on drug smugglers… legally. What the hell's going on with this country?"

I floated some greenbacks over the check and waved goodbye to Doug. "That's above my pay grade. For now, I'm only thinking about finding Boston's killer and fitting him for bracelets. I'll worry about the fate of the Union later."

CHAPTER 28

I was glad to be back in the city. Open spaces give me the willies. And all that nonsense that it's not the heat it's the humidity… it's the heat.

I was heading over to the Teekee for an afternoon tightener when a black Interceptor skidded to the curb. I stood still to see who would pop out of the passenger side although I had a feeling I knew.

Keegan.

"Pretty dramatic entrance," I said, as he bounded to the sidewalk, barely missing a parking meter.

"You've been traveling, eh?" he said.

"I got itchy feet."

"First New York, then Chicago. And what the hell were you doing in fucking Missoula, Montana? Who goes there?"

Billy Wong must have taken the GPS and pasted it on a long-haul truck.

"My phone now says you're in Reno, but here you are right in front of me. It's not cool to fool the DEA."

"I have no idea what you're talking about Keegan."

"I'm sure you don't, Marlowe."

"What have you been up to?" he said, leaning against the parking meter that nearly sliced him into twins.

"This and that. You know, trying to catch the bad guys, keeping the world safe for democracy."

"Have you found Sameer?"

"I would have told you. Remember, we had a deal to share information."

Keegan looked like someone had a gun to his head and forced him to smile. "Here's some information – just because we're buddies. Pemberton still makes you for the murder of your client."

"Really? And you know that because you were privy to our conversation?"

"Something like that."

Exactly like that. "And what do you think?"

"I've known you for a long time, Marlowe. You're not a saint, but I've never known you to kill a client."

"Thanks. That's a resume builder."

He cleared his throat. "What do you know about the Mexican border?"

"Tacos, wide sombreros, burros laden with burlap bags, men sleeping against the walls of cantinas in the afternoon. And piñatas. I love those things."

"Cut the crap, Sam. I know you've taken an interest in that part of the world."

"And you know that how?"

"I'm with the government. We know everything." His smile was no longer forced. When he realized that I was screwing him with the GPS play he must have checked the fly list. He knows we traveled to Tucson. He probably checked the car rental agencies, too, knows we skirted the border.

"Horace and I were taking a short vacation in the desert. I was hoping to stay longer but you know how it is. I just can't seem to get away for more than a few days anymore."

"Do you know a cop named Montano?"

"What's that name again?"

He let out a long breath. "I'm gonna talk and you're gonna listen." His lard turned hard. His body stiffened. I cut him off before he could open his maw.

"Is this the speech where you tell me to back off, to just walk away, that I don't know the forces that I'm up against?"

"You're watching too many old movies Sam."

"I just got a free week of HBO and Showtime."

"This isn't funny. Frankly, I don't give a shit if you end up with a bullet in your heart. But I do care about my case, and this one especially."

"Which one is that… especially?"

"I'm with DEA so, let's say… drugs?"

"And Sameer?"

"Cards on the table. Sameer, drugs, Mexican drug cartels, Boston's murder. They're all connected. You know it and I know it."

"Does Pemberton know it?"

"If I have to pin Boston's murder on you to get you out of the way, I will."

"And I thought we were pals."

"Friendship goes just so far, Sam. If you have something that can help me, tell me. Otherwise, step aside." I felt like I was in a western shootout movie where the sheriff takes off his star and challenges the gunslinger to a duel.

Out of the corner of my eye I saw a blue light flash on the dashboard of his car. "You're being paged," I said.

The driver motioned for Keegan just as he was about to say something. I opened my yap instead. "Isn't this when you're supposed to tell me that this isn't over by a longshot?"

He growled and headed for his ride. He slammed the door and the car squealed away. I had a feeling that Keegan was straight with me on one thing. He would do whatever he had to do to keep me from queering his case. Even frame me for murder.

CHAPTER 29

Why does it always have to be a dark alley? Can't people ever meet in a well-lit alley?

But here I was, 2:30 a.m., my roscoe under my left arm and wake-up joe sloshing in my gut.

The siren song that beckoned me here was a phone call. Which also chaffed against one of my rules: Nothing good ever happens after 2 a.m. I think I stole that line from a TV sitcom, but it seems to hold up in real life.

The caller said he was Sameer Patel and I believed him. I asked him a technical question about the USB that I found in his apartment and he is the only person other than Horace and me who knew about it. At least that's what I figured. Sometimes you have to take a chance even if it breaks your 2 a.m. rule.

The alley was off U Street Northwest where the bars were disgorging patrons in various states of sobriety after the weekday last call. Some were heading to their cars, some were wobbling back and forth on the sidewalk waiting for Ubers and Lyfts, and others simply loped to the nearest out-of-the-way spot and left a puddle for the morning staff to hose down.

I again felt the reassurance of the bulge under my coat as I stood flat against a brick wall. I didn't want any light from the street making me look like a body silhouette practice target with concentric circles around my heart.

A voice near the dumpster to my right said: "Mr. Marlowe?"

I turned my head and caught a whiff of rotten fruit and urine. A rat big enough to be a cat hybrid, sniffed my shoe and scurried when I lifted my foot. A swarm of flies buzzed my ear.

"Who are you? I asked.

"Sameer Patel. I understand that you're looking for me."

"Let me eye you."

He took a step into a sliver of light. He looked more like his driver's license photo than most of us do even although he appeared to be wrung out.

I began easy. "Many people are interested in your whereabouts including Sarah Felder."

His pan registered zero emotion. He shifted his weight.

"By now you've probably figured out most of it," he said. "Do you want to hear the details?"

"I'm already awake, and I have plenty of room in my ears. Start from page one. I'll stop you if I get bored or a rat starts gnawing on my ankle."

His face loosened. "I have a gambling problem. Football, baseball, horses. I was into a bookie named Maxie V for eighty-five large."

Maxie V's real name is Maximilian Valenzuela. Legend has it that he came to the states from Mexico with his three brothers, and they opened a landscaping business and made a killing. Maxie also worked for a bookie king named Rafael Vargas and made a killing there as well. He sliced and diced Vargas during an argument and scattered his boss's body parts all over the city and the coppers still haven't stitched together a complete human being. Nobody put up a fuss when Maxie took over Rafael's business.

Sameer said: "Maxie said he would lower my vig to zero if I did a favor for a friend."

"And that friend was the Sinaloa cartel?"

He gasped. "No. It was for a congressman named Phillip Metcalfe. When I met with him, he wanted something pretty simple, at least it seemed simple at the time. He needed a phone app that could encrypt phone calls. I won't bore you with the technical requirements."

"Did he say why he wanted it?"

"No. And I didn't ask. It was for a congressman so I figured it was legit. Later I learned that it was for the drug cartel, and that's when I got worried."

"How did you learn that?"

"For reasons out of my control, the app became unstable, and users were unhappy to say the least.' His eyes scanned the alleyway. "I got a visit from several of the most unsatisfied customers and… here, look."

I hadn't seen it before, because it was in the shadows, but his right arm was in a cast.

"They were all set to break my fingers until I told them that I needed them to work the keyboard in order to fix the app. That's when I decided to disappear."

"Why call me?" I asked.

"I want to stop hiding. I want to give myself up but I'm not sure how to do it. If the drug cartel has a congressman on their payroll who knows who else they're in bed with? The DEA, the local cops. I was hoping that you could, I don't know, help me get out of this jam without dying. I'm willing to name names, go all the way. Do whatever I have to."

"How much of this does Sarah know?"

"I want to keep her out of this."

"If she's involved there's nothing I can do. If she knew where you've been holed up, which I suspect she did, then she's already involved."

He let out a deep breath. “Let’s go.”

“Go where?” I asked.

“To the cops, feds, wherever you say. I trust you.”

“Why do you trust me?”

Before he could answer, I saw the god damn aura. The bright green light blazed a hole in my brain. Not now! It felt like a metal spike was being driven through my ear. The big faint was on its way. I heard Sameer call my name. The stench of puke attacked my sniffer as my noggin slammed the cobble stones. My world turned blacker than the inside of an 8-ball.

CHAPTER 30

I felt like my head was being used for practice by a power metal drummer. On the plus side, I was alive.

On the minus side, Sameer was lying next to me, a hole the exact size of a bullet in his forehead. His lamps were still open.

I saw strobing blue lights bounce off the alley walls. Their brightness made me wince each time they cycled. Before I could lean up on my left arm, a voice shouted from the street: "Put down the gun."

Was he talking to me? My peepers flowed down my arm to my fingers which were clutching a gat. Fuck. I rolled the rod out of my mitt, but I didn't have the strength to do anything else except lie on my side and wait. Heavy footsteps got louder. I knew the drill. First, he would kick the piece away from me, then he would scream to put my hands behind my back, then he would cuff me. What he did next depended upon whether or not his bodycam was on.

The pounding in my cranium was 20 on a scale of one to ten.

As I lay hogtied on my stomach, I could see the flatfoot checking Sameer's neck for a pulse. He shook his head from side to side as his partner yanked on the bracelets lifting me off the ground several times then letting me go like he was plucking a harp string. I arched my back as best as I could to keep my map from kissing the ground.

The next few minutes were a blur of radio calls, frisking and more coppers milling around. More than a few of them gave me a quick kick in the side just for fun as they walked by.

I twisted my neck to look up at the officers who was talking to me. "Is this you, Sam Marlowe?" he said, as he shined a flashlight on my driver's license.

"My PI license has a better likeness. I was more relaxed when they took it."

"You think this is funny, asshole?"

"Not funny at all, but it is, I guess you might say, ironic. There's always a bit of humor in irony, don't you think?"

"What the hell are you talking about?"

"That guy over there," I tried to motion with my head. "I've been looking for him. We finally meet and now he's dead. That's irony."

"That's murder," he said. "And I'm guessing that your gun killed him. Your shoulder holster is empty and a gun was in your hand when we found you."

"Maybe irony isn't quite the right word," I said.

A new voice pierced the alley. "What do we have here?"

"One dead, a single gunshot to the forehead. We found a gun that belongs to this guy," the copper said. I couldn't look up to see who he was talking to.

"Turn him over," the voice said.

My eyesight was blurry, but I made the pan. "Hello, Detective Pemberton," I said. "What brings you here?"

"You know this asshole?" the copper said.

"Yeah, I know him. One murder's not enough for you, Marlowe?"

"Another murder?" the officer said.

"I like him for an intentional overdose in 2D. Get him on his feet."

Two men pulled me up by my arms but I couldn't stand on my own. "C'mon," one of them said, as he poked me in the ribs with his baton.

"Easy, I got a medical condition."

"Fuck your medical condition," he said, as they pushed me against the wall and pinned me there.

"This place smells," I said, as Pemberton inched closer. "I saw some rats, too. This area could use a power wash. Know what I mean?"

Another officer approached the detective, pointed to Sameer's body, and I heard him whisper, 'no ID.'

"Who is that?" she asked me.

"His name is Sameer Patel. He called and wanted to meet me."

"Why would he do that?"

"Sameer got himself into some hot water. I've been looking for him and so is your pal Keegan."

"What does the DEA have to do with this?"

"That's a long story."

"I got time."

"I gotta sit down," I said.

She told the coppers to unlock my nippers but refasten them in front. One of them shimmied over a wooden crate and plopped me down with prejudice. She motioned for them to move away as the crime scene investigation team entered. "Swab his hands first," she ordered. "Test it in the van. I want to know now."

She turned back to me. "Okay, Marlowe. Let's have it."

"Patel was a gambler with Maxie V up his back."

"Maximilian Valenzuela, the bookmaker?"

"Patel owed him some big green but he couldn't pay. Some of Maxie's boys got physical, Patel got scared and called me to see what his options were."

"Why call you?"

"Friend of a friend of a client. You know how it is."

"Go on."

"Before we could swap business cards I blacked out from a chronic condition. When I woke up, he was iced, and I was getting booted in the ribs."

"What about Keegan? Why is he looking for him?'

"You'll have to ask him yourself. All I know is that Keegan and I found ourselves shaking down Patel's crib at the same time. He and I go way back."

"So I understand."

I didn't let on that I knew Keegan listened in on my interrogation with Pemberton. I also wasn't going to tell her all I knew about Patel and his involvement with the Sinaloa cartel. That story was Keegan's to tell – if he wanted to tell it.

The crime scene technician returned and handed Pemberton a sheet of paper. "Are you sure?" she asked.

"One hundred percent," the tech replied.

"Turn him loose," Pemberton said.

"What?" the officer said.

"You found him on the ground with a gun in his hand, right?

"Yes, ma'am."

"Was he wearing gloves?"

"No ma'am."

"The instant ID kit found no trace of GSR on his hands. He's not our shooter. I was hoping he was."

"Damn," the officer said. He stomped his feet and cracked his baton against the wall. He was angrier than a hornet in a jar.

My headache was raging full blast.

"You look like shit, Marlowe," Pemberton said. "Go home. We'll talk again."

"During the day," I said. "Not after 2 a.m. It's my one rule."

CHAPTER 31

I woke up sooner than I wanted, but I had to see Dominick LaFarge, Sameer's boss, before the cops got to him. He was my client and it was better for him to hear from me what happened to Sameer than from someone else.

I slugged down some wake-up juice and hit the road to Tyson's. Traffic was heavy. As I inched across the Roosevelt Bridge, I wondered how he would take the news. I wondered how Sarah would take the news. And I wondered why people in my orbit kept sleeping the big sleep.

All of this made me even more cynical than usual. It's not healthy to be like this but it's just how I am and what I do for a living. Many dicks, cops, doctors and anyone who deals with death handle it with booze which… yeah, that's how I do it, too. And jokes. It's all about the wise cracks. It's an immature defense mechanism. I know that. It works most of the time to keep me from seeing the ugliness in the world but when it doesn't I get punched in the kidneys, kicked in alleys, knocked on the head and generally thought of as an irresponsible asshole by those around me. If I could change it I would.

The way I talk doesn't help either. Sometimes I'm amazed I function in day-to-day society as well as I do.

This morning, I was cold sober and not feeling particularly humorous. The area behind my eyes pulsed and my head felt too large for my ears. As I replayed last night, I was certain that I wasn't being tailed so it had to be Sameer who brought the shooter. Or was it a random act of violence? No, a slug square to the forehead usually meant someone was standing in front of him at point blank range. Sameer may have been begging for his life or giving up something, or both. Either way, he now was cooling on a metal tray in the morgue waiting to be claimed. I'm not sure who would do that. According to his employment record, he had no family in the States.

I had called from my heap that I was on the way and Sarah was sitting behind the reception desk as I stepped off the elevator. She stood up to greet me. She was featuring a yellow sun dress with flowers and a pearl necklace. Sandals closed the deal. She looked more like an afternoon at the pool club than a day at the office.

"It's casual Friday," she said. "Mr. LaFarge is waiting."

"I'd like to jaw with both of you."

"Okay," she said, her lip trembling.

LaFarge was where I left him the first time we met, sitting behind a clear glass desk with not a scrap of paper in sight.

"I was concerned that we hadn't heard from you Mr. Marlowe. Have you found Sameer?"

"He was dusted last night," I said. Just as the words came out of my mouth, I knew they were wrong. Damn it, Marlowe. Focus.

"What does that mean?" LaFarge asked.

"I'm sorry. That was crude." Hold it together. Talk normal. "Sameer was shot last night. I'm sorry to say that he's dead. As far as I know, police don't have any leads."

Sarah took a step back and almost fell. LaFarge wheeled his chair around and guided her into it.

"What happened?" he asked. Sarah began to cry.

"He called me and said that he wanted to meet. We did, but before we could even talk, I had one of my blackouts. You know about them; you've seen it firsthand. When I woke up, he was dead and I was in handcuffs."

"Handcuffs?" he said.

"He was shot with my gun."

Sarah gasped. LaFarge froze.

"I didn't do it. The police let me go."

I could tell that LaFarge wanted more details about why the police let me go, but he didn't ask. "I told the coppers that I had been hired to find Sameer, but I didn't snitch on who or why. Get ready. Once they do a background search on him, they'll be over to chat with you."

"What should I tell them?"

"That's up to you." I looked at Sarah and she was still crying. LaFarge put a hand on her shoulder. "It'll be okay," he said.

"One other thing," I said. "The DEA has been looking for Sameer, too. The police will probably ask you if you know anything about that."

"Drugs? Are you serious?" he said. Sarah looked up and stopped her crying in mid weep.

"Dead serious," I said, then realizing that the 'dead' part also was a poor choice of words. C'mon, Marlowe. Stay with it.

"What do you think, Mr. Marlowe. "About the drugs, I mean."

"I don't know anything about it," I said, bracing for my nose to grow. No way I was going to spill about Sameer and the Sinaloa cartel. My inner cynic screamed that LaFarge may be part of it.

Just then the phone rang and Sarah composed herself enough to answer it. She offered a few 'yeses,' hung up and turned to us. "That was the police," she said. "They're on their way over."

"I better hit the pavement," I said. Sarah walked me out and stood with me while I waited for the elevator.

"Sam," she said. "What do I tell the police about my relationship with Sameer?"

"Like I told LaFarge, that's up to you. By the way, what do you know about Sameer and why the DEA was looking for him?"

"Nothing. Not a thing."

"Will I see you again, Sam?"

"That's flat… er, I mean I'm sure of it."

CHAPTER 32

"Have you been avoiding me, Sam?"

I was stealing about in the dark with a penlight flashlight, trying not to make any noise, looking for the gun that I left for safekeeping under a pile of art supplies in Goldie's gallery. If I wasn't trying to avoid her, I would have searched during the day. Yes, I was avoiding her.

"No, of course not, Goldie. I didn't want to disturb you. I had my regular gun glommed by the coppers yesterday and don't think they'll be giving it back any time soon."

"Why is that?"

"It was the principal weapon in a rub-out."

"Did you do it?" She said that too calmly for my tastes.

"Not as far as I know. I had one of my blackouts so… no, I'm pretty sure I'm in the clear."

She turned on the lights and stood by the window. She was one of those women who slept in an oversized football jersey thinking it was cute and sexy. It always worked on me. I continued to push aside canvases, paint pallets, frames and other debris. "Ah, here it is." I pulled out the rod from under a rag.

"I'm not going to ask," she said. "But I do want to know about the missing photographer. Have you found him yet? Are you even looking, Sam?" She sighed.

"He's a tricky one. It's going to take some time." I hated to lie to Goldie. I mean, we used to have a thing and may have it once again and this was no way to rebuild a relationship. On the other hand, these kinds of missing persons cases tend to work themselves out with the target returning home or going so deep that nobody could ever find them no matter what.

"I have some feelers out," I said. Which was true. I had a police buddy send out an APB to surrounding states. It doesn't mean that officers will actually look for him, but if he gets stopped for speeding or somehow comes into the contact with the law, they will hold him and contact my pal. I was counting on the missing fotog to have a lead foot.

She accepted my explanation. "Are you done here?"

I checked the cylinder, gave it a spin for no other reason than it makes a cool sound, and shoved it in my pocket. I nodded.

"I'm going back to bed. Would you like to join me?" she asked.

"Sleeping with a client. Is that an ethical breach?"

She frowned. "Detectives in the movies do it all the time."

"That's true and since you're not paying me, you're not really a client."

She turned out the light, and crossed her arms. "Are you coming or not?"

Of course I was.

CHAPTER 33

It's difficult to be a cynical, hard gumshoe when you wake up next to a sexy woman. I've tried.

There's a connection between Goldie and me that goes beyond our history. She's one of the most capable and smart women I've ever met. I fill in some blanks for her and vice versa. We've also had our issues, which is why we we're not together. As a couple, I mean. The fact that we're still solid friends, and enjoy being sexual with other when the occasion strikes is a blessing. Some might say it's just friends with benefits, but that belittles the unique nature of our bond. I can't quite describe it. In some ways it's magical and to dissect it, I fear, might make it disappear like powder off a butterfly's wings when you touch it. I once thought that if the powder came off on your fingers the insect could no longer fly. It's a myth, but I didn't want to risk it.

I know where all her kitchen items are located so I built some breakfast for us. Over eggs, toast and the strongest joe I could compose, Goldie showed me an invitation for an art show at her gallery that evening.

"Interested in going?" she asked. "There will be the usual Washington wonks and self-important people."

I scanned the mini-poster for the photography exhibit.

"This is the photographer who took a powder, right?"

"I'm trying to get some of my money back. Besides, this was planned before he skipped town. They'll be finger foods, beer and wine."

"I don't know..."

"We're serving real liquor, too."

"I always support local artists."

"Here's the guest list. Maybe you'll see some friends of yours."

Doubtful. I travel in different circles. Between gulps of mud I scanned the roster. No friends, but someone I'd like to get to know better. I pointed to a name. "Think he'll show up, Goldie?"

She leaned over to read the name and squinted. "Most likely. He comes to a lot of our showings. He's bought some photos and landscapes before with Southwestern themes. Tonight's showing is right up his alley. I'll make sure to introduce you."

* * *

Even though I live just upstairs, I arrived fashionably late. I recognized a few pols whose asses I saved and a few whose rears I helped fry. None of them noted me, some on purpose and some because my work stayed in the shadows.

I ankled over to the bar where a line was forming behind the pinot and bottled water. The spirits were on a table behind the bartender, a young woman whose face and ears showed the vestiges of metal which she smartly removed so as not to scare this crowd. She looked vaguely familiar.

"Yes, sir. What can I get you?"

"Any chance for a martini?"

"Of course." She reached behind her and scooped some ice into a shaker, poured an extra count of gin and gave it a wiggle. She set it down to cool and served a glass of pinot to a man wearing too much cologne and a seersucker suit. It's an outfit that no one over the age of eight should wear.

She smiled like she heard what I was thinking and poured the elixir into a proper martini glass. "Twist or olive?"

"Neither. The toothpick soaks up too much of the liquid."

"I've heard that line before," she said. "Now, I know you. You're a friend of Horace over at the Teekee, right?"

Another boozetender alum.

"I've seen you. My name is Claudia. Tell Horace I said 'hi,'"

"I will."

"And if you need anything else, don't line up. Come to the side and signal me. Okay?"

It pays to have friends in low places. Goldie sidled up. "Having fun?" she asked.

I held up my drink. "It's a blast."

"Look who's here," she said, moving her eyes to the door. It was Metcalfe, and he was alone. "Give me a few minutes and I will introduce you. Why do you want to meet him?"

"I think we could become friends. We have things in common."

Goldie didn't believe a word of it, and she gave me a look that told me to behave, not cause a scene. It's happened before. I was attending one of her showings and in front of an abstract painting, a man in a cheap suit turned to me and asked, "Are you Sam Marlowe?" Before I could answer, he shoved a gat in my gut and requested that I take a ride with him. As he herded me out, I asked if I could grab a beer for the drive. He said 'yes' and as I lifted the bottle off the bar, I made a quick turn and bashed his skull with it. Green glass shards spewed everywhere. The gun hit the floor and let off a round barely missing a patron's neck and lodging between the legs of a life-sized Venus di Milo statue look-a-like. Once he hit the floor, I recognized the man as an embezzler who did a dime because of my fine detective work. It was a federal rap, but since DC closed Lorton Prison those serving time had been scattered to federal facilities across the country. He served time in Montana, Colorado and New Jersey as the Bureau of Prisons moved him around looking for accommodations. I had wondered where he'd gone next because packing a rod busted his probation.

It took Goldie a long time to forgive me for ruining her showing despite me saying how it was not my fault. "I can't be responsible if people don't move on," I kept telling her, which was the absolutely wrong thing to say.

I kept a close eye on Metcalfe as Goldie greeted him. He looked like he could do with a beer bottle over the noggin, too, just for kicks. I had a smarter approach in mind. She grabbed his arm and guided him over to me. He looked a lot calmer than when I saw him having dinner with Montano.

"Senator Metcalfe, I'd like you to meet..."

I broke in. "Pinkerton. Allan Pinkerton. Glad to meet you Senator."

"Say, isn't that the name of a famous detective from a long time ago."

I beamed. "Yes, my parents had a warped sense of humor. Who would name their child after a famous detective? It's crazy, but that's what they did."

I watched as Goldie's lamps tightened like she was trying to crack a walnut with her eyelids.

"I was about to ask if we've met, because you look a little familiar, but I would have remembered your name. What do you do?"

The quintessential Washington query. Because it's such a transactional town people want to know right away what you can do for them. In New York City, people size you up with the question 'where do you live.' I'm not sure which is worse.

"I work in telecom. My company makes apps for smartphones."

He feigned interest. "Like games?"

"Nothing like that. We produce encryption apps mainly for the military. I'm not allowed to talk about it." Washington people love when you say that you can't talk about something and then proceed to talk about it. "Say, for example, you need to phone someone but you don't want to risk anyone listening in; that's our bread and butter."

"Anyone?"

"Anyone," I said, as I motioned for him to come closer. "Even the smartest government guys can't crack our algorithms." I've known a few con artists in my line of work and what always impresses me is how barefaced they can be when they're fishing. Amateurs are subtle. Pros are blatant. "We produced an app for a European company that was doing business in China. They were afraid that they were being wiretapped when they made calls back home, and... "

He interrupted. "And the Chinese are some of the best hackers in the world."

Hooked. "They sure are," I said. "They were able to negotiate contracts, prices, whatever, without any worry." I took a sip of my drink. "Privacy; that's my racket."

Before I could ask what he did, to show that I was a true Washingtonian, he said, "I may have need of your services."

I handed him a card that had just my name and phone number.

"Nothing else? he asked. "No company name or website?"

"Senator, do you know who Red Adair was?"

"The oil well firefighter?"

"That's right. He could cap burning oil wells when no one else could. He did it anywhere in the world, on land and on the ocean. He did only one thing, and he was the best."

"Didn't they make a movie with John Wayne?"

"*Hellfighters*," I yapped. He was paying such close attention that I thought I would suffocate. "His business card had only his name and number. His philosophy was that if you didn't know who he was, you had no business calling him." I smiled. I had no idea if that story was true or not, but it's a keeper. I may add it to my pretext rotation.

He tucked the card in his inside breast pocket and patted his coat like I had given him a valentine.

"You will be hearing from me," he said.

I'm sure I will, Senator. With Sameer gone, you need me like Deepwater Horizon needed Red Adair.

CHAPTER 34

"You're crazy to take such a big chance," the voice from behind the bar said.

I hoisted a beer. "Danger is my middle name."

Horace looked at me and laughed.

"No, really. That's my middle name."

His pan turned serious. "Oy, vey."

"Did you bring what I asked for?"

He wiped the bar then slid an envelope across, and I unclasped it. The passport looked perfect. The driver's license looked even better. "You even spelled Allan with a second 'a.' and not an 'e'."

I have long since given up asking Horace how he produces such righteous paper. Passports, drivers' licenses, medical records, college diplomas, you name it. Not only are they perfect but they come with the computer accompaniment. When the TSA officer runs a passport through their scanner everything clicks. When someone calls to check on a college education, you're summa cum laude. Horace would be a dangerous man if he were on the wrong side of the law, which he might be for all I know.

"Tell me your plan again," he said, as he held a wine glass up to the light searching for water spots. He grabbed the rag off his belt and wiped the rim.

"That depends upon Metcalfe, but I set the bait and I think he'll bite. If he doesn't, I move to plan B."

"And what's that?"

I shrugged, and as if on cue, my phone beeped. After a short exchange, I turned back to Horace.

"No need for plan B," I said.

Horace was twisting the bar rag like he was trying to strangle it to death. "What happens if he wants you to meet Montano? Have you thought about that?"

"Not really."

"And if he wants an encryption app, where will you get one?"

I stared at Horace, tucked my head and grinned.

He waited a beat. "Fuck you."

"It won't get to that. If it does, I'll finesse it somehow. Besides, he's so blinded by the money and the cartel's reach that he can't see straight. It's my guess that he found Sameer for them and he's out on a limb if he doesn't get a replacement – and fast. Whatever action they got going is on hold until they reestablish secure communications."

"When does he want to meet you?"

"Tonight. Union Market at seven."

"Want backup?"

That's what I love about Horace.

"I'll be okay. I'm the golden goose. Nothing's going to happen to me tonight."

"Tonight," Horace repeated.

* * *

Union Market sits across the street from Gallaudet University, the world's largest college for deaf and hard of hearing students, which is why

I saw so many people signing and snacking. Millennials love this place because it has the authenticity they crave but no longer see in their world of virtual everything. In the 1930s, tough men hooked beef hindquarters and carried them on the shoulders of their bloody white smocks while others unloaded wooden crates of tomatoes, apples and peaches and lauded their ripened condition to buyers. Now, after renovation, it's aisle after aisle of artisan empanadas, smoothies made from the latest, previously-neglected green vegetable and bowls of grains whose sellers promise that it's the new quinoa.

I sat at a raw bar situated in the middle of the building and swallowed a few oysters chased by an IPA. I was there for about ten minutes before I heard my name.

"Mr. Pinkerton," Metcalfe said. "Thanks for meeting me on such short notice. Can we sit over there for a bit more privacy?" I glided a few bills onto the counter, thanked the shucker and joined the senator on a high-top away from the crowd.

"I'm here to discuss what we talked about the other night." He looked like a man who didn't have any friends. "This has to be totally on the down low. Do you know what I mean by down-low?"

I'm a biracial, bisexual man. I know exactly what down-low means. "Absolutely. As I said at the gallery, privacy is my racket."

"I did some checking around and couldn't find out much about you. It's crucial that you are who you say you are."

I raised my voice but kept my cool. "I agreed to meet with you because Miss Feather said you're a regular customer, that she knows you. Quite frankly, I don't need the business and I haven't got time for interrogations. Call me after you've satisfied your curiosity about my credentials." I lifted off my seat to leave.

"No," he said as he grabbed my arm. If lasers shot from peepers, I would have been an ash pile. "I'm sorry, it's just that I have to be super careful."

I wrested my arm away. "Great," I said, in a quieter voice. "Be as careful as you want." I walked a step away.

"Stop, please!" he said. Heads turned to us, drawn by the noise.

"Way to keep it on the down-low," I said.

"Please, just listen to me. I apologize. It's just that we had some... well, you don't need to know..." Sitting there, he looked as lonely as a guy at a timeshare sales table in a resort hotel lobby.

"You're right; I *don't* need to know." I sat down. "I will listen to what you have to say as a courtesy to Miss Feather. If we can do the job, and you agree to our price and terms, then we have a deal. If not, I just ate some delicious Stingray oysters, so it's been a good night already."

His shoulders relaxed and he folded his hands in front of him. Metcalfe said what I expected, that he wanted encryption on smartphones, but it had to be done through a downloadable app and not built into the phone.

"Why," I asked.

He hesitated. "We have operatives who come and go. We need to have newcomers download the app and then supply the whatever-it-is that turns it on and off remotely."

Like the phone that Cherry snagged from the embassy traveling to the Senate office.

"I'm pretty sure we can do this for you," I said. "Let me check with my technical people first before going further. I want to make sure I can deliver what I promise."

"How long will that take?" He looked pathetic.

"I will get in touch with you tomorrow. If it's a go, we can sign the contract papers outlining what we discussed."

I thought I heard a squeal. "Papers?"

"Of course. What did you expect?"

"I was hoping that we could do this, you know, like I said, on the down-low."

I tried to compose a conspiratorial grin, but I think I just came off looking silly. Maybe I needed a handlebar mustache. "Oh, I see," I sang. I closed my eyes like I was deep in thought. "Sure, we can do that, but, well, let me check first with my tech crew before we go further. I'll be in touch."

As he walked away, I clocked sweat spots on the back of his shirt. I returned to the bar and slurped another half-dozen oysters.

CHAPTER 35

I followed a fat guy in an expensive suit through the metal detector. He smelled like a lobbyist. He emptied his pockets and tossed anything metal – phone, keys, platinum money clip in the shape of a dollar sign– into the plastic baskets so fast they almost sparked. He smiled at the guard who smiled back and proceeded down the hall.

My entry didn't go as smoothly. I was asked for ID and produced my fresh driver's license which the guard studied, ran it through a reader and handed it back after multiple taps on his computer and several up-and-downs of my face.

"Why you do that to a brother?" I said under my breath.

"What's that sir?"

"I said have a nice day."

His eyes burned a hole in my back as I headed for the elevators.

I had called Metcalfe and said it was a 'go' but I needed to learn more about his requirements. I announced myself to the aide at the front desk. Her nameplate said 'Jennifer Morgan,' and she looked young enough to still pass notes in gym class. Jennifer offered me coffee, tea or water. I said I was fine and settled into an overstuffed chair that looked like the one in my grandma's living room. The wall boasted a splatter of photographs: Metcalfe with the president, Metcalfe with the vice president, Metcalfe with people I didn't know. One black frame showed the senator hugging the Washington Nationals' mascot *Screech*, a costumed enthusiast supposed to be an eagle but looked more like a chicken. A photo at the far end seized my interest. It was Metcalfe in a 'grip and grin' stance with a white-haired, soldier whose uniform I didn't recognize, but they were posed in front of a flag that I did know: Mexico.

Metcalfe stepped out of his office to greet me. He wore a dark blue suit, white shirt and red tie. An American flag pin pierced his lapel. It tilted sideways, but no one in his office told him.

"Mr. Pinkerton," he said, "Come right in." He turned to Jennifer and told her to "hold my calls." Who says that anymore except in the movies?

He offered me a seat as he landed in his executive swivel behind a mahogany desk the size of an aircraft carrier. The walls were a larger version of the anteroom, photos covering every square inch, and his two bookcases had more tchotchkes than the Grand Canyon gift shop. Two flags flanked him, the stars and stripes and the flag of West Virginia. A miniature flag with a W and V sat on his desk and held my attention.

"West Virginia University," he said.

"Go Mountaineers," I piped. I'm not sure how I knew their nickname. I never watch football.

Metcalfe smiled. "I'm going to be honest with you Mr. Pinkerton. We had someone do these apps for us but he didn't work out. The truth is that he was untrustworthy."

The truth is that he got bopped. "I understand completely. Based on what you told me we can do the job and here's our fee." I handed him a sheet of paper. He put on his glasses, unfolded the paper and I detected a tiny gasp. I purposely wrote an outrageously high figure to gauge how desperate he was.

"That's fine," he said, removing his spectacles.

He was hanging-by-his-fingernails desperate. I must admit that I enjoyed his discomfort.

"This may entail some international travel, Mexico mostly. I assume that your passport is in order."

"I've got the goods."

He squinted. "Er… Okay."

"I will get my techs on this right away, but they do have a few questions."

Metcalfe looked up.

I opened a folder, made believe I was reading. "They'd like to know where the calls will be going."

"Mexico, as just mentioned."

"And how many apps will you need to download?"

"I'd say under 50."

"Good, and last question. Is any of this related to illegal activity? I like to know where I'm sticking my smell… er… nose."

"Fair enough. I'm on the Senate's International Narcotics Control Caucus and we're involved in helping nations combat the drug trade especially when those drugs end up in America. Let me show you something." He produced two maps with arrows showing drug routes into the United States. "This map is how it used to be." His finger followed the arrows. "Drugs came from Medellín, Colombia through the Caribbean, Central America and Mexico. The Medellin cartels ran the show. That's all changed." He pointed to the other map. "The center of drug trafficking has moved north to Mexico." The map had different hues for each area where each cartel operated. Except for a section of white – the inset labelled it 'disputed areas' - that arced down the middle of the country, it was carved up in a colorful tie-dye like rainbow. Each color touched the US border. Equal access.

"Why?" I asked.

"One reason is to be closer to their market." He poked at the US. "Drugs like cocaine are still largely produced in Bolivia, Colombia, and Peru, and then transported through Mexico. However, Mexico has now come into its own. The Mexican gangs shifted from being couriers for Colombian cartels to being wholesalers. They're one of the largest makers of Fentanyl, a synthetic opioid which is much more dangerous than heroin."

He stood up and walked over to the far wall unhooked a photo and handed it to me. What do you see?"

"Looks like a baby submarine."

"That's right. The Colombia cartels have their own small fleet of 30-foot submarines that can carry up to six tons of drugs. They have a few larger ones, too. The vessels carry their contraband to Mexico, the Bahamas, elsewhere in the Gulf of Mexico, where it is transferred to a cigarette boat bound for Miami. Now that cigarette boats have become common the Coast Guard and Navy often stop them on sight. The cartels have switched to low-profile vessels that ride right just below the waterline. They are undetectable on radar. They still use these methods but we're seeing a shift to land-based transit. The Mexican cartels control it all and we made it happen."

"What do you mean?"

"The war on drugs, backed by the US military and the DEA, focused so heavily on the Colombian cartels that they were destroyed. In one way, you can say that we succeeded but, in another way, we failed. We forced them to move the center of the drug trade closer to the US and it's only a matter of time before it spills over the border. Actually, it's already spilled over. You won't see this in the news but we're seeing drug cartels fighting it out on American soil especially in Texas and Arizona."

"I had no idea." Yeah, I did.

"Our committee is tasked with acting as a liaison between American authorities and the Mexican authorities. The main problem is that we don't always know who to trust. The cartels have so permeated the government and the military that we have trouble separating our friends from our enemies. That's where the encrypted communications come in. We allow only those people who are completely vetted to have access to our intelligence communications, to know where and when the authorities are planning raids."

He sat back satisfied with his presentation when a phone buzzed. He fingered a key, unlocked a drawer in his desk and retrieved a phone. He pressed a few buttons and said "One moment."

He put the phone down. "I will wait to hear from you, Mr. Pinkerton."

I was dismissed.

CHAPTER 36

I met Senator Metcalfe at National Airport at the stroke of seven a.m. We walked together to the general aviation area and stood in front of a Learjet which was painted white but had no other markings save the tail number.

"This is our ride," he said. "DEA has about a hundred aircraft. Most of them are in the US but we have some in Afghanistan, the Bahamas, Colombia, and Peru. This one," he pointed proudly, "is based in Mexico."

He used the word 'we' as if he were part of the DEA.

I handed my briefcase to the co-pilot who introduced himself as "John Smith." He tipped the visor of his cap. "Good to see you again, Senator," he said, as he gripped Metcalfe's briefcase and motioned for us to ascend the stairs.

The cabin seated eight with a set of four seats surrounding a table. We settled into two cushiony, white leather chairs on opposite sides. The air carried a hint of jet fuel and cleaning products. The engines were already running and co-pilot Smith informed us that we would be taking off within six minutes after which he would offer us breakfast.

He stepped into the cockpit as the captain came out. "Captain James Jones," he said, shaking my hand. "Welcome aboard. Senator, and good morning, sir." He read from a sheet of paper with small holes down the sides and said, "We should have a smooth flight."

After he left, I turned to Metcalfe. "I know that the DEA thrives on secrecy, but are those their real monikers… Smith and Jones?"

"What's in a name, Mr. Pinkerton?" Metcalfe said, as he snapped his seatbelt.

What indeed. Metcalfe reclined his seat and closed his eyes. I retrieved my tablet and read the latest edition of *Men's Health*. The cover showed a muscled giant with tribal tattoos and words in large letters promising to "Build Abs," "Cut Your Gut," and "Find Out Why Jerks Get More Sex." I found myself leading toward a story titled, "Worst Ways to Die" in case I needed to be prepared.

The jet steeply powered for a short time then leveled off. As soon as the upward trajectory ended and the engines no longer strained, Metcalfe opened his eyes. Smith exited the cockpit, headed for the rear and returned with plates of eggs, bacon, sausage and a small fruit cup. "Coffee?" he asked. We both nodded.

Metcalfe ate quickly and silently then placed his empty dish in a far corner of the table. He kept his coffee cup in front of him, took a file folder from his briefcase and handed it to me. "This is who we'll be meeting."

The first page resembled a job resume with a small photo taped to the upper right-hand corner. It looked to me like a mug shot but without the numbers. His name was Fernando Jose Martinez Santiago Villanova, aka "Pachuco."

According to the dossier, Pachuco was a slang term for a Chicano who dressed in flashy clothes. 'The pachuco look was an important part of the young Chicano scene in the 1940s and 50s…' the report stated. I read: 'The LAPD considered this youth subculture gangsterish and troublemakers although it was not necessarily the case. Groups of pachuco were arrested and harassed by law enforcement culminating in the 1943 Zoot Suit Riots which only served to embolden the group, set it apart from other immigrants and cemented bigotry among authorities against them. Villanova was born in Mexico and raised in Los Angeles in the 1960s, and this history hardened his anger against US law enforcement.'

The report noted that the now 72-year-old Pachuco relocated to the 'Free and Sovereign State of Sinaloa' in 1981 and has remained there ever since. 'Pachuco is suspected of involvement in at least 197 murders. He was fifth in command of the Sinaloa cartel and is now considered *emeritus* in status.' Imagine that; tenure in the drug cartel.

The dossier went on for several more pages, but I had seen enough. I turned to Metcalfe. "Why are we meeting with him?"

"He's on our side now."

"Get outta here," I said.

"I'm serious. He has been working with the DEA for two years. He's an informant."

"And why would he stoolie out his own people?"

"The story is that his wife and two sons were gunned down by the Sinaloa. It was a case of mistaken identity or part of some internal struggle. We don't know. He wanted revenge but knew that he couldn't accomplish it on his own. One of our DEA agents turned him and now he informs for us."

"He's a fakealoo artist."

"What now?"

I focused. "He's a conman."

"I didn't believe him either, at first, and neither did the DEA until he proved himself by supplying some intel that led to the capture of several high-ranking Sinaloa commanders. He was one of El Chapo's inner circle. No one suspects him."

"Why am I the meat?" I blurted, then said "What's his interest in me?"

"He's one of those fellows who lives by his gut instincts. He wants to meet you, feel you out."

"You're taking orders from a rat?"

"It's not like that. We want to keep him happy. He wants to meet you. That's all."

I kept my concerns to myself, but I felt as safe as having a surgeon cut on me with steak knives from Dollar General. I slumped in my seat and continued to read the report. It didn't include the part about him being an informant for the DEA, and there could be only two reasons for that. The first is that I was reading an unclassified version. The other is that he wasn't really an informant, but still a working member of the Sinaloa cartel. Either way, I felt like I was being measured for a wooden kimono.

CHAPTER 37

The room smelled of damp cement and charred wood. There was nothing left of the windows except empty squares that allowed light to hit the floor but venture no further. Picture hooks dotted the walls but any artwork they held had long since escaped. Graffiti expressing romantic relationships - real or imagined - took up most of the remaining space. It offered the only colors in a room of gray.

In the middle were three chairs that rightfully should have been destroyed by vandals or kids letting off steam but were untouched.

Metcalfe looked at his watch. "He's always on time."

I spotted a zinc-topped bar with a curve that seemed to vanish into infinity. "What was this place?" I asked.

"At one time this was the finest club in Mazatlán. The Esquire Club. It attracted celebrities from Hollywood, politicians from Washington and royalty from Europe. They came here in the late 1940s and early 50s to drink, gamble and dance all night. Some people called it Vegas South. It was a wide-open town." Metcalfe tilted his wrist for a smattering of light to read his watch.

"What happened?"

"By the mid-60s, the world no longer wore tuxedos and gowns for a night out. Cruise ships dropped off people wearing tank tops and flip-flops. McDonald's and Burger Kings sprang up, and …"

We both heard footsteps and froze. A voice, as if from above, said: "Who is here?"

"It's Metcalfe with the man I told you about, Pinkerton."

"Bueno." The footsteps got louder, and I felt like I was in a slasher movie, the dark abandoned building, the voice without a body, and I swear the air felt chillier.

In an instant, a tall man swinging a lantern was upon us. "Sit down, my friends." He relocated a chair so that he could face us both. The lantern went on the floor casting long shadows on the walls.

"I am Pachuco," he said. "I am happy to meet you both, but I wish it could be in a more lively place."

"We understand," Metcalfe said.

The man before us had thick hair the color of a battleship. He had a high pompadour. His ears were larger than they needed to be and his face resembled a relief map. Despite the low light, I could make out ocean blue eyes that probably once had a twinkle but those days were in the faraway past.

"As Senator Metcalfe has probably told you, I like to know personally the people that work for me. He also told you that I go with what you Americans call 'your gut.' We call it 'ir con tu instinto,' and I place a high value on it." He twisted in his chair to face me squarely. "Hold out your hands."

He took both of my paws in his and closed his eyes like he was reading my fortune. Pachuco held for a count of 20 then turned to Metcalfe. "He is alright with you?"

"Yes."

Pachuco let go of my hands. "Let me tell you a story, Mr. Pinkerton." He leaned back in his chair. "In the organization to which I belong…" I immediately noted his perfect diction and use of grammar. He could have been raised in Iowa. "… has little regard… let me rephrase that… no regard for life. It is all about the money and nothing else. I was taught to believe that and live that. I'm sure you've seen my dossier." He smiled as small a smile as he could while still having it officially considered a smile. "Yes, I killed all those people or had them killed. It's how I lived. It's how I rose in the ranks. Now, as I get on in years, I find that way may not be the way to heaven. Quite frankly, I had what you might call a come to Jesus moment.

"What brought me to this new line of thinking? They say nothing is personal until it becomes personal. Several teenagers, professional assassins they were." His words turned louder. "They worked for my organization. They were not even in their 20's. They shot my wife and children while I was away. I found these two men, boys really, had them brought to my boat and we went for a ride." He cleared his throat, found a flask in his pocket and took a swig. He didn't offer either of us a shot. "They said it was a case of mistaken identity. Was it? I don't know. I chopped of their fingers and dragged them behind our boat for several miles on a tuna hook in their mouths." He became animated, flailing his arms left and right, taking another jolt from his flask. "I had them pulled up, and they were still alive, begging for their lives even although they couldn't talk because their mouths were hooked. I saw them both, squirming around on the boat deck, just children but like fish, and then a divine spirit entered me."

I glanced over at Metcalfe and his headed ticked forward like he was about to puke.

Pachuco sat back, relaxed. "My life was all wrong, and it took the death of my family to realize it. I heard a voice, the voice of god telling me to honor life and so… " He took another swig. "I ordered the captain to take the two boys to the nearest hospital and have them taken care of. They are maimed but they will no longer assassinate anyone. They have no fingers in which to pull triggers." He let out a larger smile.

"Since that time, I have devoted my life, in Jesus name, to repair the hurt that Sinaloa has done. I am what you call paloma mensajera, a stool pigeon. And I have done nothing but good, have I not, Senator Metcalfe?"

The senator looked like he barfed in his mouth and had choked it down. He managed a 'yes.'

"And so, Mr. Pinkerton, you and I and the Senator are on the same team, working for the same goal, to bring hurt to the Sinaloa cartel where it hurts them the most. In their money. I devote the rest of my life to doing this."

He was so sincere and his speech so moving but I didn't believe a word of it. I have gut instincts, too.

"Yes, Pachuco," I said. "We are on the same team. I will not disappoint you."

He took my hands in his and, softly as a butterfly's sigh, whispered, "Bueno, bueno." He sat back. "There is someone that I want you to meet. I want everything in the open between us," Pachuco said. "No secrets."

Out of the darkness entered a figure sweeping a flashlight from side to side.

"Hello, Pachuco. Hello, Senator Metcalfe and you are Mr. Pinkerton, I presume."

He shook my hand. "DEA Agent Harry Keegan. A pleasure to meet you."

CHAPTER 38

"I like to think of Mazatlán as a demilitarized zone," Keegan said, after ordering us drinks at a restaurant. We were seated in a corner. "We're in Sinaloa territory and they keep it safe. After all," he said, letting out a muffled laugh, "they control the labor and every truck that comes in or out. They take their piece of the action and the hotels, bars and restaurants are happy to pay for protection. Look at this," he said, his arms opening to the ocean. "This is fucking beautiful. It's like Disneyland."

And it was. The buildings were colored pastel, the beach was pristine. The people who walked by looked like they fell off travel posters.

Keegan spied a look on my face that he rightly interpreted as concern.

"Don't worry about being seen with me or Senator Metcalfe. Everyone knows who I am and why I'm here. As for the senator, he's a fixture. Metcalfe raised a glass in a mock toast to himself.

"So, Mr. Pinkerton. How did you and Senator Metcalfe meet?" I felt like a wayward husband having lunch with his unknowing wife and mistress. Keeping my story straight was taking a lot of brain power and having just met a chap who cuts off fingers and gaffs teens wasn't helping my focus.

"We met at an art opening of a friend of mine." Keep it simple, Sam.

"And?" Keegan asked.

He was really enjoying this. "We discovered that I offered services that he needed."

"Keegan knows what we're up to here," Metcalfe said. "As you probably figured out, Keegan turned Pachuco and he has become an enormous asset for us."

"I can't take all the credit," Keegan said. "Pachuco was already hooked; I just reeled him in." Metcalfe looked like he was going to barf at the reference.

I was living my dream or nightmare – depending upon at which minute you asked me. This case was turning into a spider web story like the Maltese Falcon. As great as that book is, and the movie was super, too, I can't believe I'm not the only one who has had trouble following the intricate story line. I didn't know if Metcalfe knew that Keegan was investigating Sameer, but I was going to find out now.

"This operation has been going on for a while," I said. "What have you been doing for communications services?" I turned to Keegan. "That's why I'm here. I'm sure the senator told you that."

Keegan interrupted. "Senator Metcalfe doesn't tell me everything about his operations and I don't tell him everything about ours. Different branches of government and all that. He does know that you're helping with communications."

As far as Metcalfe knows, Sameer just disappeared into thin air and doesn't have a clue that he has a third eye the size of a bullet. And he certainly doesn't know that he was meeting me in an alley. Nor does he know that Keegan has been on to the now-dead Sameer's trail for quite some time. I could use Humphrey Bogart right about now to recap the action while pressing a gat against someone's temple.

"We offered the senator's committee access to the DEA's secure communications network but he turned down our offer. He does enjoy our planes, though." Metcalfe was trying to look cool and reserved at that dig but he wasn't built for it and his face turned to mush.

"I understand that you're located in Washington, Mr. Pinkerton. My office is there. Even though I spend a great deal of time in Mexico. Perhaps we could have lunch."

"Sounds good," I said, "and call me Allan."

"Harry," he said.

A young man ferried our lunches to the table. Metcalfe attempted small talk but neither Keegan nor I cared about responding with more than a nod or a 'yes.' Keegan couldn't stop smiling and laughing between bites. I thought he might spit out his food.

"What's so funny, Harry?" Metcalfe asked.

"I'm just happy to be here, senator. Look around. I've got the best job in the entire DEA."

Scenic-wise, there was no dispute. The sky was cloudless and the air felt smooth and warm. The breeze bussed your face and left a tickle that you could carry with you all day. But that wasn't what was amusing Keegan.

"Harry," I said, between bites. "Let me ask you something. The DEA was successful in destroying the Medellin cartel in Colombia. Did you have any inkling the drug dealers would move north to Mexico?"

Keegan frowned. Metcalfe leaned in. "Just between us, I think it was a bad idea to eviscerate the cartels in Colombia. The further the cartels are from our borders the better off we are. We should have worked on containment. That's just my opinion. To be honest, I don't think this was thought through at the highest levels. We knew that the cartels would have to move somewhere. Nobody gives up that kind of money, and users still want supply. Some in the agency thought they might relocate to the Caribbean, but why should they? The logistics infrastructure can't support the weight they want to handle. All we've really done is make it easier and cheaper for drugs to reach the US. Not only are they closer to their market, but the cartels were easily able to easily compromise the Mexican local cops and even the army.

"And we would be naïve to think that the violence in Mexico will not seep into the US big time," Keegan finally said. "The cartels already control the drug trade in major US cities. They are well established."

I had always heard about drug gangs in Washington and that some were associated with The Salvadoran MS-13. I never made the connection to the Mexican cartels. Keegan took out his government-issued Toughbook and lit up a US map showing which cities are controlled by the Mexican cartels. The heading said: 'Areas of Influence of Major Mexican TCOs' and every city with a colored dot had a cartel presence. It looked like a smallpox victim's back. Sinaloa mango-orange was the most used color and their reach spread to almost every city in the country and even to mid to small-level sized burgs.

"TCO means transcontinental criminal organizations. It sounds less scary than Mexican drug cartels," Keegan said. "Many Americans think that gang wars are still among homespun groups, but the landscape has changed. The Mexican cartels are fighting among themselves and the public doesn't realize the extent. They hear about the cartel wars in Mexico and think that's all there is. Newspapers in southern California write about these gangs but the public seems to think it's because they're close to Mexico." He pointed to the map. "Look here: Sinaloa controls Oakland, San Francisco, Sacramento and San Jose." My eyes went north to see more Sinaloa dots in Salem, Oregon and Yakima, Spokane and Seattle, Washington. "The public just doesn't know."

"Or care to know," Metcalfe dropped in.

Keegan gave him the side-eye and continued. "Police know it but no politician wants to acknowledge how deep the foreign cartels have dug in.

So far, they haven't compromised any police departments that we know about."

"There are exceptions," Metcalfe said, looking at Keegan.

Keegan threw a dirty glance at Metcalfe like a parent telling another parent not to say something in front of the children. He closed his laptop and announced that he was late for an appointment. We shook hands and with a wide smile handed me his business card. "See you in Washington, Allan."

"I look forward to it."

"Senator," Keegan said, "See you as well."

Metcalfe eyed Keegan's plate. "He hardly touched his food. That's odd. He and I go out all the time and I can barely keep up." He took a sip of water. "He seems happier than I've ever seen him before."

And why wouldn't he be happy? Keegan had me three ways to Thursday. He still was capable of fixing a few murders on me, depending upon which one he chose to put at the top of the list. He could also jam me up with the Capitol Police or the local coppers for bunko even though my Pinkerton persona deserved an Emmy. Or, he could decide to burn me with Metcalfe. He had more leverage on me than a Sumo wrestler on a seesaw. I could only guess what he might do with his power and the guesses all ended bad for me.

CHAPTER 39

I was standing on line at Starbucks when the first bullet shattered the front window and knocked my latte out of the barista's right hand. A second slug hit my left shoulder and corkscrewed me to the floor where I saw 'Zam' instead of 'Sam' written in black Sharpie on the fallen cup. What was so fucking hard about getting my name right?

I screamed for everyone to get down and watched as several people insisted on typing on their laptops before diving under their tables. A woman with neon blue hair complained that she couldn't get any work done under these conditions. It was only after she clocked me and the blood spurting from my body that she screamed and squeezed into a corner by the unisex bathroom. A twenty-something man wearing business casual khakis aimed his phone at me and recorded my puss twisting in pain.

I managed to unholster my pea shooter and point it at the door.

I waited.

Silence.

Nobody said a word. Nobody moved.

Then, sirens.

The door opened and the shooting end of an M-16 rifle poked through. I couldn't see the gunman. Not yet.

Everyone was hiding, eyes down.

The sirens grew louder and the muzzle retreated, but not before I got off a round in its direction. I dropped my gun and used the counter as a crutch and looked out the broken window at the fleeing gunsel. He was wearing a black ski mask and squeezed himself into a baby blue Mercedes before roaring away.

I've been shot a few times before but never from an M-16. I won't go into the ballistics signature of the .223 bullet except to say that it hurt like hell. The barista who had my latte shot from her hand, threw me a towel which I held over the hole in my shoulder. "I may need that latte to go," I said.

People started for the door but were met by a dozen cops who shooed them back inside. "We'll need statements from everyone," a sergeant, shouted. "Please return to your seats."

"You okay?" he said to me.

"Couldn't be better," I said. He spied my roscoe on the floor. "Don't move."

He pushed it away with his foot while another copper held his service rod on me. He motioned for another flatfoot to pick it up which he did by poking a pen in the muzzle. He held it in the air as if it was a flag not knowing quite what to do with it.

"That's mine," I said.

"Now it's mine," the sergeant said. He jammed it into his belt. As I scanned the room, the scene looked like a convention of iPhone videographers. Most were pointing at me. Others seemed to be taking B-roll of the café.

The patrons were getting restless and the sergeant screamed for everyone to stay where they were. He ordered the uniforms to take statements before releasing anyone. Several people shouted, "Take me first. I have to get back to the office," but from what I could see most of them were already at their workplace.

I described to the sergeant what happened but left out the part about how my name on the cup was mangled. I thought it was irrelevant.

Paramedics arrived and two of them looked familiar. It was the team that rolled up on Helen and didn't administer the Narcon because the doctor at the hospital told them not to.

"Oh, it's you," Amanda said. She sounded disappointed.

"I get that a lot."

Her partner Carl removed the towel covering my bullet hole and aimed a flashlight at the wound. He perused it from several angles. "There's a cavity just below the clavicle. The round went clear through and didn't hit anything important except muscle. I bet it hurts like a motherfucker, though." He was almost laughing.

"What amuses you, the pain or that it's me?"

He thought about it. "I was thinking about when you came into the firehouse and we told you about Doctor Nahal. Did you ever find him?"

"No. He was a ghost."

"Yeah, we know. We couldn't track him down either." He looked at Amanda who was setting up a saline drip for me.

"I'm fine," I said, waving her away with my good wing. "Just patch me up and I'll be on my way."

Amanda looked startled. "Are you refusing hospital service?"

Carl said: "Okay, tough guy. Let me toss some antibacterial gel on the wound and cover it in gauze. You can have some morph if you want it, but I really recommend you get a few stitches - on both sides."

I'm sure he was right, but I wasn't in the mood for stitches although the morphine sounded pretty solid. I had things to do. I knew I'd be spending time with the coppers explaining why people with guns seem attracted to me. Besides, I'm not a fan of hospitals especially when they have phony baloney types like Nahal hanging around and giving orders that allow people to die.

I spotted Pemberton before she saw me. "Detective. Hi, it's me, Sam. Over here."

Before the sergeant could open his mouth, she said: "Yeah, I know this guy. Unless you actually saw him pull the trigger and someone fell to the ground, he's okay."

The sergeant's mouth now was open but nothing came out. He handed Pemberton the pistol retrieved from the floor. "What the fuck Marlowe? You're a shit magnet." She sniffed the gun barrel and handed it back to me. I moved my head toward my holster side and said, "How about it? Can you do a brother a solid?"

She jammed the gun in my holster so hard I almost lost an inch of height.

"Hey, I'm the aggrieved party here. An assault rifle no less."

I expected a bit of sympathy but got none. "How is he?" she asked the paramedics. "The bullet went through his shoulder area," said Carl. "He'll live."

"Patient refused hospital service," Amanda repeated quickly.

Pemberton looked back at me. I said, "If you take a gander at the counter, you may even find the slug that tagged me."

Carl set me up with an arm sling and patted me on my good shoulder. He slipped some pills in my pocket along with a note. "I mean, if you're interested," he said. Why not. He was pretty good looking.

Pemberton stood with her hands on her hips and did a three-sixty around the café. "What a freaking mess. Any idea who did this, Marlowe."

"A guy who gave me five grand."

"Why did he do that?"

"So he wouldn't have to shoot me."

"That didn't work."

"No. Not so much."

CHAPTER 40

I slept like a dead man.

The combination of the adrenaline rush followed by the inevitable letdown, along with the pills - whatever they were - that Carl the flirting paramedic slipped me insured that I lost a day of my life.

I was able to stand and look in the mirror half expecting to see a Vise-Grips squeezing my shoulder. Instead, I saw the reflection of a man with bags under his eyes, a day-old beard and blotches of red oozing through white gauze. My left arm was cradled in a sling.

I wiggled my fingers to see if there was any damage that I couldn't see. Check.

I twisted my head in both directions and felt only a slight twinge in my left shoulder. Check.

Then I eased my arm out of the sling. No check. I felt myself being lifted to my toes just to get further away from the pain. My arm hung lifeless as a salami in a deli, and every time I tried to bend it, pain careened around like white-hot coals in a pachinko machine. Using my right hand, I secured my left arm back into the sling, and the electric pain became a dull throb that traveled north and formed a lump in my throat.

I heard a knock on the door.

"Sam, are you okay? It's Goldie. Can I come in?"

Without any response from me, the door opened.

She gasped. "What the hell happened to you?"

"Got shot."

"Holy crap. Let me take a look."

She peeled the gauze of my shoulder. "You need stiches."

"So I've been told."

"We're going to the hospital."

"Nope. Too many doctor Nahals."

"What?"

"I'm not going."

"You don't have a choice. The bleeding started as soon as I lifted the bandage. The hole is too big." She looked at the back of my shoulder. "Why is there a bandage… For fuck's sake, Sam. Did you get shot in the back, too?"

"Same bullet."

She grabbed my good arm and pulled me towards the door. "Wait," I said. "I know a guy."

"You know a stitches guy?"

"He's a sawbones, too, kind of."

"That's a plus," she said. "Don't you need an appointment or at least call him first? How do you know he's even in?"

"He's always in."

We waved down a cab, and I gave the hack the address. The ride took six minutes during which time we hit two potholes that sent me into the throes of exquisite pain.

"You're kidding me, right?" Goldie said, when she saw the name on the door.

She opened the portal and we walked in on three people playing Scrabble on a coffee table.

"Gold Feather," I began, "I'd like you to meet Doris, Jeannie and Dr. Zinowitz."

They all smiled. Zinowitz stood up and said "Ron. Call me Ron." He eyed my arm. "What happened to the wing, Sam?"

Doris retreated behind the reception desk and Jeannie began putting away the game.

"Shot," I said.

"Is the slug still in there?"

"It drilled through."

"Do you need sutures?"

"Yes," Goldie piped in. "He doesn't trust hospitals."

"I don't blame him. I had a patient whose wife recently died. She was just 36-years old. Lovely woman. She suffered a traumatic brain injury in a car accident and they didn't give her any chance of recovery. Every day, the husband visits her, sits with her, reads to her. She couldn't speak. She couldn't even open her eyes."

Goldie was fixed on Ron.

"Even though the doctors told him that she would never recover, he still visited her until one day her eyes open and she started to speak. She improved, sitting up, eating and the doctors were surprised yet perplexed. She remained in the hospital for another week just to make sure they didn't miss anything, until the husband finally got the call that he could take her home. He decorates their house, invites friends and neighbors... did I mention that they have two teenaged girls? Anyway, an hour before he's to bring her home the hospital calls him and says that she may not be discharged. She vomiting and can't keep anything down, not even water.

"He rushes to the hospital and by the time he gets to her room, they're pulling back the curtain. She's gone."

"What happened?" Goldie asked.

"The doctors had no idea but the husband thinks something's fishy. One day she's fine and the next day she dies so he has her autopsied." Zinowitz reached into the reception desk area, behind the glass partition, and pulled out a tissue. He blew his nose and put the tissue in the pocket of his white lab coat.

"Well?" Goldie said.

"In her stomach and bowels, they found unopened ketchup packets."

"Ketchup packets?" I said.

"Yes."

"Zinowitz shrugged. "The hospital settled with the husband for over seven million dollars. He bought a house in Martinique. The kids are doing fine. I got an email from him the other day." He took out his phone and scrolled. "Doing well here, Ron. Come visit. We have plenty of room. P.S. They could use a good dentist here." He opened the door to the exam room. "Follow me. You can come, too, Miss Feather."

"Call me Goldie, and yes, I will come in. I want to make sure he gets stitched up and there are no ketchup packets around."

I sat back in the chair. "I don't have a local that will work on your shoulder so breath in. He placed a mask over my mouth and nose and the next thing I remember is waking up and seeing Goldie. Ron walked in and stood behind her.

"Looking good," he said. "No infection. I put two stitches in the front and three in the back. I would recommend physical therapy to get your mobility back, and I would do it sooner rather than later." He handed me a mirror, and I could see that the front bandage was smaller than what was there. I couldn't see the back.

"Put it on my tab, Ron."

He laughed, handed me a small, brown envelope with bumps. "Dosing instructions are inside." He announced to Doris and Jeannie that it was time for lunch.

We all walked out together, and they waved goodbye as they walked in the other direction.

"How are you feeling?" Goldie said.

"Surprisingly good," I said, although I was a tad woozy from the anesthetic. I tested my arm again by shimming it out of the sling. Big mistake. We walked back to our building.

Pemberton was waiting by the door. 'I'll see you later," I told Goldie. She gave Pemberton the side-eye and left.

"Would you like to see the shooter?"

"The mook who ventilated me and murdered my latte?"

"You know those lion statues at the entrance to the Taft Bridge?"

"On Connecticut Avenue? What about them?"

"The man who shot up the Starbucks sped north on Connecticut. We had two cruisers in pursuit and they hit 70, 80 easy. He lost control and hit the concrete pedestal of the lion on the right side."

"How's tabby?"

"The lion is unharmed but the pedestal needs some patching. The man is dead. Would you like to see him?"

"I never saw his face. I can't ID him."

"How about taking a look anyway." Unlike our previous encounters, Pemberton appeared civil, even solicitous. This could mean only one thing. She wanted something from me.

"Who is he?"

"We'll get to that," she said, as she opened the passenger door for me. She started to cup my head like coppers do so perps don't hit their head on the car's headliner and scream police brutality. She caught herself and pulled her hand away and closed the door. She scuttled around to the driver side and we took off.

"So, Sam, how are you feeling?"

"Considering that I had a hole in my shoulder that you can stick a pencil through, I'm doing peachy keen."

"Had? I thought you refused a trip to the hospital. Who sewed you up?"

"The drugs are winding down and I'm in no mood for small talk. What's on your noggin?"

She swerved the car over to a bus stop and killed the motor. "I don't like people shooting up my city. Why was this guy after you?"

I decided to tell it all, well, most of it. "This gunsel came into my crib while I was taking a nap, middle of the day. He pointed a gun at me, threw some dough on the bed and told me to back off the Helen Boston murder and… "

"Murder? How did he know that it wasn't an accidental OD?"

"Maybe because he was the one who cooled her."

"Go on."

"That's it. Except that he knew enough anatomy to abuse my kidneys. I pissed red for several days."

"Why didn't you report it to the police?"

"You're kidding, right?"

A bus driver wanting to pull into the space blasted the horn several times before Pemberton gave her the 'go around' hand signal. The operator pulled alongside, swung open the door and yelled that it was a no-standing zone. Pemberton badged her and the driver cursed before pulling out with an angry whoosh of air brakes.

"Then what?"

"Then yesterday happened."

"Why would the shooter fire at you in a public place?"

"I asked myself that very question and the only answer is that he wanted it to look like a random shooting. You know, a good old American massacre."

"But there's another possibility," she said. "This *was* a random shooting and you just happened to be in the line of fire."

"If you believed that we wouldn't be sitting here, and I'd be home chomping pain pills."

She started the car and we drove silently to the ME's office. We passed Jaime de Castro in the hall and he purposely made like he didn't know me.

The body was on a metal tray. Pemberton asked the technician to leave us alone. She pulled back the sheet. "Do you know this man?"

"He wore a ski mask. Did I leave out that part?"

"He didn't lose control because he was speeding. He was shot in the neck, bled out and lost consciousness. "Did that shot come from you?"

"Did you find the bullet?"

"No," she said.

"Then it didn't come from me."

She put the cover back and asked the technician for the man's belongings. She put on latex gloves and emptied the bag's contents on a table. Any of these look familiar?"

She showed me a ski mask with the eyes cut out but not the mouth. Then she showed me a belt buckle belt with a bald eagle stooped to conquer on an American flag background. "That's him," I said. "Who is he?"

"He didn't carry any ID but his prints came back. Name is Victor Faucheux. Former French military. When he couldn't get enough killing to suit his moods, he became a hired gun. He works for multinational companies, mostly in Africa and Asia."

"Mower."

"What?"

"Faucheux means mower, harvester. It seems appropriate. Is he French? He had a perfect Midwest accent."

"American. Born in New Orleans. According to Interpol, he attempted to join the US Marines but they found him unsuitable due to his mental state."

"Which was?"

"They didn't elaborate. The French didn't have a problem and he joined the Foreign Legion. He speaks French. He did tours in Gabon, French Guiana and Afghanistan but then he was reassigned to France where most of the Legionnaires are now garrisoned."

"Let me guess. He found it too tame."

"When his hitch was up, he left the Legion and turned freelance. Interpol has been looking for him ever since he did some wetwork in Africa."

"Why would anyone send him to off me when you could hire any kid with a gun in DC to take me out?"

"It does seem like overkill," Pemberton said laughing. "But seriously, that's what I'd like to know, too."

"Have you asked yourself why Keegan was so interested in Helen's Boston's OD. Didn't it seem a little small potatoes for the DEA?"

"He told me that it was part of a larger drug case he was working on."

"And you believed him?"

"Why wouldn't I?"

"Because he's a fed, that's why. You think he gives a rat's ass about our city and its drug problems?"

She went silent, looked down at the white tile floor. "You think he's playing me?"

"Like a baby grand. And another thing. Why was he so interested in the disappearance of Sameer Patel?"

"He said it had to do with a case he was working on. We never made a connection to drugs but we weren't looking for one."

"And here's another question: If Interpol's been looking for Faucheux how did he enter the U.S? Someone gave him a green light. Any idea who that might be?"

Pemberton laughed. "Or maybe he just walked across the border from Mexico."

You have no idea how close you may be detective. "One last thing. When were you going to tell me about his M-16?"

She shrugged. "Under the 1033 Program, it was sent to a federal law enforcement agency for their use."

"This is getting too easy. It went to the DEA, didn't it?"

She lowered her head and nodded.

"I need to hoof. I have to meet Keegan for lunch."

"After all you've said about him do you still trust Keegan?"

"I didn't say that. It's Washington. You can't trust anyone, but I will get a free lunch."

CHAPTER 41

"Keegan," I said, "are you trying to bump me off?"

"What makes you say that?"

"You're not Jewish. You can't answer a question with a question."

"Oh, and you can?"

"You did it again, and yes I can. I'm one-eighth on my mother's side."

"Half-black, half-white and one-eighth Jewish. God bless America," he said.

"If we're done with the ancestry lesson then answer my fucking question."

"If I wanted you dead, you'd be on a slab," he said. His pan was granite with the sharp edges left on.

"Then how do you explain that the M-16 that drilled me was gifted to the DEA and the shooter was a freelance gunsel who works for the government?"

"I heard about that," Keegan said. "How's your arm?" he said, pointing to my sling. Before I could answer, the server came over and took our drink orders. I asked for a Laphroaig neat and Keegan went for a Hendrick's martini, straight up with a twist.

"It's not my arm, it's my shoulder, but that's not the point."

"What's this guy's name?

"Victor Faucheux."

Keegan thought for moment. "I don't know him. To be honest, that doesn't mean he's not one of ours. We have some real characters on the payroll." He laughed. "But I don't know him. Think about it. Why would I want you dead?"

I hate it when people say, 'to be honest.' "Because I'm interfering with your case?"

"On the contrary. You know more than you're telling me and I want to know what you know. I want you around until…"

"Until I am no longer of use?"

He didn't answer.

"Look, Helen Boston is in the middle of a drug investigation. I'm not sure how or why she's involved, but I have a feeling you know more than I do. She's the nexus of drug activity that starts in Mexico and ends in the US. We're on the same side, here Sam, we just have different goals. I want to bust a drug cartel's operation and you want to find Boston's killer. I want you around. That's why I didn't burn you with Pachuco or Senator Metcalfe."

"You want me to play my hand and see where it leads?"

"Something like that."

Something like that, my ass. There's an old saying that if you're in a poker game and you don't know who the patsy is… it's you. "Are you proposing an alliance?"

"I thought we already had one, but it didn't seem to take. I don't think you trust me," Sam."

"Back at ya, Harry."

"As a show of good faith, how about we tell each other something new. You go first."

Why not. "We agree that Boston was murdered, right? There's no question."

He nodded.

"Did you know that the ER doctor who the paramedics called said specifically that they were not to administer Narcon."

"Who was the doctor?"

"He said his name was Nahal but there's no record of anyone with that name working at Georgetown Hospital. Whoever wanted her stiffed, covered all their bases. They went to a lot of trouble to install a phony medico just at the right time and in the right place. It spells big-time operation to me."

Keegan's eyes widened and he settled back into his chair like he was exhausted.

"Now you," I said.

"The Mexican Embassy is mixed up in this."

"I know that," I said.

He squinted. "Did you know that Senator Metcalfe has been in touch with the embassy?"

"Yes, I know that, too."

"How did you… never mind."

I could almost hear the wheels turning inside Keegan's skull.

"Did you know that Metcalfe has received a large amount of money recently?"

"How much money?"

"We're not exactly sure. Could be over five million."

"How do you know?"

He smiled. "We have our source."

"Where is it coming from, the embassy, the cartel?"

"We're not sure. We have to tread carefully. If we have a senator doing some kind of deal with a foreign government and there are drugs involved then… I don't have to tell you that I have to watch my step. It has to be locked down before I can bring this to my superiors."

‘I don’t have any superiors, Harry.”

“I was hoping you’d say that. Go ahead and order the lobster,” he said. “It’s on the taxpayers.”

CHAPTER 42

"What the hell happened to you?" Horace asked as he stood behind the bar and clocked my arm.

"M-16." I kept my answer purposely short because I knew that a history lesson was coming. "Before you say another word, how about a beer?"

I was the only customer. He pulled the tap on a Stella.

"It looks like the bullet did what it was supposed to do."

I was afraid to ask so I didn't. Didn't matter. Horace began, "When the M-16 was invented it went a different way than other rifles. It used a small bullet at high velocity instead of a large bullet, like the AK-47, at a lower velocity. It's 223 caliber which is just a little larger than a 22 caliber that kids use for hunting squirrels but the muzzle velocity is over 3,000 feet per second."

I knew all of this but I let him continue. Horace's teaching complex must be fed. I pulled on my beer and the cold froth made me shiver.

"Where'd you get hit?" he asked.

"Shoulder. Went right through."

"The exit was larger than the entrance, right?"

I nodded.

"The bullet tends to tumble when it enters the body, but the most important aspect is that it doesn't kill you but injures you. For one thing, the high energy shock wave messes up your organs. You sustain internal injuries. This means that your buddies risk their lives to get you out. This puts two people out of action instead of just one. Very smart business model for war." He smiled like he just completed a satisfying lecture.

"I was in the military, remember?"

"Of course." He pulled two shot glasses from the shelf, poured in tequila and said 'salud.' We clinked and I drained my glass and followed it with a swig of beer that emptied that glass, too. It was starting to become one of those afternoons. But before it did, I needed to catch Horace up. When I got to the part about my being Pinkerton, he laughed so hard that he couldn't catch his breath. "And Keegan kept his mouth shut? That's fucking amazing. Have another."

He loaded two more tequila shots and toasted to our good health. "You're gonna need it," he said. "What's your next move, Sam?"

"I was just noodling something. Could you modify Sameer's app so we can listen in to conversations? I owe Metcalfe and his partners an app. The one that Sameer made was pretty good and…"

"It had some glitches," Horace said. "Isn't that why he was murdered?"

"Well, kind of. Maybe. Not sure."

"Can you be more vague?" Horace said. "When the Sinaloa cartel doesn't like your work, they don't contact the Better Business Bureau."

"I don't think that was the only reason. Can you do it?" I asked.

"Probably. Maybe. Not sure." Horace smiled. "I was fooling around with the app the other day and I found the problem, but the wiretap feature may take a few days - if I can even do it. I'm not promising anything."

"Great. Drop a dime when you got something."

"What will you do in the meantime?" he asked.

"I have to figure out Pemberton's deal. She blows hot and cold. One day she wants to jam me for a murder or two and the next day she's my best buddy."

"One for the road," Horace said, as he launched tequila into our shot glasses.

As I ambled out, I heard him crooning the *Parting Glass*. I had a feeling he wouldn't be working on the phone app today.

CHAPTER 43

"A copper who doesn't drink," I said. "Are you a friend of Bill W?"

"I had a father who drank, used to beat my mother when he was loaded," Pemberton said. "I saw what it did to him and my mother and decided that I wouldn't touch the stuff."

She looked at me, waited for a response. "What happened to your father?"

"The abuse went on until one day he came home drunker than I had ever seen him. He had just lost his job. He began beating on my mother. I tried to stop him, but he was too strong. He pushed me aside like I was a feather. I was only thirteen. She landed in the hospital with a broken nose and a broken rib that nearly punctured her left lung. I was sitting by her bed when he finally came to see her. He brought flowers and begged her to forgive him and she almost did."

"Almost?"

"She told him that everything would all be okay, that she wouldn't press charges. She told me to go to school as if nothing had happened but to lock myself in my bedroom when he was around. He went out every day, where, I don't know. Some nights he didn't come home at all. I made my own meals, did my own laundry until she was discharged about a week later. My father promised not to drink anymore and for a week he kept his word but then he came home so drunk he could barely stand up. He put hands on my mother and in the scuffle, she pushed him out a window. We were on the fifth floor. After the ME checked his BAC level, they pronounced it an accident."

She sipped her coffee and her mouth became a thin smile. "I had to stand on a chair to open the window all the way," she said. "But, as they say, that's not why you asked me here."

I cleared my throat, and looked around the diner. It was a basic eatery in Adams Morgan, open all night. They served the best BLT in the District and it wasn't crowded. I wanted to take another hit of my beer but felt reticent about doing it after hearing that story. I didn't. "Do you still make me for those murders?"

"If I did, we wouldn't be sitting in his booth. Like I said before, you're not a murderer. We have three murders: Helen Boston, Sameer Patel and Victor Faucheux and they all are connected. You know it, I know it and Harry Keegan knows it."

Our food arrived. She had ordered breakfast for dinner: eggs, sausage and a toasted bagel. My BLT was a triple decker and the lettuce was unnaturally green.

"Speaking of Keegan, how was your lunch?" she asked, while cutting her over-easy eggs with a fork.

"If he wanted to frame me for the Boston murder, he could do it."

"I know," she said. "For a while, he had me convinced that you were the prime suspect."

"Is that why you allowed him to watch my interrogation?"

She looked up. "I'm not sorry about that, Sam. I was doing my job, but I had to ask myself why he was working so hard to lay it on you. He had some strong evidence, though."

"And your answer?"

"I don't know. Somebody tried to hang you for Patel, too, but that wasn't as elegant a frame. Plus, you had no motive. I had the feeling that Keegan didn't necessarily want to frame you right away, but that he wanted to keep both of these charges in his back pocket just in case he needed it."

"For what reason?" I asked even thought I knew why. He wanted someone like me who works outside the rules to do his dirty work.

"No idea. Why do feds do anything?" she said. "Right now, I know that your bullet hit Faucheux, made him bleed out so he drove into the lions. I couldn't give a shit about that," she said, smearing butter on her bagel. "Hell, the ME would be glad to say that he hit the statutes during a high-speed pursuit. But I do care about the unsolved murders on my plate. By the way, mind the toothpicks."

"What?"

"The toothpicks holding your sandwich together."

"Ah, you do care."

"I have a proposition," she said. "How about we work together on this. We'll share information."

This is great. I will have deals with two people I don't fully trust instead of just one. "Sure," I said. "How about we tell each other something that the other doesn't know. I can go first."

She put down her fork, and looked at me with the focus of a border collie.

"Did you know that when the paramedics were working Boston's OD call they were specifically told not to deliver Narcon?" Her eyes opened wider when I told her that the doctor didn't exist. "I couldn't find him and neither could the paramedics."

"Must be a big-time operation to put logistics like that in place," she said.

"My thoughts exactly."

"Here's mine," she said. "Sameer Patel had worked for the CIA at one time."

I'm guessing that Keegan knew that but decided not to tell Pemberton or me.

"What was he involved in?"

"It's not clear. All I know is that he was stationed in Colombia and then Mexico."

"I smell drugs," I said.

"It gets better. We did a background on his boss, a guy named LaFarge who runs a Beltway Bandit shop in Tysons. He worked at the agency, too. He was a CIA pilot."

"How did you get that info? The CIA doesn't confirm or deny agent's identities."

"I'm not just another pretty face, Marlowe. Do we work together on this?"

"Sure. Get some descolumbsert. It's on me."

CHAPTER 44

I was determined to free my wing no matter the pain. It had been only a few days since the shooting and the wound was still weeping and my shoulder thumped like a car running on turpentine. The first time I tried to lay my arm straight I almost passed out. I sat on the bed this time just in case.

By the time I had flattened my arm against my body then flexed my elbow a few times everything seemed to be working, but I couldn't be sure if I was screaming out loud or it was all in my head. I bounced a handful of pain pill down my gullet and followed it with cold joe that had been sitting on the kitchen table since breakfast. It was now after noon.

I jangled Metcalfe's office to let him know that I had the crypto phone app ready for him, and the person who answered the phone told me that the senator was attending a drug conference at the Ronald Reagan building and I was welcome to attend. I replied that I would. Sitting in an audience of policy wonks while I was high on goof balls might be exactly what I needed to push the day along.

I had arrived after the introductory remarks but just in time to hear someone from the Portuguese government describe how they handle the drug situation in their country. I remembered reading something about how Portugal had decriminalized illegal drugs, but I didn't know anything else. As I watched the representative walk to the podium I looked out at the audience from my seat in the last row. The place was packed but I saw a familiar face sitting up front. It was Metcalfe.

This was a serious subject but the pills made it all seem pretty damn hilarious so I sat in the back and hoped he didn't turn around to see me smiling.

Galenia Faracho, an official in the Ministry of Health, said that there were many misconceptions to what some have called "The Portuguese Experiment." Drugs were still illegal, she said, but that drug use is handled as a medical issue and not a criminal matter. She put up a slide that showed that since 2000, when the country had about 100,000 heroin users, the number now was cut in half and most of these addicts are under treatment. She compared the country's drug induced death rate to three per million residents compared to the European's Union rate of 17.3 per million. The distinct murmur in the audience was so loud it sounded like it was part of a sitcom laugh track.

Faracho paced back and forth on the stage as she pointed a hand laser at the screen to emphasize each point.

The other effects seemed too good to be true or maybe it was just my drug-addled mind. Crime was down, incarceration rates were down, communicable diseases like AIDs and hepatitis were down. "And the money saved from putting people in prison and paying police to go after drug users is now spent on prevention of drug use and other medical priorities," she said. She continued showing charts and graphs.

When it came time for questions, the room buzzed.

"Are there any downsides to the program?" a voice in the audience asked.

The presenter walked to the front of the riser. "Yes," she said. "We have found that the drug cartels no longer want to use my country as a destination. Because there is no longer any severe risk being caught with drugs, and use is down, so the price is down. There is no profit motive anymore for large drug dealers. How do you say… It is not worth their while."

"How is that a downside?" the person asked.

"For those who made money from illegal drugs it is a downside. They had to find honest work."

The audience laughed.

"We do still have some drug dealers," she added, "and they are prosecuted, but there are far fewer than before."

A few others asked questions and when invited to wrap up her presentation, the speaker said: "It is not a perfect system, but it is working."

The audience applauded. As Faracho walked off the stage, Metcalfe met her, shook hands and they exchanged business cards. I ran out before he could see me.

The pills were wearing off and I was in no mood to talk to anyone especially Metcalfe who thought I was someone else.

I bounced uptown in a cab hoping to catch a few zzz's before Metcalfe got the message that I had called and dialed me back. No such luck. My phone rang, and I let it go to voicemail seeing as how I gobbled a few more pills to relieve the pounding pain produced by letting my arm dangle loose like most humans who hadn't been pierced by a bullet. The pills acted fast and I was once again everybody's best friend.

In my daze, I thought about what the Portuguese health expert said about their success with legalizing drugs and whether it could work in the United States. Cynical me said 'no.' The cartels would figure out a workaround. I fell asleep to the sound of city life outside my window. Cars honking, people yelling and sirens wailing soothed me more than pain pills ever could.

CHAPTER 45

Metcalfe was leaning back so far in his executive chair that I thought he might tip over. The pain pills were almost done working through my system so imagining him slide to the floor with the chair landing on his head, Three Stooges style, didn't seem as funny as it should be.

"I went to a meeting yesterday and one of the speakers was from Portugal. He handed me a loose-leaf binder. "Read for yourself," he said. He didn't know that I was there, too.

The front cover read: *Drug Decriminalisation in Portugal: Setting the Record Straight.* "The main point is that they moved to a more health-centered approach to drug use. Just as important, they also instituted a guaranteed minimum income for all citizens. These factors in concert, I believe are what lowered drug use, not just the decriminalization."

"What's your interest in the Portugal experience?"

He stood up and walked toward the window. "One of our mandates is to look at best practices, and for that matter, all practices around the world having to do with drug use and the crime that flows from it. Quite frankly, we don't know what will stem drug use in the US, but what we have now certainly isn't working. We have more drug use than ever before and every time we crack down on one drug another appears. It's usually more virulent, more addictive and cheaper."

His face turned red. He picked up a pen from his desk and threw it at the wall. "It's almost like we're helping the drug cartels grow their business. We cracked down on heroin so the drug cartels moved to fentanyl which is fifty times more addictive and less expensive. Here, look at this." He produced a chart showing that a kilo of heroin costs about $55,000 and fentanyl costs less than $10,000 a kilo. "To extend the heroin they mix it with fentanyl, charge less and addicts want more. The cartels sell lower quality products, and users need more of it to be satisfied."

His arms made sweeping gestures. "Now we're seeing the precursor chemicals to fentanyl coming from China which is allowing the Mexican cartels to manufacture it themselves and push it over the border. The Chinese used to impregnate the chemical into paper products like greeting cards and clothing, but now they just ship it in small packets hidden among other goods going to the US."

"If it's shipped to the US how do the cartels mix it with heroin?"

"That's the part that really gets me angry. The cartels in the US ship the fentanyl to Mexico where it's mixed with heroin, cocaine or whatever and they send it back to the US." His arms were moving around so fast I thought his hands would fly off. "Can you believe that?"

"How much moolah is involved?" My hold was fading, but Metcalfe was so animated that he hardly noticed my choice of words.

"One kilogram of pure fentanyl from China is about this size," he said holding up a large plastic water bottle," and costs about three to five thousand dollars to produce. Once it's turned into a diluted powder and sold, say in San Diego, it has a street value of around $300,000. As it moves further from the border towards the east coast the value skyrockets."

He composed himself and sat down again. "That's why our work here is so important and why we need such secrecy in our communications. The stakes are so high, the profit motive is so strong that we don't know who we can trust."

"I dig," I said, although I tried to muffle the words. I handed him a thumb drive and a cable that hooks up to iPhones. "Installation is a breeze."

"Thank you, Mr. Pinkerton. Your country thanks you," he said, as he extended his hand.

"One thing doesn't jibe Senator. How are the cartels able to launder all the dough they make?"

"That's a discussion for another time," he said, hustling me to the door. "I will call you if I need you."

I waved to Jennifer Morgan who looked at me and said, in a hesitating voice, "Um, goodbye." I'm sure she was wondering what all the loud voices were about and whether her boss was angry at me.

All I had to wonder about was when he would have his minions install the new app and what gems Horace would get off the wiretap. I figured I had a few days of R&R before this happened. I could use the rest and a few more pills from my favorite dentist.

CHAPTER 46

I heard from bike messenger Cherry Lane that packages now were moving from Senator Metcalfe's office to the Mexican Embassy, a reverse flow than before. This meant that he was installing the crypto app on phones and sending them to his contacts in the Sinaloa cartel. I had to give Metcalfe credit for taking matters into his own hands.

It wouldn't take long for the phone taps to yield some information and perhaps I could find out why the hell a US senator got north of two mil from the Mexicans.

One of the saws about investigations is follow the money. Great idea in theory, but sometimes the trail stops dead especially when the lettuce gets tossed into an offshore bank or some other black hole. The feds track it as best they can, but sometimes they hit a wall like when a foreign bank doesn't want to cooperate and their government backs them up. There is one exception. When the US Treasury screams narco-terrorist funding it tends to make banks more cooperative. I have a couple of pals at Treasury, and I decided to chow down with one of them. It cost me lunch in an expensive eatery.

Alyce Fleming was one of the good guys. She could double her wage as a forensic accountant in the private sector, but believed in public service. She walked into the restaurant wearing a dark blue, well-tailored business suit and flat shoes. If she had the lapel pin of the day, she could pass for a Secret Service agent. She wore minimal makeup and glasses with thick, smart-girl frames. Her tightly-scrunched ponytail rode high on her head.

"I've always wanted to dine here," she said.

"PIs are rolling in dough. The sky's the limit, Ally."

"You always were a charmer, Sam."

Which was true. I charmed her for about six months before the magic wore off.

"What's with your shoulder?" she said. "You seem to be favoring it."

I didn't realize I had a tell. Noticing small details is what makes her good at her job.

"Someone shot me."

"A politician's wife exacting revenge?"

"Something like that." I didn't want to go into the specifics. We both ordered the risotto with mushrooms. Alyce asked the server about the white burgundies and she ordered a 2014 vintage after mumbling to the server something about excellent density and concentration. She smiled at me and said, "Life is too short." She placed her napkin in her lap, leaned forward and widened her eyes.

"So?"

"It's a been a while since I've dealt with washing geetus. What are the smart boys doing these days?"

"If you're asking about money laundering, it's all changed in the past several years. Even we're having trouble getting a handle on it. For one thing, the amounts are bigger than ever. We're talking in the billions. And the subterfuges are becoming more convoluted and difficult to trace."

"Because of FinTech?" I wanted to show her that I knew something.

"Blockchain, cryptocurrencies, robo-investing, artificial intelligence, peer-to-peer lending and the list goes on. Financial Technology is being sold as bringing financial services to the underserved but that's nonsense. It's really about the haves getting a larger piece of the pie and hiding it from the have-nots. Remember the algos who caused the 2008 financial crises?"

"The gonifs who invented those obscure real-estate derivative products until the last one holding the bag brought everyone down, including the companies that insured them?"

"One and the same," she said. "These same FinTech actors now are money-laundering rock stars. We had an unfortunate convergence, Sam. Since 9/11 the FBI, CIA, ATF, NSA, all of government law enforcement agencies shifted their focus to terrorism. Almost nobody's doing large domestic cases like fraud, stock market manipulation, organized crime, human trafficking unless there's a connection to terrorism. In order for me to work on a case, I have to show my supervisor that the suspects may be funneling money to terrorists."

"That's a wrong number."

"For sure. Why do you think nobody was keeping an eye on the bankers that caused the crash? Everyone was looking for Al Qaeda, the Islamic Jihad and whoever else showed up on radar. Overseeing financial institutions just wasn't sexy - or rewarded. Sometimes I have to stretch the truth to work on a case that I know is in the public's interest. It makes me want to quit."

The wine arrived and Alyce taste-tested it. She sipped and swirled and nodded her approval. The server refilled her glass and she took a gulp. "That's better, she said. "Now, what was I saying about money laundering?"

"What the FinTech crowd is doing."

"First, let me tell you what they're not doing. There's a Netflix show called *Ozark*. Have you seen it? It's about this money manager, not into FinTech by any means. He still reads paper readouts, and has to launder millions of dollars for a drug kingpin or his family gets killed. Very entertaining. Anyway, he moves from Chicago to Lake of the Ozarks in Missouri and buys or becomes a partner in cash businesses like restaurants and strip clubs. He works hard to mingle the dirty money with clean money by overpaying for products and repairs. It's old school. There're even episodes where he literally washes the uncirculated drug money in a washing machine to help it mix in with what the businesses take in. It's a great show to watch, but it makes me laugh. That's not what is going on these days."

Our entrees arrived and we began eating. The risotto was warm and creamy.

"What's the latest? Spill," I said.

"It's all about Foreign Trade Zones, aka Free Trade Zones. There are thousands of them around the world. The original idea was that a company, say in Michigan, could import raw materials, turn them into manufactured goods, like a car, and sell it overseas by paying no import taxes or tariffs."

"Sounds like hooey."

"These FTZ's are like special islands within a country's borders, but they're not part of the country for taxation purposes. They've been around for hundreds of years, designed to even the economic playing field among countries, but that's not how they're being used today. Very little manufacturing is going on in these zones except maybe China. In the US, they're used to hide assets. For example, let's say I buy a Van Gogh painting at Sotheby's in New York for twenty million dollars. Normally I would have to pay sales tax, right?"

I nodded.

"But if I ship the painting immediately to an FTZ in Manhattan, and keep it there, it's as if I really didn't buy it for tax purposes, because it's not located in New York State or the US for that matter, in a legal sense."

"What happens to the painting?"

"The buyer can keep it there indefinitely and never pay taxes until they sell it in the US. And maybe not even then if they wait long enough. Why? Because by that time, the IRS has lost track of it and might not even know it has been sold. Or, the owner could ship it overseas and not be liable legally for any taxes. It ends up hanging in some rich dude's mansion in France and no one is the wiser."

"On the level?"

"It gets better. There's an ongoing uproar in the art world about masterpieces stored in these FTZs that will never see the light of day, never exhibited in a museum. They're sitting in a box in a warehouse until the owner decides that it has appreciated enough to sell it."

"I was always wondering why you hear about a famous painting that was just discovered somewhere and nobody can say how it came on the market."

"That's right. It probably came out of an FTZ storage building. But there's more," Alyce said, lowering her voice. "These FTZs are not policed by customs or the IRS to any degree. Goods come in and go out without going through any kind of usual accounting or searches like when a container comes into the harbor. Compliance is assured through audits and spot checks under a surety bond, rather than through on-site supervision by Customs personnel. This makes it ideal to launder money or hide any other asset."

She took a spoonful of risotto and continued. "There are so many opportunities to wash money using an FTZ; here's a simple example. A drug cartel from Mexico sells drugs worth one million dollars to dealers in the US. Another company, let's call it Drug Inc., in an FTZ in a different country, let's say the Cayman Islands, acts as an intermediary. Various people deposit funds into Drug Inc.'s bank account. Drug Inc. exports goods, it doesn't matter what, to the drug cartel in Mexico where they're sold for one million dollars. That money goes to the Cayman Islands bank, supposedly for the goods and is sent to the drug cartel in cash. On paper, it looks legitimate. With banks keeping their depositors' names quiet, the money looks clean. Add to that the lax security and oversight of the FTZs and the schemes are rarely if ever uncovered."

She refilled her wine glass. "Want some? she asked.

"Please. It sounds like it would take a long time to launder large sums."

"For sure. With this most basic example. In real life, the transactions use more intermediaries and multiple FTZs so you can scale up the amount laundered. You sell a product for twice, three times what the real value is and there's no easy way to find records of the transactions. Every state has FTZs, every country, even the poorest, least industrialized ones, and they're especially common near our borders, south and north and in Mexico and Canada. They were established for making cars and machinery to save on taxes, but now… "

She dabbed the napkin on her mouth, took out her phone and read. "In 2015, the Treasury estimated that what we call Trade Based Money Laundering, TBML, hit $276 billion between 2004 and 2009. I would guess that it has at least doubled, maybe tripled since then."

"Where is all this dough?"

"Some of it is sitting as physical dollars, yens, euros, whatever, in crates in FTZs, some are in offshore bank accounts and some are continually moving around in cyberspace. Why the interest, Sam, or shouldn't I ask?"

"Can I drop in on one of these FTZs?"

"Well, that's the funny thing. There's one only a few blocks from here but you wouldn't know it. Some FTZs are on acres and acres of land, some encompass whole cities, but the one near us is in a non-descript building with more security than a nuclear power plant. Although it's government sanctioned, it's privately owned. The owner decides who enters. They set the rules. You have to be a customer or potential customer and call ahead for access."

"Can you badge your way in?"

"I would have to submit a request to my supervisor who would then request access. It would have to be for a case I was working on. Because it's not considered land within the US, per se, we cannot execute a search warrant in the usual way or just barge our way in with a SWAT team. There are procedures we can use to gain access if we think something isn't kosher, but I've never heard of it happening. I've been inside this particular building, and there's nothing to see but steel cages with crates inside. The cages don't even have names on them, just numbers to identify the user."

"Could a drug cartel own one of these FTZs?"

"I don't see why not."

CHAPTER 47

Maybe I've been thinking too small. With a string of strategically placed FTZ buildings in the US, Mexico, China, and who knows where else, you could ship large quantities of drugs, physical money and anything else you wanted anywhere you wanted without the law finding out.

Could this really be true?

I started noodling all sides of the argument. What about the mules carrying drugs in their backpacks, trudging through miles of Arizona deserts? How do they fit in? Seems like small potatoes.

And another thing, if the US is awash in drugs how come we hardly catch the bad guys except at the street level? El Chapo was the exception, but he probably never heard of FinTech or FTZs. He used to bury tons of shrink-wrapped hundred-dollar bills in the Colombian jungle for safekeeping.

On the other side of the ledger, how could a worldwide network like this really exist? Why aren't legitimate governments and law enforcement doing anything about it?

I leaned back in a booth at the Teekee, sipped a cold one and pondered these scenarios. I went back and forth and my head began to hurt. Horace was sitting behind the bar doing the crossword puzzle in the

Wall Street Journal. After a few minutes, he pronounced it finished, slashed a big check mark on the page and joined me.

"This answers a lot of questions," Horace said, after listening to my theory. "It never made sense to me that the estimates of how many tons of drugs entered the US synched with how much they caught at the border or on the street."

He grabbed two beers.

"And neither does the government line about a parade of Mexicans with backpacks supplying all our addicts," I said.

"Oh, my god," Horace said, "the government is lying to us."

Horace can be a sarcastic chap. Worse than me.

"Check this out," I said, pointing to a Wikipedia page on my phone. I read: "There are over 230 foreign-trade zone projects and nearly 400 subzones in the United States. It says here that a subzone is an area approved for use by a specific company instead of a shared zone. That means even less scrutiny and fewer strangers walking around."

"And look at this," Horace said, scrolling to a list of FTZs. "Most of them are in the southern border states. Texas has the most. I remember that Mexico used to ship car parts to the US, then the car companies would build them into cars and export them back to Mexico or South America. That saved a ton of taxes and tariffs. I can't imagine that they're building many cars anymore for export."

"But the FTZs are still there," I said.

"A worldwide string of warehouses protected by the law and used by the one-percenters to hide their wealth from the rest of us. This is approaching Trilateral Commission, UFO and Illuminati shit," he said.

"Let's not forget the Freemasons," I said.

"I'm serious," Horace said, tapping on his phone then walking into the back room. He returned a few minutes later with a stack of papers, plopped them on the table. "Sam, old pal, we are really late to the party on this one. The top sheet was a report that read: *Trade-Based Laundering: Overview and Policy Issues.* "It's from the Congressional Research Service." He turned to the next piece of paper which read: *Money Laundering Vulnerabilities of Free Trade Zones.* "This is from the… it says, the Financial Action Task Force, an inter-governmental body established in 1989 by the Ministers of its Member jurisdictions. In other words, government regulators. It says they represent about 40 countries." He fanned more than a dozen pages. "And these are just the front pages of reports. Some of these studies go back 10 years or more. Even then, people saw that these FTZs could be exploited."

"That's what Alyce told me."

"Alyce Fleming?"

I nodded.

"What happened to her? She was smart, pretty and…"

"Focus, Horace."

"What else did she say?"

"She said that a drug cartel could own and operate an FTZ. All they would need is a few shell companies to hide their ownership and Bob's your uncle."

"Bob's got a lot of nephews," Horace said. "Perhaps we could narrow it down."

"I'd prefer to do it sooner rather than later. You may have noticed that people have been using me for target practice and it's getting annoying."

"Are you feeling lucky, Sam?"

"Lottery lucky or not getting rubbed out lucky?"

"The phone taps should be bearing some fruit. Let's give it a day or so and see if anything comes in."

"Good idea. In the meanwhile, I'm going to work at not getting shot at."

"You realize that the more we look into this, the more you'll be in the crosshairs. This is much larger, more dangerous and more significant than finding out who killed Helen Boston."

I got up to leave, swish-shot my empty beer bottle into the recycling can. "Not for me it isn't."

CHAPTER 48

My shoulder felt aces, and I was able to gig up my cross-draw holster although I didn't tug the straps as taut as I usually did. Between the heater that Helen Boston gave me, the one that the coppers gave back to me after the shootout at the Starbucks ranch and a few other possible switcheroos along the way I lost track of which gat I was toting. I know that old time dicks are supposed to cherish their shooters like lovers, but I just can't get that worked up about a hunk of blue steel especially because it may leave me once again. There's some cosmic power at work here, I believe, because the universe always makes sure that a rod comes to me when I need it.

I had a gut feeling that such a time was coming.

I walked out of my building into a cool, sunny day, and headed over to the FTZ building that Alyce told me about. I knew the building. For a time, I played poker in the sixth-floor offices of a lawyer whose name I no longer recall. Marvin, something or other. I do remember, though, that he often lost but continued to host the games because it was the only way he could get a night out from his wife who kept him on a short leash. She would call several times during the game and we all took turns saying 'hello' to allay her fears that he was dogging around with another woman. Which, as far we knew, he wasn't. The weekly game rumbled along for about a year until one night we all decided that it would be funny not to talk to Marvin's wife despite his pleas as he passed the phone around. We played on and when we broke up around an hour later than our usual 11 o'clock time his wife barged in, wearing a bathrobe and slippers, and without saying a word stabbed him in the neck with a bread knife.

As he bled out, Marvin's last word were "Marjorie, I love you." His wife's name was Gladys, and we held her until the coppers arrived. The group never played cards together again.

I scanned the lobby directory and most of the tenants sounded like law firms but I found the name I was looking for: Tiber Creek, Inc. It was the name Alyce gave me. They were on the 4th floor.

I checked in with the lobby guard. He was on his late 50's with hard, angular features. His eyes were tired and the color of blue raspberry ices. His hands shook a bit and the first two fingers on his right hand were yellow-brown from years of smoking.

"Who are you seeing?"

"Tiber Creek."

"Do you have an appointment?"

"No."

"Sign here."

No ID; no nothing. That was easy.

I entered the elevator and pressed the button for the 4th floor. The elevator door did not close. I pressed again. No dice.

I stepped out and called to the guard. Is this elevator broken?"

He looked up. "No, sir."

"But it won't go to the 4th floor."

"Not supposed to. Step over here please, sir."

I walked to the front of his desk. He checked his bank of cameras before looking back at me.

"Entry to the 4th floor requires an elevator key which I don't have. Only the tenant has it, sir."

"Why didn't you tell me that before?"

"Sir, you are not the first person who has wanted to visit the 4th floor unannounced. I used to tell people that they couldn't enter without an appointment, but they didn't believe me, thought I was hiding something from them, gave me a hard time. Some folks got downright nasty. This way, I let them find out for themselves and it saves me having to argue. I don't need the hassle. Know what I mean?" He took a sip from a straw impaled in a diet Coca-Cola can.

He handed me a card. "Call this number, ask for this person."

"Do you know what kind of business it is?"

"Don't you know?"

"I was cold calling."

"Anything else, sir?"

I was just about to walk out when he said. "By the way, sir. I should probably tell you that the stairwell doors to the 4th floor are dead-bolted, the floors and ceilings contain four inches of steel, the windows are barred and they have their own private alarm system different from the rest of the building's tenants." He smiled, and I saw a hint of dimples.

"Why did you decide to tell me that?"

"You look like a man who doesn't like to waste time. I'm the same way. Have a nice day, sir."

CHAPTER 49

"I want to be Canadian, Horace."

He looked up from his Kindle. "Who doesn't? They're polite, have national health care, and they've legalized pot nationwide. And they have poutine, an excellent hangover cure."

"I need another identity. A Canadian. I'll need a passport and driver's license. How about British Columbia?"

"Geeze, Sam. Like I have nothing else to do?"

"Well, do you?"

"That's not the point. Do you want a French or English type name?"

I had to laugh. Only someone who has falsified Canadian documents before would know to ask that.

"English," I said. "Let's keep the British Columbia theme consistent."

"This could take a day or two. By the way, how did it go at the FTZ?"

"Couldn't get passed the guard. Invitation only. Anything from the wiretap?"

"Just one thing, didn't seem important." He rifled through some papers. "Metcalfe is supposed to meet someone at the Tiber Creek. I'm guessing it's a restaurant"

"Holy, crap. Do you know what Tiber Creek is?"

"Of course. I was born in DC. It's the creek that fed into the Potomac where the National Mall is. They widened it into a canal before turning the whole thing into a tunnel for drainage and as a storm sewer. There was a pub named Tiber Creek but they changed their name and… "

"No. It's the company name of the FTZ that Alyce told me about. The one that I couldn't get in."

"I guess that is important."

"When are they supposed to meet?"

"Eight p.m."

"Who is he meeting?"

"Didn't say. All she said was to meet her."

"Her? A woman?"

"Sounded like it."

"I'm going to see who that someone is. Wanna come?"

"I have some IDs to work on."

I started to leave. "Do you still have the Washington Gas gear?"

"It's in the basement. Help yourself."

I pulled a string on a lone ceiling lightbulb. It cast such dark shadows on the piles of junk that lived in the basement that I could barely see behind some of the large boxes and crates. I pulled out my flash and wandered around. I pushed aside hunks of wood, metal cabinets with wires sticking out, and equipment that looked like it came out of airplanes, boats and trucks. I spied a jackhammer leaning against a far wall and headed in that direction. I found what I needed, and it took several trips to bring the equipment to street level.

"I guess you want to borrow my van," Horace said as he watched me carry metal tubes on my shoulder. He threw me the keys.

Around 7:30, I set up in the street outside the building. I had on a hard hat, reflective vest and began building a small barricade. I hung a lantern from a yellow safety bollard. It took about 15 minutes to complete the job and damn if it didn't look like a real Washington Gas job site unless someone was curious enough to ask why the manhole was still closed.

I had the perfect view of the building entrance and the lobby.

At exactly eight Metcalfe emerged from a government-issued town car. The driver had purposely turned off the dome light, but I was sure it was the senator when the street light hit his face. He was pulling wheelie luggage large enough to carry a baby whale. He rolled it to the building doors and looked at his watch.

A minute later, another town car, this time a private job, pulled behind the senator's ride. A woman got out and she also had luggage with wheels. She wore jeans, a white shirt and a baseball cap. I couldn't see her face. She walked towards the senator and without a handshake or greeting the two opened the glass doors, waved to a guard who I hadn't seen before and walked to the elevator.

All I could do now was wait until they left and try again to see her face.

I was on 17th and K Street, less than a block from the Farragut North Metro, and people were walking towards the station on their way home. Some were working late; others had stopped for a quick drink hoping the train would be less crowded after a few. I looked up at the buildings, office lights still shining, cleaning crews arriving, cars detouring around my little island.

Except for the police car that stopped. The spinner came alive, and the copper yelled out the window. "Problem?"

"Routine," I said, walking to his car. "We got a funny reading on a pressure gauge. I'm here to check it out. I don't smell gas, do you?"

He held his head out the window and sniffed. "Nothing."

I checked the lobby door and saw the duo leaving the elevator.

"You alone?" he asked.

"I got two more guys coming. They're late. You know how it is."

"Yeah. I used to have this partner..."

"Oh, crap. Now I smell it," I screamed. "I ran to the van pulled out a random metal box, held it over the manhole cover. "Shit."

I screamed into my phone. "I need a shut-off a block north of my location. That's right. Now!"

I looked over at the lobby. They were almost at the guard station. I had less than a minute before they would exit the building.

I moved towards the cop. "Any chance you can cut the traffic until we get this sorted out?"

Without saying a word, he swung his car around and blocked the lanes. He exited the car and directed traffic around us.

I had my chance to focus on the two as they walked into the street light. They shook hands and parted. Metcalfe reached his car first. The woman stopped for a second to take in the night air.

I strained to see her face, which was still partially covered by her baseball cap, but I finally saw her clearly as the street light reflected off the car roof.

Sarah.

CHAPTER 50

Sarah. What the hell.

If she was dirty then so was LaFarge. That also meant that they knew what Sameer was doing. Did I have to spell it out for myself? Apparently. All three of them are or were working for the Sinaloa cartel. Sameer was doing the communications end of it, Sarah was helping to launder money and LaFarge… what was his role? I knew that he was a former CIA pilot so maybe he was working the logistics angle, flying drugs into the states. Or maybe he was moving product among the FTZs.

Did LaFarge think I wouldn't learn about their link to the cartel? I try not to take things personally in my business, but my professional snooper ability had been insulted. Of course, this wasn't the first time that I had been hired by someone who hoped that I wouldn't dig too deep. This shows me in spades just how desperate LaFarge must have been to find Sameer that he was willing to risk being exposed.

The cartel probably had LaFarge in their gun sights. Now that I think about, I'm surprised they didn't croak him when Sameer took a powder. The Sinaloa cartel doesn't take too kindly to failure. Metcalfe saved LaFarge's life when he took it upon himself to replace Sameer with Pinkerton. When they learn that Pinkerton is not who they think he is, LaFarge will end up as a smear on the sidewalk. So will Sarah. I won't be buying any green bananas for Metcalfe, either.

I snagged a bottle of rye, sweet vermouth, bitters and built a Manhattan. I put in a slice of orange instead of those crappy cherries that I see too often. I sat back and waited for the coolness to bathe my throat. I went on line and checked Tiber Creek on a web service that holds incorporation papers. The majority of private stock in Tiber Creek, Inc. (DC) is held by another company, Tiber Creek Partners which is registered in Delaware. When I checked their papers, it turns out the majority shares are held by a company, MBI, Ltd., in Nevis. This Caribbean island, half of the federation of St. Kitts and Nevis, is an independent country. Nevis is famous for being home to banks that keep their books to themselves and resist attempts by government investigators worldwide.

I got in touch with a friend on St. Thomas which wasn't that close but at least in the same neighborhood. Cyril Willingham is a Brit who moved to the U.S. Virgins after a stint as a British economic attaché in Washington. That was his official title. He was essentially a spy from an allied country who kept tabs on U.K. economic interests in the States both overtly and covertly. He retired after winning a million dollars in the DC lottery. The last time we spoke, he told me: "Sammy boy, I gotta get out of this fucking city."

I emailed him asking if he wanted a short hop to Nevis and he responded within minutes saying that he was getting a tad bored sitting on the beach and would welcome a trip. I emailed the information that I wanted and he replied that he would leave on the next plane. He wrote: "I can be there in time for Happy Hour at Sunny's," which I guessed was a popular watering hole. I expected that Cyril would find several companies in the chain of ownership. Eventually, if we got lucky, it would end in a physical address, usually an ordinary looking building with offices that act as what's called registered agents.

If you look long enough and exercise patience you can eventually reach ground zero and it usually lands in an ordinary-looking building with offices that act as official registered agents for corporations. Their job is to be a physical address as required by law and to accept mail, usually government communications like tax forms, and on occasion, a court subpoena.

It's all very efficient, clean and legal.

I finished my Manhattan, built another, and thought about FTZs and this network of underground wealth that most of the world knows nothing about. Alyce said that some people have dubbed it *Moneystan* because it functions almost like a country unto itself with its own rules and regulations separate from the rest of us.

I fell asleep reading incorporation papers on line and dreamt that I was a citizen of Moneystan. I was piloting my sailboat, drinking champagne out of the bottle and heading into the sunset.

In my dream, I was being poked in the temple by the playful pecks of a sea bird with a cartoonish grin. When I awoke, the bird's beak was a gun barrel, and the holder wasn't smiling at all.

CHAPTER 51

Waking up to someone holding a gat to my noggin was getting to be a chronic habit, one that I'd prefer to twelve-step my way out of.

"You were given five grand to back off," the voice said, through the woolen mask. "And you didn't."

I started to get up out of my chair, but the gunsel pushed me down.

"Stay put," he said.

"Do you guys get a discount on those masks?" I waited for a gat slap that never came. "Who are you?"

"There's no reason not to show you," he said, ripping off the mask in one move. "You're going to die anyway."

His face was pockmarked, with a nose that went a little further to the left than it should. His eyes were bloodshot, rheumy. He had the look of a man who sleeps only a few hours a night and makes up for it with espresso shots scattered throughout the day. There was something familiar about him, but I couldn't pull it up.

"You don't know who I am, do you," he asked.

"You're the guy going to off me? I thought that's what I heard."

"And I heard that you're a wise-ass. Always a funny comment."

"Who told you that?"

"My brother, Victor."

Victor Faucheux. The hired gun who offered me five grand to walk away from hunting Helen Boston's killer. The guy who tried to shoot off my head in Starbucks. The guy who died when his car sped into the lions statues on the bridge. That guy.

"Is this about revenge?"

"Yeah, it's about revenge. You killed my brother."

"Not technically," I said. "The police were chasing him after he shot up a Starbucks. He lost control of his car."

"He lost control of his car because he was bleeding out and lost consciousness. Because you shot him."

"Okay," I said. "When you put it that way… but he did try to kill me. That should count for something."

"What is with you?" he said, waving the gun back and forth. "You don't seem to take this seriously."

"I know. It's an unhealthy part of my personality."

"Shut up," he yelled. "There's nothing funny about you killing my brother."

"Since I'm a goner anyway, tell me something. Are you and your brother in the same line of work? Is it a family business?"

"Not that it's any of your concern but I'll tell you. Victor left the military but the military never left him. It was the only world he knew. It was the only way he could make a living."

I started to speak and he put the gun to my neck. "Shut up. No more jokes. As for me, I'm not a killer. I'm a roofer."

"A roofer?"

"Fifteen years. I have my own business, I employ a couple of guys, I have a wife, two kids."

"And you're willing to give all that up just to teach me a lesson?"

"A lesson? It's my fucking brother we're talking about."

"Okay, then," I said. "Shoot me."

He leaned back and took aim. I wanted it to end like a *Lifetime* special where the avenged person's hand starts to quiver, and they can't quite pull the trigger, so they hold the gun with two hands. They start to squeeze the trigger, can't do it, and drop the gun to the floor and sob.

That wasn't happening.

He held the weapon straight at me with hands as solid as granite. He was aiming at my head. He squeezed the trigger.

I watched as the cylinder turned.

The technical term is hang fire, the time between when the trigger is pulled and the propellant is ignited forcing the bullet out of the shell, then out the barrel and, in this particular case, into my face. All of this went through my mind in nanoseconds. I considered the poor odds of a malfunction and fell to my right side while hitting the gun with my hand as I went down. The gun went off and missed me by a hair. I came up with a fist to his jaw that knocked him back on his heels. He backpedaled and couldn't get a purchase. He skittered on the floor like a tasered crab.

The rod actually flew up in the air and spun around a few times like in a *Yosemite Sam* cartoon and I caught it on the way down. My index finger even slid into the trigger guard.

I pointed it at Victor's brother while he gained composure in the corner. As if written into the script, he began sobbing.

"Who was your brother working for?"

He hesitated. "He said the DEA."

That tracks. Now, I felt as if I needed to punish him for trying to kill me, but I just didn't have a heart. He was confused, overwrought by his psycho brother's death; he seemed like a family man caught up in… Fuck it.

I pointed the gun at him, pulled the trigger knowing the slug would miss him by an inch – which it did. I left him in a heap, a yellow stain blotching his pants.

I spun the magazine and collected the bullets. I threw the gun in his direction, said: "I have enough guns," and walked out the door.

"Be gone by the time I get back."

CHAPTER 52

When I returned home, Victor's brother was gone, replaced by two beat cops standing in my office and the booming voice of Pemberton barking orders. As usual, when she's involved in anything having to do with me, she's angry as a teen who sat on their smartphone.

"We got a 911 call about gunshots," she said. I thought I heard her molars grinding. "Where have you been for the past hour?"

"Remember that Starbucks where I got shot? They owed me a latte. The barista bumped it up to a Venti size. Nice people."

If we were in the 1930s, she would have the two coppers drag me into the alley and dance a Samba on my face. She was digging out the second bullet from the wall. I watched as plaster dust dribbled on the rug. I was tempted to use the dust buster I got as a white elephant Christmas gift but decided that would really piss her off, and a visit to the alley might become a real possibility.

"What happened here?"

"Victor Faucheux's brother dropped in for a visit."

"And?"

"He waved a gun around, threatened to kill me, took a shot and missed. I fingered his heater, squeezed off a shot and also missed. That's all there was to it."

She mumbled something that I couldn't make out, but I thought I heard the phrase 'lousy shot.'

"Discharging a weapon within the District of Columbia is a misdemeanor," she said, scratching her cheek, then holding up two baggies containing the slugs. "I haven't known you to miss, especially at close range."

"Off day," I replied. "Victor confirmed that his brother was working for the DEA. Why do you suppose they would want me dead?"

"Because Keegan finds you as annoying as I do?"

"That's quite possible," I said.

She put the baggies in a manila envelope, sealed it and wrote her name across the flap. She handed it to one of the officers and said: "Evidence room, then you can go back in service."

She looked out the window and watched as the cops curved away from the curb.

Out of nowhere, she asked: "Who do you think killed Sameer?"

"I can't say for sure, but I'd guess it was the cartel who were unhappy about his work." I dropped a few more details about Sameer. "They don't send pink slips to employees; they send shooters."

"If Sameer produced this app, which didn't work to the cartel's satisfaction, they would still need a new app, wouldn't they?"

Before I could respond, she asked: "Who was on the other side of the conversation? Who were the cartel people talking to?"

"I don't know," I lied.

"I'm sure they had no problem finding someone else to replace Sameer. This app, is it complicated?"

"Not for the right person."

"Your friend Horace," she said. "He's could be the right person, couldn't he?"

"What do mean?"

She smiled. "By the way, what were you doing pretending to be a Washington Gas employee and shutting down the street the other night?"

I started to answer but she stopped me. Again.

"I will save you the trouble of lying. The officer who cordoned off the street filed a report about the incident. I didn't think anything of until I happened to run into a friend who works for WashGas. I mentioned what happened just in passing and he told me that he didn't see any possible gas leak reports in that area on that evening. If there was, Fire would have been notified and then we would have been notified and we weren't. Our officer thought that having a white van with no markings was a bit unusual so he logged the tag. I ran it and turned out to belong to your pal Horace or whatever his weird number-name is."

"256-L12."

She blew a raspberry. "What were you doing in the street playing gasman? Which is, for your information, a few more misdemeanors that can be added to your list."

"They are adding up," I said. "I was watching the building across the street - for a client."

"Who's the client?"

I gave her a smirk. "Let's walk out together."

When we reached the sidewalk, I spied Senator Metcalfe heading towards me. I quickly tried to reroute our direction but he caught up.

"Mr. Pinkerton. Hello."

"Hello, senator. This is Detective Janice Pemberton, MPD, an old friend. This is Senator Metcalfe."

They shook hands. "Lovely to meet you. How do you two know each other?" he asked.

She said: "We were on a community recycling committee, a mixture of public and private practitioners." The tale fell so easily out of her mouth that I almost believed it myself.

"And you," she asked. "How did you meet?"

"Mr. Pinkerton is doing some consulting work for a committee that I'm on. He's as honest as the day is long. Delivers what he says he will, a refreshing trait these days."

"He's quite the pillar of our community." She lightly squeezed my arm. "He's such a dear. We love working with him." She squeezed my arm again.

Metcalfe's phone vibrated. "Sorry, I have to take this. Nice meeting you, detective." He turned and walked away.

Pemberton looked at me. "Pinkerton? Impersonating someone else is also a misdemeanor. It could even be a felony. Is Metcalfe mixed up in all this?"

"A senator and a Mexican drug cartel? That'll be the day," I said.

CHAPTER 53

The call came in early, before I even had time for my morning meditation. Hell. Why do I delude myself? My meditative sessions usually come from the open end of a glass.

Metcalfe was on the horn and his voice was shiny.

"Mr. Pinkerton. Would you be interested in a plane ride to Arizona? I have an associate I'd like you to meet."

Montano. Shit.

"No thanks. I'll have to pass. I have several appointments today." Damn right I have to pass. If there's any hope of keeping my multiple personas straight and staying alive long enough to find Helen's killer I need to keep different worlds from colliding. Metcalfe knows me as Allan Pinkerton, Montano thinks I'm TV producer Chick Gomez and the LaFarge and Sarah duo know my real moniker… what is it again? … Sam Marlowe, which, when you really think about is a phony baloney handle thanks to my parents.

I may need to keep a who's who index card in my pocket.

"Maybe another time," I said.

"I understand," he replied. "I see you as a long-time associate and… "

I heard a click which meant he got another call. He rushed a goodbye with me and the line went silent. Long-time associate. That's fucking great.

I put my feet up on the desk, staring at the Maltese Falcon statue hoping that it might offer me some clarity. What would Bogie do besides light up a fag and straighten the brim of his fedora?

Thankfully, the phone beeped. It was Cyril.

"Sammy boy, I have to tell you about this place I went to that..."

"Cyril. I would love to hear about your tippling experiences, but I'm under a squeeze here."

"Alright, Sammy boy. MBI, Ltd. as you suspected is a holding company. I located them in a new building just outside of Charlestown in Nevis and that's all I could get – for now. They're one of about eight companies listed on the door. I knocked and nobody answered. I found a phone number and called them. It went to voicemail. But wait, there's more, as you Yanks say in your late-night infomercials."

"C'mon, Cyril."

"Sorry, mate. I went next door where a chartered accountant works. I charmed her with my good looks and asked about MBI. She told me that she had tried to get their business once but was unsuccessful. She said they are a shell company - that St. Kitts/Nevis was loaded with them - and they have their own accountants. She rarely sees anyone going in or out of the room; maybe once a week somebody picks up the mail. I had the feeling that she didn't like what was going on."

"Why not?"

"She was born and raised on Nevis and says that their reputation as an offshore banking haven is unsavory, gives the island a bad name. She hates it. And get this: St. Kitts/Nevis is one of those countries that sells passports for money. It costs about a half million and Middle Easterners and Chinese buy them so they can travel with some impunity. It's how they bring cash in and out of the country."

"Don't other countries have citizenship by ownership and investment?"

"Yes, but it's usually tied to investments or employment that help the country's economy. Here, outsiders start to build condos and never complete them. They start companies and never employ anyone. It's a bloody scam."

"Where does the passport money go."

"According to her, the money goes into the pockets of politicians."

"Ain't that the way. What's your next play, Cyril?"

"She gave me the name of the bank that MBI does business with. I'm going to visit and see if I can find out who owns them. Her cousin works there. Everyone has a cousin who works somewhere who can help you out. It's like a small town."

"Small towns can be more dangerous than big cities."

"I will be on my toes, Sammy boy. And by the way, they have this moonshine rum here called Hammond that is supposed to blow your knickers off. Sometimes, they add marijuana to it, Green Hammond they call it."

"Be careful, Cyril."

"I will, Sammy. I have a Nevisian-born escort for dinner tonight. I think I'm in good hands."

CHAPTER 54

I had trouble understanding the West Indian accent on the other end of the blower. Maybe it was because I didn't really want to hear what he had to say.

"Sir," the voice repeated. "I am calling from the Royal Saint Christopher and Nevis Police Force. My name is Sergeant Isaac Halbert. To whom am I speaking?"

"That depends. What do you want?"

"I am calling to ask if you know a Mr. Cyril Willingham. I am inquiring because this number is the most recent outgoing call on his mobile."

"I know him," I said, still not wanting to hear.

"And your name, sir?"

"Sam Marlowe. What's this about?"

"I regret to inform you that Mr. Willingham was the victim of an apparent robbery and killed."

"Dead?" The job was supposed to be fun in the sun. Easy peasy. "Are you sure?"

"Yes, sir. What is your relation to him, may I ask?"

"He was working for me."

"In what capacity, sir?"

"Consultant," I said.

"Do you know of any next of kin whom we may contact?"

"Cyril was not married. I believe he has a sister in Devon, England."

"The UK authorities have informed us that she was deceased last year. They know of no other family."

I told the sergeant that I would take care of Cyril's remains. I wasn't sure how, but I owed him at least that much.

"Thank you, Mr. Marlowe. We will meet you upon your arrival." He hung up without asking which plane I would be taking or when I would land.

I called the British Embassy and their HR person told me that Cyril also had listed his sister as next of kin, but that was three years ago just before he left his post. They referred me to a lawyer also listed in his records. I hoofed it over to his office. It was just a few blocks away.

"I am Johnathan Nye. We do a lot of work for embassy personnel. I am sorry to hear about Mr. Willingham. How can I help you?"

Jonathan Nye, Esquire, wore a dark blue suit, white shirt with initialed cufflinks, a hand-tied paisley bowtie, and a wrist watch with four subdials on the face. He saw me eye it and smiled. "It's not a watch, it's a chronograph."

I told him what the Nevis copper said, and Nye shook his head. I showed him the death certificate that the authorities had faxed to me, and shook his ahead again. "Bad business, some of these islands." He proceeded to tell me in great detail about how his wife had her purse stolen as they walked back to a cruise ship in Nassau. "We gave them what they wanted. You can't spend money when you're dead, am I right?" Then he lectured me about how the formerly British slave islands were better off under direct rule. "Look at Jamaica with all their violence and drugs. It's a shame. Such beautiful beaches."

I wasn't sure if I could make it through our meeting without slamming him against the wall a few times. First for his racist rant, second for his chronograph and one more for his stupid bowtie.

He opened a folder, perused it and gave a few "aha's" and "I see's" before closing it.

"As wills go, this is straightforward. His assets will go to his two nieces, his sister's daughters, after my administrative costs, of course."

Mr. billable hours asked why I was willing to take on the task of handling Cyril's remains.

I could have schooled him about honor, integrity and doing the right thing but he wouldn't understand. I managed: "He was a friend."

"I am the executor so I authorize you to fly to Nevis and make arrangements for his body to be transported to Devon where it will be buried in the same church cemetery as his sister. Those were his wishes." He handed me a slip of paper with the church address, folded his arms and leaned back. "That should conclude our business. Any questions?"

I held my peace for the sake of Cyril's memory.

"One last thing, Mr. Marlowe," he said, picking up his phone. "Fly coach, and keep your receipts."

* * *

I thought about flying first class just for spite but realized it would take money out of Cyril's nieces' inheritance so I booked a knee-squashing seat to St. Kitts. I took a taxi to the ferry in the capital Basseterre where my luggage was placed on deck along with crates, boxes and three cars. Most passengers took advantage of the shade offered by the upper deck flooring. They sat on folding, wooden chairs in neat rows and columns like an outdoor graduation on a sports field.

I stayed outside on the main deck in a lawn chair which allowed the wind to scrape off the recycled airplane air still clinging to my skin.

It started to drizzle but none of the people sitting near me on crates, along the railing or just standing and yakking with friends seemed to mind. Despite my pigment, the other passengers knew that I wasn't a resident and one of them turned to me and said: "It will stop raining in a minute. Beers are inside."

I walked by rows of wooden chairs, past men playing dominoes, searching for some sign that beers were being sold but didn't see a counter, table or anything resembling a beverage vendor. "You looking for beer, mon?" a young man asked. I nodded and he pointed to a large blue cooler with an even larger man sitting on top. As I walked over, he lifted the lid, popped the cap off a Carib and handed it to me. "Two dollars," he said.

"All I have is American dollars."

"No problem."

The boat sidled to the dock smoothly. I stepped off and watched as the deckhands unloaded the cargo onto the cement pier. I found my luggage, and wheeled it under a sign that read: "Welcome to Nevis. Birthplace of Alexander Hamilton."

Several people asked me if I wanted a taxi before a man in a well-pressed, gray uniform approached me. 'Mr. Marlowe," he said. "I am Sergeant Halbert. We spoke on the phone." He had a pencil-thin moustache, high cheekbones, round face and pockmarked cheeks. His shoulders were straight and solid.

I didn't ask how he knew what ferry I would be on. The sergeant said 'may I,' and took my rollaway. We walked a short distance to a police car where he opened the passenger side door. "Please," he said. There was no jibber-jabber.

"This is Charlestown," he said, as we drove through a town that looked like it hadn't changed in 100 years. Most of the buildings were constructed of dark stone blocks. Some had wooden second floors. They all had shutters. A handful of men staggered about the main square while several women carrying white plastic shopping bags tried to avoid the tipplers. Knots of people in office attire stood on the narrow sidewalks and chatted.

"With your permission," Halbert said, "I would like to take you to identify Mr. Willingham."

I nodded.

We drove a few miles to a hospital where we parked in the emergency room driveway.. Halbert shook hands with an attendant and they spoke softly for a few minutes. "This way," he said. They stood beside a stainless-steel table with a white sheet over a body. He asked if I was ready, and I said 'yes.'

He pulled back the sheet, and I recognized Cyril's face immediately even though his skin was drawn, pallid and sagging. This was not the first time I've had to ID a body and it doesn't get any easier. But this was sadder than others. I thought I was sending Cyril on a slam dunk, an easy gig. Did I unwittingly put him in danger? Is Nevis that dangerous an island that I put him in harm's way and didn't know it?

We walked outside and it was hotter than before. My shirt smelled from sweat and I needed a shower. "I understand you're staying at Montpelier," Halbart said as we pulled away from the hospital.

"Does everyone know everyone's business"

Halbert laughed. "It is a small island, and we are all cousins. Nevis was a sugar cane island, and after slavery ended, many of our families took the last name of their plantation owners. That makes us cousins. I was a police officer on St. Kitts and moved to Nevis about 10 years ago. I was hoping for a quieter life for my family. To Kittians, Nevis is the country; we're considered bumpkins. Nevisians will never totally trust me. I'm still not fully accepted even though my family is from only a few miles away.

In one way, that makes me a better policeman. I'm not afraid to arrest someone."

"What do you mean?"

"Nevisian police officers are reluctant to arrest cousins, friends of cousins, cousins of cousins. People won't turn witness against a relative or help us in our investigations. We have had people witness a cold-bloodied shooting and refuse to ID the shooter. They know that if they do, their extended family will disown them - or worse." He patted his forehead with a handkerchief. "Nevis has recently become a route for drugs heading for the US and Europe and we're seeing an increase in gang-related crime tied to these drugs."

"Can you bring in police from the outside?"

"We have ongoing programs to recruit police from other islands like Jamaica, and even from Guyana in South America. Both were British colonies and the people speak English. This initiative helps, but not enough."

"Is that your way of telling me that you probably won't find Cyril's killer?"

He didn't answer. "We will be at Montpelier in a few minutes," he said. "I suspect that you'll make arrangements for Mr. Willingham's transportation tomorrow and then leave us shortly thereafter."

"I may stay a few days, Sergeant. It all seems so pleasant here." I looked out the window at palm trees, goats and donkeys. I saw small monkeys climbing tamarind trees.

He handed me his card. "Call if you need anything," Mr. Marlowe, "and be careful. Paradise can be deceptive."

CHAPTER 55

The giant weeping fig tree is the first thing you see when passing through the iron gates of Montpelier Plantation. The massive above-ground roots splay across the bottom and threaten to burst through the brick-lined base that struggles to keep it contained.

Just like Nevis, the tree is beautiful and deceiving.

"Everyone asks about it," Donna the receptionist said. The constant breeze kept the office comfortable, and she looked cool in her neatly-pressed, conservative blouse and skirt, which was hemmed below the knee. Her hair was pulled back tightly behind her wide face. "Sandy, one of our groundskeepers, planted it in 1966, the year that we opened as a resort. He was just 13 years old." She pointed to a photo of a young lad holding a watering hose. "He is still here. You will see him around."

She pecked the keyboard, then turned to me as she described the amenities: the pool, the bar and the breakfast that is included. "If there is anything you need, just let me know."

I asked her to arrange a rental car, found my room and took a shower. Afterwards, I napped for about an hour before entering the Great Room for cocktails. The space consisted of overstuffed but fashionable chairs, couches with pillows and small tables. A rounded bar with a few stools resided in the corner. The weeping fig filled the view out the front door.

Looking out the side door you could see the brick remains of the windmill where sugar cane was crushed into juice. Several copper boiling pots had been turned into planters.

I wondered what it must be like for the descendants of slaves to work in a place that was once a setting for economic and social oppression, not to mention physical atrocities. My ancestors had been slaves in South Carolina, but I'm not reminded of their horror every working day.

The young bartender concocted a rum punch that I downed too quickly for my own good. I ordered a second.

I was staring at the remnants of the windmill atop a slight hill and realized that the cane juice must have flowed down sluices into the boiling room, now the Great Room. I was sitting and enjoying a cocktail in the place where slaves toiled in the dangerous heat, stirring copper pots until the liquid evaporated, eventually producing brown sugar or molasses which was turned into rum. Enjoying the punch in such luxury today made me feel guilty.

At that moment, a woman about 35-years old sat down on the opposite sofa, and said: "Are you Mr. Marlowe?" She sported a gray pantsuit over a white shirt which opened into a V and was sided by wide lapels. She wore a gold crucifix around her neck and wire-rimmed glasses with lenses that seemed exceptionally clear. Her shoes were beyond their prime.

"And you are?"

"My name is Valma Halbert. Isaac… Sergeant Halbert is my brother." She resettled herself on the sofa. "Mr. Willingham and I met when he was in my building. My brother told me about the robbery. I offer my condolences."

"Thank you. Cyril said that you and he had spoken. He appreciated your help."

"Can we go somewhere private to talk?"

We walked outside to the veranda. There was no one around us. Based on what I know about Nevisians, it took a lot of courage for her to contact me, a stranger, a foreigner at that. Nevisians can be reserved, especially women, in the old-school, British style of etiquette.

She began: "I don't know how much you know about offshore banking, as you call it in the states, but it is almost impossible to learn ownership of assets on Nevis. Even our corporate registry doesn't know who owns what. And while the U.S. authorities force Swiss banks and financial institutions in other Caribbean countries, like the British Virgins to divulge their customers, Nevis resists it and there's nothing that the American authorities can do about it. The U.K. government forced all British island banks to open their books, and other European countries did the same for their territories, but we're an independent nation. They can't do a thing to us."

"Not even under court order?"

She laughed. "In Nevis, you must file a bond of $100,000 with the court to show that your case isn't frivolous. Even if you win, you won't be able to confiscate assets because you won't be able to find them. Even if you did, which is highly unlikely, you must have filed your suit within a year of the trust or whatever entity was formed."

"It sounds foolproof."

"Not only that, but anyone caught disclosing financial information without a court order can be put in prison for a year and fined $10,000."

"This leaves out greasing the palms of bank officials."

"Pardon?"

"Never mind."

"I had given Mr. Willingham the name of MBI's bank and the name of my cousin who works there but I wasn't sure what he could do with it. I warned him of the danger."

"Danger?"

"I don't believe the robbery that led to his death was a random occurrence. In fact, I even risk talking to you."

"Why are you?"

"I love my island and I think all this corporate secrecy is wrong. We are outliers in the financial world and it degrades our nation. We have only been independent since 1983. We're a young country and traveling down the wrong path. Our leaders have set up a system that is stealing from us and the world."

"Does your brother feel the same way?"

"He does, but in many ways his hands are tied. He has to work within the law enforcement system that we have."

"What about your cousin at the bank? How does she feel about it?"

"Angry, frustrated and scared. Just like the rest of us."

CHAPTER 56

I spent the following morning making arrangements for Cyril's body to be shipped to England. The undertaker in the white guayabera and black slacks welcomed me with a reserved smile. He asked me how I knew the departed and said: "The Brit retirees almost always have their remains shipped back home. They come here for the sun, but they do not mix with the local people, not even in death. The only contact they have with us is when we maintain their pools, mow their lawns or sell a casket to their next of kin." He didn't sound bitter, just matter of fact.

"Why do you think that is?" I asked.

He laughed. "It's the color of our skin, my brother." He handed me a sheet of paper. "Here are the charges and the transport schedule. The recipient will send you an email when the deceased's body is received at the airport in the U.K. We shook hands. "Good luck to you."

As I turned to leave, he said: "Wait; I almost forgot. I have a message for you."

It was from Sergeant Halbert, and he wanted to meet at a bar named Sunny's on Pinney's Beach. It was the same place that Cyril had talked about. The Four Seasons resort anchored one end of the beach and the other end was held down by local joints where tourists visited to have an authentic island experience – at least to their minds. I parked my car on a grassy spot just off the sand and found a hut that offered beer and music. I downed a few Caribs then wandered toward Sunny's one of the more built-up establishments. On the way, a Rasta offered to take a photo of me and his organ grinder-type monkey. Another entrepreneur suggested I buy some sea shell necklaces. Still another showed offense at my disinterest in a taxi tour around the island.

"I am Sunny," the smiling man said to me as I entered the restaurant. The walls were plastered with photos of celebrities. Flags from various countries and colleges hung from the rafters. Seating consisted of brightly-colored wooden chairs mingling with comfortable couches. There were several red-skinned, U.K. frat lads who had gotten an early start on their passing out from rum punches, beer and too much sun.

"Are you here for lunch?" Sunny asked. He was about six-feet tall, sported dreadlocks to his waist, a yellow caftan that only a select group of men can pull off and a beaded necklace with a gold medallion in the shape of a lion. He didn't appear to have a worry in the world.

"I'm meeting someone," I said.

He looked around and pointed. "Would that be him? he said, his index finger aimed at Halbert. I nodded. "The waitress will be right over."

The sergeant was in civies and had a Skol in front of him.

"Are you concerned about being seen with me?"

"No, sir. People know why you're here, to retrieve your friend's body. It's only natural that a police officer will be talking with you."

The server arrived at the table. "I'll have one of those," I said, pointing to Halbert's bottle.

"I will have another," Halbert added. When she left, he said, "Mr. Marlowe, I know what you do for a living. I am not offended that you told me on the phone that you were a consultant instead of a private investigator, but I'd like to know more about what Mr. Willingham was doing here."

His comment didn't take me by surprise.

"Perhaps my sister told you. I don't think that his death was random. He was targeted."

"Then you know that he was looking into a company called MBI. He was trying to learn the ownership."

"Which my sister also probably told you is nearly impossible to discover."

Our beers came and we both sat back until the server walked out of earshot. We leaned forward. "Who knew he was here besides you?" he asked.

"Not a soul," I said.

He motioned for Sunny to come to the table.

"Sunny is my cousin," Halbert started.

"Who isn't?" I said.

"Really. He is my mother's, sister's son. We grew up together. He may have been one of the last persons to see Mr. Willingham alive."

I focused on Sunny's face which didn't have a single wrinkle except around his eyes. He began: "Your friend was asking a lot of questions about offshore banking. We were short a bartender so I was making drinks, and I overheard his conversation with a white guy. He said his name was Nigel something or other and he worked at WIBC."

"West Indian Bank of Commerce," Halbert interrupted.

Sunny continued: "I had never seen him before. I would have remembered. He looked like the actor Patrick Stewart. Spoke like him, too. I noticed that he was wheezing, you know, like he had trouble breathing."

"Did they leave together?" I asked.

"We were very busy, but I'm sure that Mr. Willingham left a few minutes before this Nigel fellow. I did not pay much attention. Two white guys talking to each other. You know…"

A server motioned for Sunny, and he excused himself.

Halbert said: "Mr. Willingham was found just outside of the WIBC bank in Charlestown. He was in his rental car, a single shot to his temple." I started to talk but he stopped me. "His wallet was on the passenger seat. Cash was missing and we could tell from the tan line on his wrist that his watch was taken."

"How do you know it wasn't just a robbery?"

"The only people who shoot each other on Nevis are local gang members and anyone running drugs or evening out a personal vendetta. Despite what you may have heard, black on white crime is rare. And when it does happen, the guy takes what he wants and leaves the person alive knowing full well they won't go to the police. They just want off the island as fast as possible." He sipped his beer. "My sister told me that MBI has an account at WIBC. That's the connection."

I looked at the waves. "A stranger visits the island, making inquiries about MBI and WIBC and unfortunately he runs into a person who works at WIBC. That's some bad luck."

"Small island," Halbert said, "but why would Mr. Willingham drive to the bank when it was closed?"

"My guess is that Nigel lured him to the bank, perhaps saying that he was willing to help him get the information that he wanted. Did you talk to this Nigel?" I asked.

"We tried, but there's no one named Nigel working at WIBC. And nobody fitting his description works there either."

"What does your supervisor think?"

Halbert smiled. "He says the incident looks like an accidental, self-inflicted shooting by a drunk visitor or maybe a suicide. He said that sometimes the island doesn't live up to visitor's expectations."

He waved to Sunny on our way out.

When I returned to my rental wreck, the temperature inside must have been over a hundred degrees. I opened the windows, cranked up the AC, leaned on the bumper and stared at the ocean. A scrum of men was playing cricket on the beach. Several tourists were staggering their way from the Four Seasons hoping to find cheaper booze.

And a guy looking like Patrick Stewart jabbed a gun into my side and insisted that we take a ride.

"I already have a ride."

"I have a gun."

"I'm tired of people sticking guns at me. Besides, driving is on the left here and that means you'll have to keep the gun on my left side, and that's my bad side."

He jabbed it again.

"Owww. That's not sweetening the invitation. Holy crap," I said. "You really do look like Patrick Stewart. Say something from Star Trek or X-Men."

He wheezed.

"Shoot me now, if you want. A white guy killing a black guy on Nevis with all these people around? That's a career ender, worse than getting a face tattoo. By the way, Sergeant Halbert from the Nevis police department is standing right behind you."

"I'm not falling for… "

Halbert sliced a karate chop into the man's neck. I had never seen that move before except in the movies. The man dropped the gun and I retrieved it. Halbert slammed him against the car and placed him in a hammer lock. The man groaned as Halbert kept applying pressure to his arm before he retrieved handcuffs from behind his belt.

"Sergeant," I said, "do you know an out of the way place, something not in the tourist brochures?"

CHAPTER 57

All of this was a lot of drama and travel just to find out who owned a company. Knowing that Sarah was dirty should have been the end of the case because I could have leaned on her and LaFarge even Metcalfe, but then… there was Cyril's death. He was not merely a loose end but a friend whose retirement I was trying to fund with what I thought was an easy gig. I felt sick to my stomach thinking about it.

We motored up a dirt road. I could see the cloud-covered Nevis peak in front of us. The road narrowed and we got out. I dragged Nigel or whatever the hell his name was, out of the car and pushed him forward.

"There are some great views further ahead," Halbert said, "and some steep drops."

The man dropped to his knees. I hoisted him up. "Keep walking," I said. "You don't want to miss the vistas. I understand that you can see Montserrat from the top."

"We're going to the top?" he asked, clearing his throat several times. He had trouble breathing.

"Well, maybe not all of us," I said.

He started to hyperventilate which made his wheezing worse.

We trekked about a mile to a clearing that allowed us to see across the island to the ocean. "Beautiful," I said. I threw a rock the size of a baseball over the edge and heard it bounce a half-dozen times before it stopped.

"What do you think, sergeant?"

"A visitor has to be very careful of falling over the edge. Sadly, it happens from time to time." He pulled at his nose. "I remember one incident where a hiker, umm about your age," he said looking at the man, "accidentally tripped and went over the side. He lay in the ghaut for I would say about a week before anyone found him. He lived but he was never the same. They had to amputate his arm, and remove a leg that was stuck between boulders. Lost an eye, poor fellow."

The man began blinking like someone squirted lemon juice in his eye. He couldn't stop. "What do you want?" he pleaded, between gasps for air.

"I don't want anything. How about you sergeant?"

"I just want tourists to enjoy themselves on our lovely island. Some people call it the 'Queen of the Caribbees.'" This copper was worse than me with his wisecracks. Maybe we're long-lost cousins, too. "So fitting," I said. "Sergeant, I think it's time that we removed the handcuffs."

"No," the man shouted before coughing.

Halbert unlocked the nippers and we each held the man by a paw. He had no fight left in him, and we were able to swing him back and forth like a jump rope. His feet were useless, just stumbling along to keep from falling face down.

"One," I said, as we sling-shotted the man toward the cliff.

"Two." Another swing. "Ooops, sorry. I almost let go."

"And..."

"Stop!" the man yelled. "I did it. I shot the man at the bar, Willingham."

We pulled him back from the edge. I almost lost my footing on the loose gravel. He collapsed and we leaned him against a pine tree.

"Who are you?" Halbert said, "and how did you get on my island?"

"My name is Steed, and I work for a private group that does security for the government."

"What government?" Halbert asked.

"Your government, for god's sake. St. Kitts and Nevis."

"I don't believe it," said Halbert.

"It's true," he said. "It was just coincidence that I was sitting in the bar next to Willingham. He was asking questions, the kind of questions that my bosses want to know about. I called my boss, and asked what I should do. He said to drive him to the bank and someone would be there to take over. Well, nobody was there." The man caught his breath. "Willingham got scared, realized that it was a trap and we got into a scuffle. I held him at gunpoint to keep him from escaping but he fought back, and I shot him. It was an accident, and that's the truth. I took his money and watch to make it look like a robbery."

He was sweating more than before. I threw him a bottle of water.

"Who pays you? I asked.

"I told you. A private company working for the government. My job is to make sure that anyone asking questions about certain companies would be dissuaded from further, you know, inquiries."

"And how were you to do that?" Halbert asked.

"We weren't supposed to kill people, if that's what you mean. Mainly we would pay people to go away. You would be surprised how many lawyers, investigators and even foreign government agents will take a bribe if it's large enough."

"Who's behind the money payoffs?" I asked.

"I don't know. The cash is supposed to come by courier, but I'm new on the job. I haven't had to pay off anyone yet so I can't say exactly how it's done."

I pulled Halbert aside and we spoke for a few minutes.

"Sergeant Halbert is going to arrest you for murder."

"Is there any way we can make this go away?"

"Are you offering me a bribe?" Halbert asked.

"Well, I..."

"There is one way, that maybe, you could fade the beef," I said.

He cocked his head, not sure what he had heard.

"Call your boss, make up a story, say you need ten-thousand as a payoff. No, make it twenty. Tell him that the man was snooping around the bank, that he knows about everything,"

The man sat upright. "And what's in it for me?"

"We can always take you for another walk if we don't like how things work out."

The man coughed again. "I'll do it."

"I have one more question, Steed," I said. "I'm sure your boss told you that it's almost impossible to get access to corporate information let alone bank assets on Nevis. Why would someone pay hush money to keep snoopers away?"

"There's always a first time. My boss said the people who employ us believe it's cheaper and easier to pay money than risk exposure and possible prosecution. There has been chatter that the U.S. and European authorities may be getting close to piercing the islands' corporate veil."

I let that sink in. If that happens, it could bring down global crime organizations, oligarchs, corrupt governments, and drug cartels that are keeping their spoils hidden in the island banks. Twenty large was a small price to pay. We walked down the hill to the car and drove in silence to the police station in Charlestown. I dropped them both off, went on to Montpelier and sat at the pool bar.

"Are you having a relaxing vacation? the bartender asked.

"Relaxing is not the word," I said.

CHAPTER 58

I ate dinner at Montpelier with a couple on holiday from the north part of London. Afterward, we settled into the Great Room where the husband and I matched each other drink for drink until he became loud and began spouting about cricket being fixed. His wife apologized and directed him to their room. I didn't catch their names.

I flopped onto my bunk after a last gin and Ting and didn't get up until sunrise when I heard donkeys or monkeys or who knows what making unearthly noises outside my room. I'm a city kid. I only know wild animal sounds from cartoons so I'm not sure what they were.

At breakfast, I sat at a table next to last night's couple minus the husband. The wife smiled at me and read her tablet.

I ankled over to the buffet to grab another cup of joe and when I returned Sergeant Halbert was at my table. "I called my contact at the airport," he said.

"Your cousin?"

He smiled. "There is a non-commercial jet arriving around eleven this morning from Washington, DC."

"Does your cousin know who the plane is registered to?"

"An organization called 'AD Services;' he gave me the tail number."

I texted Horace with the number to see if he could track down the plane's owner. "They are expecting Steed to greet them," I said to Halbert. "Let's not disappoint them."

He chatted for a few minutes with everyone who worked there, including a kitchen staffer who hadn't seen him since they were in high school, then headed to the parking lot. "I will collect you at ten-thirty," he said.

I sat by the pool and watched as clouds played peekaboo with Nevis Peak. I saw pale guests wander in and out. Some of them spoke German or French but mostly English of the British variety. The husband from last night sauntered by and asked if the chaise next to mine was taken but sat down before I could answer. He carried a towel in one hand and a Bloody Mary, speared by a celery stalk, in the other.

"How are ya, mate? Say sorry about last night. My wife said I was a bit of an arse, so no hard feelings, I hope."

"None."

"I get passionate about me sports. What's your game, mate?"

"Hockey." I was hoping that would be a conversation stopper.

"Don't know anything about that," he said. "On holiday?"

I'm sure we covered this territory last night. "I'm visiting a cousin."

"I'm here on business," he said. "I was supposed to meet an associate from London the other night in Charlestown but he never showed. We must have gotten our wires crossed. Now I can't reach him by phone." He laughed. "I will run into him sooner or later." Without notice, he downed his drink and dove in the pool.

Hate to tell you, mate, but he's been pinched.

Halbert showed up in his private vehicle. Steed was sitting in the back seat. His mitts were handcuffed behind him. I got in the front and turned around. "I met a guy last night. I think he was your contact. What was he supposed to do when he met you?"

"His job was to evaluate the person's information then have me call it in to my boss."

"Why not just have you do it?"

"I'm new. This was a shakedown run."

"Was he supposed to call your boss?"

"He doesn't even know who my boss is. The operation is compartmentalized."

"So, your boss doesn't know that you two didn't meet?" He nodded.

"What about the people bringing in the hush dough. Do they know you?"

"All they know is that someone from London will meet them at the airport. We have a password: Piccadilly."

Halbert took a call, hung up and looked at me. "The plane is twenty minutes out."

I rehearsed with Steed what Halbert and I had planned. He nodded and said: "I understand." We drove through the gate and waited far down field. Halbert removed the handcuffs and made sure that Steed understood that he would face a murder rap or a header down a cliff if he didn't follow exactly what we had discussed.

The white jet landed, the door opened and a customs officer boarded. He walked off a few minutes later. Even with binoculars, we couldn't see inside the plane from our location. Heat waves rose from the tarmac engulfing the plane like ripples in a pond.

I handed Steed my phone. He placed it in his breast pocket and walked inside the terminal, then outside again towards the jet like a man heading for the electric chair. He went up the gangway. Halbert pressed the speaker button on his phone and we listened to the conversation.

"What is the password?" a man's voice asked.

"Piccadilly," Steed replied.

A few seconds later, Steed departed the plane with an aluminum attaché case. He walked through the terminal and outside again into our car. He was sweating. I opened the case and flipped the stacks of hundred-dollar bills.

Steed returned the phone, and I asked, "What did he look like?"

He coughed, had trouble forming words and catching his breath. "I couldn't see him. He left the case on the floor and talked to me from the front. He was in the shadows. I didn't see anyone else. The pilot's cabin door was closed."

Halbert looked at me. "Any idea who he was?"

"I might recognize the voice if I heard it again, but I can't be sure from just one sentence." My phone buzzed. It was Horace texting me who had registered the tail number.

"Now, I have a pretty good idea," I said, as we drove away.

CHAPTER 59

I couldn't get rid of that gnawing-rat noise in my brain. Why fly in a plane just to drop off 20K in hush money? Why not withdraw it from the local bank? Why all the secrecy, passwords and cut-outs for a few leaves of lettuce?

I left my rental car at the hotel and glommed a ride with Halbert to the ferry dock. "What will happen to Steed?" I asked.

"I will keep my promise, an accidental shooting, and we will throw in an immediate plane ticket to London. As for the man he was supposed to meet, I will pay him a visit at Montpelier."

"Catch him before cocktail hour," I added.

We pulled up to the dock and the scene was a jigsaw puzzle with extra pieces. "Those two white guys don't look like they belong here," I said. Without missing a beat, Halbert drove passed the drop-off area and pulled into a parking space a half-block away. "Civilians don't talk into their sleeves. Are they yours?"

"We don't have white officers, but I know the two men standing next to them - Special Services Unit from St. Kitts."

"Somebody doesn't want me to leave Nevis."

"I haven't seen any alerts today," Halbert said, checking his phone.

Who would know I was here? The same people who flew in the money plane; that's who. They checked the commercial flight manifests.

I get weary of internal dialogue. It makes me feel like I'm going nuts. Next thing you know I'll be thumbtacking photos of suspects on the wall and connecting them with red strings.

"Is there any way to get off the island without being tracked?" I asked.

Halbert worked his phone, speaking in a rapid patois that I couldn't understand. "Let's go," he said.

We drove to a dirt road that looked north to St. Kitts just across the channel. The sign read Sea Bridge ferry with an arrow to the right. We veered to the left. We sat under a tree at Cades Bay beach near a sign promising a restaurant and accommodations. Halbert's phone buzzed. "Your ride is here," he said to me.

We looked out of place on the beach in our long pants and shoes but the tourists drinking Mai Tai's and beer didn't seem to notice. A fishing boat was rocking in place about 50 yards out.

Halbert lifted his car's hatchback, rummaged through the storage area and handed me a large plastic bag marked EVIDENCE. I emptied my pockets and grabbed a few items from my luggage, removed my shoes, pants and shirt, and headed toward the surf with the plastic bag between my teeth. Now the beachgoers noticed.

"Good luck," Halbert said.

My sidestroke was pretty damn solid.

The captain looked to be in his 60's. His face was weather worn, his shirt had fish and oil stains and his cap looked like it had gone through a shredder. His mug displayed a hobo scruff. He tossed me a towel, pulled up the anchor and tore out like we had stolen the tub. The engines rumbled and strained. Once past the swimming zone, we slammed even faster.

"Did my cousin Isaac tell you where we are going?"

I shook my head.

"Montserrat. It's about 40 miles. We will be there in about an hour and a half. It should be dark by then." He pressed a few buttons on the autopilot, then a few more finger stabs on his iPhone and Soca music shouted from speakers attached to the ceiling. He placed both feet on the wheel and leaned back. "There is food in the galley. Make yourself a sandwich. Beers are in the cooler."

I sat on the deck watching Nevis Peak slide into the horizon. We were now in the open ocean with no islands in sight. I found a sleeping bag in the forward cabin, dragged it on deck and laid it flat. I fell asleep after seeing the first evening star.

I woke with a start when the engines slowed and changed pitch. I peeked my head above the gunwale and saw lights twinkling through the palms.

"We're here," the captain said.

I leaned on the rail as the boat nudged the pier. A man waved to the captain and then at me. I hopped onto the concrete. "You should be able to make the next flight to Antigua," he said, as he hustled me into his car. "They leave all day at fifteen-minute intervals. Since the volcano destroyed more than half of the island about ten years ago there are no direct flights to the states, but once you get to Antigua, you should be as good as home."

The orange and green John A. Osborne airport building looked more like a suburban library or middle school than an air terminal. One small plane sat on the field with its engines idling. I showed my passport to the ticket agent.

"Thank you for flying Air Montserrat, Mr. Taylor," he said. "I guess you will miss our warm weather back home in Vancouver."

"It was much hotter than I expected."

CHAPTER 60

I had to get inside the Tiber Creek Free Trade Zone and see what's what. I dialed the number that the lobby guard had given me, and a woman's voice sang through the wire.

I closed my eyes and focused on my words. "Good morning. My name is William Taylor, and I have need of your services."

"What services would that be?"

"I just bought some artwork, and I am seeking storage space."

"I am sorry, but we only take customers based on client recommendations. Who may I ask suggested us?"

"A colleague who works at a government agency."

"Which agency would that be?"

"They deal with special imports."

A pause. "When would you like to meet?"

"How about today? I will be taking possession of the artwork tomorrow, and I would like to have a storage space ready."

"Certainly. I can meet you in the lobby of the building at four pm. My name is Celeste Owen, and I am the general manger.

"That's fine, but one last thing, Ms. Owen. I would like to tour your facility, of course, and I don't want to run into any other clients. Would that be possible?"

"That shouldn't be a problem."

All that concentration gave me a headache so I headed over to the Teekee for a healing remedy. The bar was empty save for Horace and Kerry the bartender. She was buffing wine glasses.

Horace let out a laugh. "Pretty good stuff having the DEA plane delivering hush money."

"It's a helluva tickle," I said.

"It's not like I haven't seen this before," Horace said. "The CIA delivers drugs, weapons and pallets of cash all over the world. Why should the DEA be any different? Was it the same plane that you flew with Keegan to Mexico?"

"Check."

He laughed again. "What a coincidence."

"Do you have what we jawed about?" I asked.

Horace stopped laughing and his eyes sparkled. "I sure do. It's downstairs." I thought I saw him click his heels in the air as he left.

Kerry looked at me, and smiled. "I didn't hear a thing you fellows were discussing."

Horace returned with a brown paper bag. He poked inside with a screwdriver and gave a few twists. He folded the mouth of the bag and handed it to me. "Use it in good health."

I waved goodbye to Kerry and headed back to the office. Just as I stepped inside, my phone buzzed. It was Keegan.

"What's new partner?" he asked.

"Nevis."

"What's that?"

"Don't fuck with me, Keegan. What about the plane that you sent there?" I repeated the tail number.

"That's one we've used before, but I don't know anything about sending a plane there."

"Have it your way," I said.

"Is that something you want me to check?"

"Swell. You do that."

I clicked off the phone, and walked downstairs to see Goldie. She was standing in front of a large white table and framing some paintings. She barely looked up even though she knew it was me.

"Hi, stranger," I said.

"Where have you been?" she said, even though she didn't seem interested in the answer. "I'm not going to ask you about the photographer anymore."

"You don't need to. I'm getting close."

"No, you're not. You're a son of a bitch. Do you know that?"

"Goldie, c'mon. You know how these missing persons cases work. You have to let them percolate."

She let out a sigh that could melt a ball bearing. "I'm not mad, just disappointed."

Ouch. That's what my mother used to say when I got into hot water as a kid. It was worse than when she yelled at me. "I always keep my promises, Goldie. You know that."

"You should leave. I have work to do."

I left, and heard a piece of wood bounce off the closed door.

* * *

The lobby guard recognized me immediately and smiled. "Back again, sir?"

"This time I have an escort."

"Excellent, sir." He sounded like a snooty butler in a 1930's movie where, if you said your head was on fire, he would respond quite calmly with a nod and a "very good, sir."

Ms. Owen appeared out of nowhere. "Mr. Taylor?"

Once again, I worked hard to sound normal. Having a jacket and tie helped sell it. "William," I said. "Pleased to meet you."

The guard had been right. The fourth floor was a fortress: two thick sets of steel doors set as a mantrap when you departed the elevator, two sets of alarms that the general manager deactivated before we entered, and a motion sensor in each ceiling corner. And these were the tripwires that I could see. I had a feeling that the floors had imbedded pressure sensors, too.

She led me to a barebones office with a desk, three chairs, a computer, fax-scanner- printer-type gizmo, and file cabinet. There was a calendar on the wall showing a panoramic view of the Grand Canyon. "Please, sit down," she said. "May I see your identification?"

I handed her my Canadian passport and British Columbia driver's license. She ran them both through the scanner and handed them back. She typed something on her keyboard then turned to me. "So," she said, "how is the weather in Vancouver these days?"

"We get a lot of rain," I said. She kept staring at the screen as we made small talk, obviously waiting to see if my credentials were kosher. It didn't take long. "Follow me," she said, as she stood up abruptly. "I will show you around."

The setup was essentially a warehouse with metal cages like holding cells you see at police stations. Each cage had a number. As we walked through the rabbit warren of corridors, lights triggered automatically. She rattled off the security features, most of which I had guessed but a few that were new to me including a thermal sensor that could detect a person's body temperature. "That's an extra feature that we can add to your storage area," she said. "Let me show you several spaces that might be suitable for you."

Every occupied cage was filled with either wooden or metal crates. None of the containers had any markings on them besides numbers or letters that didn't spell any words. Looking at them, you had no idea what was inside.

She pointed to a 10 by 15-foot cage marked 17. "This is available," she said. "And there's another one down there that might be suitable." As we rounded the corner, I retrieved Horace's thingamajig from my coat pocket and rolled it under the gate of a nearby cage. I hurried to catch up and glanced at my watch. "This one is larger, fifteen by fifteen," she said, in front of a cage marked 21. We have a few others, as well."

"The smaller one will suit my purpose."

"Of course," she said. "Then seventeen it is. Follow me to my office and we'll complete the paperwork."

As she opened her office door an alarm sounded. "Please stay here, Mr. Taylor while I see what's going on. She dialed her phone as she stepped out. I smelled smoke.

I had only a few minutes to find what I wanted. I searched the filing cabinet but didn't see anything but boiler plate contracts, floor plans and blueprints. The real action was in the computer. It was unlocked, and my fingers were a blur as I raced through the files.

I bit my lip. I was sweating.

There it was. The owners of MBI, Ltd.

Damnit, Marlowe. You should have known. You should have seen it.

I clicked the ESC button a nanosecond before the door opened. "Something in one of our client's containers must have, I don't know, let off some smoke. There's nothing to worry about. There's no fire." She spoke rapidly. "Something like this has never happened before. I do apologize. I know this doesn't look good. Our clients sign an agreement that there is nothing volatile in their containers... but something... I don't know... We can't open the storage area until the client arrives."

"Let me think about it," I said.

"I totally understand." She shuffled her feet and coughed. "Seriously, this has never happened before, Mr. Taylor, and... "

"I will be in touch," I said, as I walked out of the office. I tried to feign an entitled, rich-man outrage, but I wasn't good at it. The smoke was thick and smelled like success.

As I walked past the guard station, he was standing in front of the camera bank. "The fire department is on their way, but we really don't need them, do we, sir?"

He smiled and I smiled back.

CHAPTER 61

I stood across the street and watched as fire fighters packed up their gear. The huge exhaust fan they brought still was expelling smoke from an upstairs window which they broke out. The battalion chief strode out of the building, clicked off the flashlight attached to his helmet and handed the fire marshal an object the size of a tomato paste can.

A few minutes later Detective Pemberton arrived. The fire marshal and Pemberton were chatting as the last of the fire fighters walked out holding the large fan. About ten minutes later, the trucks pulled away, and the area was clear.

"Marlowe," Pemberton said. "No gas company gear this time?"

"Didn't need it."

"Should I add arson to your suspected felony and misdemeanor tab or do you plan a few more crimes?"

"An open tab sounds jakeroo. How would you like to sit in your car with me and enjoy the evening air?"

Before she could respond, I hustled her to the unmarked cruiser, opened the door and squeezed her inside the back seat. "Marlowe, what the hell…"

Sarah Felder appeared carrying the same aluminum attaché case as before, but this time two men carrying bankers' boxes stacked on hand trucks trailed behind her. Another jumped out of their white van with his hand truck and boxes and slipped into line behind them as they entered the building. Pemberton didn't notice the entourage because she was focusing on belting me. I scooted out the car door just as she cocked her arm. I removed the expandable baton from my pocket, whipped it to full extension and crushed both rear lights of the van.

I returned to Pemberton's car. "What, vandalism, now? she said.

"Probable cause. This is where you're supposed to say to me, 'this better be good.'"

"I'm not in the mood for your black and white movie memes, but yeah, this better be good."

I knew now that I could trust Pemberton, even though she kept looking at me like I was nuts. "Watch this," I said, pointing to the building.

Nothing. Nothing. And more nothing.

Pemberton huffed in my direction. "Okay, smart guy. What am I watching?"

We sat in silence for another ten minutes. Finally, Pemberton got in the front seat, started the engine and told me to get out or she would arrest me.

"There it is," I shouted. Sarah was leading a hand truck parade out of the lobby and into the van where the boxes were loaded into the back and the double doors slammed.

"Holy crap," she said. "That's the woman who worked with Sameer Patel, the homicide victim from the alley. What's she doing here?"

"Sarah Felder," I said. "You might want to radio for backup."

The detective wailed the siren and cut off the van before it could pull away from the curb. Pemberton went through the routine of asking for license and registration while waiting for other officers to arrive. She pointed to the rear of the van obviously explaining about the broken tail lights.

In less than a minute, several cruisers hemmed in the van. A couple of officers opened the back doors and helped each man to the sidewalk. Pemberton shouted to one of the officers that she would give them a hand, and as she helped the last passenger to the sidewalk, she accidentally knocked one of the boxes onto the street.

Damn, she's good. She accidentally kicked it, and bricks of plastic-covered Franklins spewed out. When the other officers saw this, they began handcuffing the men and sat them on the curb. Sarah was handcuffed, too, and she sat on the sidewalk with a thousand-yard stare. She still hadn't seen me sitting in the back seat of the cruiser.

Pemberton returned to her car and asked, "How did you know that she would show up?"

I gave her a short explanation of Free Trade Zones, and how they're used to store artwork and keep money away from the prying eyes of government. I told her that Sarah was one of the owners of the FTZ. "I figured that the general manager would call the owners about what happened. Because they couldn't risk an arson investigation that would reveal all of the cash they stashed, they had to get the loot out of there fast."

"What about clients using the other cages?"

"I don't think they were notified at all. The general manager owes her allegiance to the owners. Everyone else would have to take their chances. The FTZ can always say they aren't responsible for what clients put in their spaces, and they would be right in saying so. It's like a bank safe deposit box. The bank doesn't know what customers stash in them. I don't think the general manager knew what was in the owners' storage."

"Let me get this straight. The owners of the FTZ..."

"MBI, Ltd.," I interrupted. "An offshore corporation."

"… is owned by a group of people, one of whom is Sarah Felder. And the others?"

I rattled off the names.

"You gotta be fucking kidding me," Pemberton said. "And you can prove it?"

"It'll be a lulu," I said.

CHAPTER 62

I stood on the other side of the one-way glass as Detective Pemberton interrogated Sarah about twenty million in one hundred-dollar bills covered in Saran wrap and stacked neatly in cardboard boxes. She was quiet as a street mime with laryngitis.

Sarah had the nonchalant look of someone who knew she would skate, the kind of aloof expression you see in the face of company presidents who overcharge dying patients for medicines and then fault them for having cancer. This was not the Sarah I had dinner with, a woman I once thought, well, maybe… Perhaps you never really know a person until they're caught hiding a half-ton of Franklins.

Pemberton did everything but go old school: shine a light in her eyes and dangle a glass of ice water in her puss. I turned up the sound when Sarah looked like she was about to speak. "I want my lawyer," was all she uttered.

Pemberton joined me in the viewing room. "There's no law against having twenty mil in cash although it does raise a few flags," she said, grinning.

"You're kidding," I said.

"Of course, I am. She's a cool one, like she doesn't have a care in the world. Let me talk to the DA's office. See what they want to do."

I cabbed it to the Teekee where I tossed Rudy the Beggar a fin. "Where you been hiding, haven't seen you around."

"I was visiting my sister and her family in Baltimore," he said, folding the fiver and sliding it into his pants pocket. "I just got back into town." We all need to get away sometimes.

Horace greeted me like a child excited to open Christmas presents. "They're burning up the airwaves. The wiretaps are going gangbusters," Horace said. He pulled me towards the end of the bar and whispered. "They're using some code words but as far as I can make out, they're arranging a DEA plane at Dulles ASAP.

"What about Sarah?"

"All they know is that she got busted."

Along with the money. That's gotta hurt. I called Pemberton and filled her in.

"I'm guessing there's another stash of money around somewhere and they won't be leaving without grabbing it first," I said. "That gives us a little extra time."

"I will pick you up in ten minutes," she said. The detective made it in eight.

We screamed out the Dulles Access Road, and passed other cars like they were glued to the pavement. We hit eighty miles per hour and an Airports Authority cop car signaled for us to pull over. Pemberton hook-shotted a blue spinner on the rooftop and the car backed off, but the copper didn't look happy about it.

When we reached the general aviation area, the jet with the same DEA tail number was being fueled just outside a hanger. We parked the car out of sight and watched the plane from behind the edge of the building. I spied a bunch of maintenance workers hosing down the area. "Be back in a minute," I said.

When I rejoined Pemberton, she asked about the two men walking up the gangway. "Pilots. Smith and Jones," I said. "Yeah, I know."

"Here, put these on," I said, handing her a maintenance jumpsuit uniform. It has reflective trim. It will look aces on you."

"Why can't you wear them?"

"They know me. Let them take off. I will do the rest."

"Shit." She squeezed into the coverall, and headed toward the plane.

"Don't forget your cap," I said, tossing it to her. "Looking sharp, Janice."

She disappeared into the plane, and I hoped, into the cockpit.

Over the next few minutes, three cars arrived, each dropping off a person who entered the plane. I could only see outlines and shadows. No faces. The engines cranked and that was my cue.

"Mr. Pinkerton," Senator Metcalfe said. "What the hell are you doing here?"

"Pinkerton? That's Sam Marlowe, the private investigator I hired to find Sameer Patel," said LaFarge. "What the fuck…? What's going on?"

"I'll tell you what's going on," Keegan said, pulling out his gun. "We're going for a long plane ride." He kept his gun trained on me while he closed the door and locked it." He spoke into the intercom phone. "Gentlemen, let's get going."

The plane taxied and Keegan motioned for me to sit down. I could hear Metcalfe and LaFarge breathing from six feet away. "Drop your piece and kick it over," Keegan said. I did. "Well, pick it up," he said to Metcalfe, who held the gun between two finger tips like it was covered in Covid.

"We're heading to Morocco," Keegan said. The Moroccans have strict drug laws and the DEA has been working with them to help stop the smuggling. I'm a goddam hero there, because I helped set up a joint European task force in twenty-fifteen. It makes the country look to the rest of Europe like it's trying." He rubbed his eyes, and I thought I might have a chance to grab his gun, but he abruptly moved his mitts away from his face.

"As for these two," he said pointing to LaFarge and Metcalfe, "They're fine. Any friend of mine... The cost of living in Morocco is low and the weather is warm. There's no extradition treaty with the US, and it's a liberal Moslem country. We'll live happily ever after. You'll be detained on my say-so, Sam. After that, I couldn't give a rat's ass what they do with you. "

Once we reached cruising altitude, Metcalfe and LaFarge seemed slightly less nervous, even though they kept bouncing their attention between Keegan and me.

"Since I'm going to a Moroccan crossbar hotel anyway, would you mind filling in some of the blanks for me?"

"Sure, why not?"

"When did it go sour for you, Harry?"

He laughed. "When I realized that drug smuggling was never going to stop. People all over the world want drugs, and the more we fought it, the more people we put in prison, the bigger it grew."

"What about Portugal? They seem to have figured out something that seems to work," I said, looking at Metcalfe.

"Phil?" Keegan said, like it was a panel discussion.

Metcalfe began slowly. "As I mentioned to you, Mr. Pink ... er, Marlowe, my committee was studying the feasibility of a Portuguese-type system for the US, you know, a medical solution instead of a criminal response. We actually were making some headway in convincing others in Congress and even a few forward thinkers at the DEA. But the more we looked into it, the more research reports we wrote, the more pushback we received."

"Coppers?"

"That's right. There's lots of money in drug seizures..."

"Like Feliz Montano's department in Piedra Viegas?"

"How did you... Never mind. We cut her in when she found out about what we were doing, but I also got pushback from even more dangerous actors."

"The drug cartels?" I interrupted.

"It's simple economics. If there is no risk in selling drugs, the price plummets. The Mexican cartels would lose billions. They approached me with an offer."

I kept my eye on the gun hoping for a chance. "All you had to do was make sure that the legislation never saw the light of day and they would pay you through... let me guess... the Mexican embassy."

"Okay, smart guy. Tell me what happened next." His tone turned combative.

"I figured that you got in touch with Keegan, because he was the DEA liaison to your committee. You caught him at the just the right moment in his professional life. He put you in touch with Pachuco who would clue you in on just enough shipments to keep Montano and other coppers happy and also let the DEA make enough busts to look like they were doing their job. When I visited Montano, someone was trying to spook us. One of Montano's sharpshooters, no doubt. Why? Because she had a sweet deal with seizure money, but it was also a vital part of your plan. She would allow smugglers to come into the U.S. and alert the DEA when a caravan of drugs was on its way. ICE and the DEA could nab these carriers on a regular schedule, and tout the busts on the six o'clock news. Tables with drugs, guns and cash all laid out neatly. They overestimated the street value and everyone was happy, even the drug cartels. They were willing to throw these decoys to the G-Men to throw them off the trail of the big shipments that came in trucks, planes and even submarines. These poor souls braving desert death for a few pesos were expendable. It was the cost of doing business, wasn't it?" I took a breath. "Whose idea was it to use the Free Trade Zones?"

They all stared at LaFarge.

"I'm proud of that," he said. "When I flew for the CIA, we set up zones in foreign countries which we used to store weapons, drugs, money, whatever. Whenever we needed to move anything around, we flew from one FTZ to another around the world. If you want to be rich, you have to do what rich people do."

"And Sarah? Where did she fit in?"

"She and I worked together as you well know," LaFarge said. "She also took care of special jobs."

"You mean like Helen Boston?"

"I take responsibility," Metcalfe jumped in. "She was bugging me about a phone and I gave it to her, but something went haywire with the app and well… she called the police when she received those threatening texts and we were afraid that someone would get a hold of her phone and link it to us and the operation would be in jeopardy."

"Sarah killed Helen?"

LaFarge nodded. "We were protecting our interests. It was just business."

"You picked her up in your car a few blocks away didn't you? I said.

LaFarge didn't respond.

"Harry, one thing is bugging me," I said. "Why did you tell me that Metcalfe had gotten payola from the embassy?" Metcalfe's eyes narrowed and he snarled at LaFarge.

"I figured that no one would believe that a senator was taking payoffs from a foreign government to kill legislation."

"You also figured that I might be dead or in the joint on a frame job."

He smiled. "You were a little more difficult to kill or finger than I thought."

"One last question: The cartel gave you millions to make sure that the Portuguese idea went sideways. Where is that moolah now?"

Keegan said, "We lost some in an unfortunate accident last night. You wouldn't know anything about that would you, Sam?"

"How would I?"

"Ummm. We still have enough left for the three of us."

"Three? What about Sarah, Montano and Pachuco?"

"They're not our concern," Metcalfe added.

"Sit back and relax," Keegan said. "It's going to be a long and smooth flight."

"I hope we don't hit any turbulence," I said loudly.

Keegan's head ticked at my loud voice and it took him a second to figure out what I was doing. The plane took a quick dive and I leapt at Keegan punching him in the puss. He dropped the rod and it slid toward the cockpit. He came up with a hook, but we were too close for it to have any oomph. I weathered the strike and returned with an upper cut. I heard his jaw snap and he landed face down on a table.

Pemberton swung open the cockpit door. "Everybody be cool," she said, pointing her rod at Metcalfe and LaFarge.

"Tell the pilots that we're heading home," I said.

I felt the plane make a wide turn.

CHAPTER 63

The scene around the perp walk was crazier than a twenty-four-hour Walmart on Christmas eve.

I stood in front of the US District Courthouse as reporters from all over the world were hustling to get comments, videos and photos of the group who were being called 'The Cartel Four' by the media. I hope they think of something more colorful when the trial starts. X already offered a few decent monikers: The Sinaloa Senator, The Beltway Femme Fatale and the Drugtastic Four.

As they marched into the building, wearing bullet-proof vests, none of them said anything. Mostly, they kept their heads down, but Keegan sneered at me as he passed by, and I was glad he was handcuffed. Pemberton escorted Sarah, holding her by the arm. The rest walked in with other agency coppers. Everyone wanted a piece of this one.

As the doors closed and the crowd of reporters dispersed, I spotted someone who looked familiar. He wore a flak vest with a thousand pockets. He had three cameras around his neck, one with a telescoping lens. He had been part of the scrum angling for clear shots.

"Chuck Lasser?" I asked.

"Who are you?" he said, clutching his most expensive camera to his chest.

"My name's Marlowe. I'm a private dick, and your ex-wife hired me to find you."

"Which wife?"

"Gold Feather."

I called Goldie and told her that I found her photographer ex-husband. This case worked itself out without me doing a thing. In the missing persons biz, luck counts. I'll take it.

"We can go see Goldie or I can take you inside. I know a copper who hit her quota for the day but wouldn't mind another collar for possible larceny."

"The lesser of two evils," he said. "Let's see Goldie." I didn't like that he called her Goldie.

Pemberton walked out of the courthouse, and I introduced her to Lasser.

"He's Gold Feather's ex-husband?" she said. "How modern of you all to get along so well." She pecked me on the cheek. "Call me from time to time, Sam."

I delivered Goldie's ex to her gallery like he was a pizza: drop off and bolt. I could tell by her expression that there was still some juice left in that relationship, and I didn't want to deal with it or what I thought I had with Goldie.

"Thanks, Sam," she said. I started to make a joke, but stopped myself.

"You're welcome. See you around the building."

I swung by the Teekee.

"I saw it on the news, Sam," Horace said. "What a hoot. The FBI says that Sheriff Montano drove to Mexico, and they don't know where she is. They were also were some execution-style murders in Mazatlán."

"I have a few calls to make," I said, as I footed over to a corner table. I texted Sergeant Halbert in Nevis and asked that he send the twenty grand hush money to Cyril Willingham's nieces. He said he would. As I searched for the next number, Kerry brought me a rye Manhattan with an orange slice, just the way I like it.

I took a deep breath before I dialed Helen's sister.

Headshrinkers, social workers, DAs and even private dicks swear that bringing a killer to justice brings closure to a family. Murders and murderers are accounted for, and loved ones can start to grieve. For me, closure is overrated. It never seems to make me any feel better except that I kept my word and that's something to be proud of these days. Honestly, I don't know what else to do except keep my promises, crack wise to stave off my demons and try not to be so cynical about my fellow human beings. Oh, yeah, and drink too much.

Life ain't never a smooth drive on Easy Street, pally.

End

Made in the USA
Middletown, DE
10 September 2024